History, Mystery & LORE
Of
Rhode Island

By Kelly Sullivan Pezza

This book is dedicated to my beloved grandfather,
Roland Kenneth Baton

Your example is my inheritance,
Your love is my legacy...

Published by:
Finca Publishing
P.O. Box 340
Wyoming, Rhode Island 02898
www.fincapublishing.com

Printed in Canada

Acknowledgements

I have spent the last fifteen years of my life obsessed with history. Researching the people, the places and the stories of days past has become my hobby, my career, my passion. I have collected boxes and folders filled with bits and pieces of information which, over time, if enough pieces are collected, start to form a puzzle. Those puzzles are completed to tell fascinating stories.

But before the pieces can be put together, they must be found. I am eternally grateful to the many people who provided me with pieces, ideas and inspiration. For without them my work would be seriously lacking. I am eternally grateful to:

Lorraine Arruda and Gayle Waite, who have perhaps done more to preserve history than anyone I know. Painstakingly seeking out old burial grounds and immortalizing those who have gone before us are what these two women have devoted their lives too. I am so proud to be able to call them my friends.

Hope Greene Andrews, one of the most beautiful human beings I know, has also done so much to preserve our local heritage. Her interest in history and her unfailing encouragement of my work has not gone unappreciated.

Larry Webster, another wonderful friend who was generous enough to provide me with an over-flowing box of historical letters and documents, from which I obtained literally dozens of story ideas. Throughout the years, he has been my sounding board and a constant supplier of new subjects and information.

Carla Ricci, who I greatly admire for her dedication to the preservation of our rural lands, and for her overwhelming kindness in letting me borrow her entire collection of old newspapers.

Scott Bill Hirst, for his quick networking ability and unfailing ambition to help get any job done.

The Hopkinton Town Hall Staff, who have never failed to go above and beyond in their efforts to assist me in my research.

Dave Panciera, for never sighing when I bring yet another stack of library books up to the counter.

Heather Chevalier, for her generous sharing of information.

Florence Madison, for taking me closer to a tragic event and an amazing man.

John Shibilio, for renewing faith in the kindness of the human race.

Christine Perkins, for bestowing upon me her beloved late father's treasured collection of postcards.

Ginger Woodmansee of Woodmansee's Oil, *Pat Perchman* of The Narragansett Vistor Center & Chamber Of Commerce, & *The Staff of the East Greenwich Free Library* for all their help.

The Cranston Historical Society, for the use of their wonderful photographs.

Craig Anthony, Registrar of The Pettaquamscutt Historical Society, for giving me one of the most interesting tours of my life.

The family of Robert Peabody, for preserving the legacy of a man they dearly loved.

Teri Sheppard, for being my confidant, my friend, my angel.

Eric White, for opening the door that made life as I know it possible.

Alecia Keegan, my Editorial Coordinator and Research & Photography Assistant, for her help with this project.

Katherine Lowenstrom, my Marketing and Copy Assistant for all she's done to get this book out there.

Marylou Fiske, my Manuscript Editor and also my mom, for her sharp eye and for teaching me that our lives are built on the foundations of our past.

Helen Baton, my grandmother, for helping me write my first book at the age of three and still reading every word I write 33 years later.
Tatiana Pezza, my daughter, for being the most beautiful reason I live and breathe.
Greg Pezza, my husband, who continues to illuminate dark rooms.

And a special thanks to those organizations which make public domain photographs and images so readily available, especially *http://wikipedia.org*
Support of free Internet encyclopedias such as Wikipedia ensure that our history belongs to all of us.

If I have forgotten to thank anyone, it is merely the oversight of an overcrowded memory right now. I can only hope that all those I am grateful to already know it.

Author's Note: Every effort has been made to provide the greatest accuracy possible in this book. Often, where history is concerned, names, dates, locations, spellings, and even details of a story differ among sources. When historical sources contradicted each other, during research for this project, I relied on the power of numbers and accepted what information was most commonly given, or what could be undoubtedly proven.

My Own History...

All history is built upon a foundation. We all root back to something. We all grow from somewhere. The stories of the past get added to the stories we create ourselves and are handed down to the next generation. One can not truly know who they are unless they know where they are rooted. Once you know, you carry within you a sense of pride that nothing can ever diminish.

When I was in the fifth grade, we were given an assignment to write a speech about our "hero". On the day we each had to recite our finished product to the rest of the class, I sat at my desk listening to the other kid's speeches about Abraham Lincoln and Martin Luther King. By the time it was my turn to stand up and read my speech, I realized that I was the only person whose hero was not immortalized in the pages of history books. My report was about my grandfather.

Much of my childhood was spent at my grandparents' house where I had a playhouse in the woods, all my dolls piled into corners of the living room, and a whole half of another room had been allotted to me by my grandfather to set up my four dollhouses in.

My grandfather had always seemed larger than life to me. Even at such a young age, I was mesmerized by his stories of being overseas during World War II, and of having to quit school so that he could take the train to a farm where he worked in order to help support his family of 18. I listened to his tales about "peddling grain", cutting ice out of ponds and hauling it to the ice house, and how he once made a record that was put into every juke box in town. I couldn't hear these stories enough.

I remember being put into an after-school group in elementary school for kids who did not have fathers. The other kids would cry and talk about the deprivation they suffered. And I would sit there and wonder why in the world anyone thought I belonged in this group. No, I didn't have a father. But I had something better. I had my grandfather.

I spent most summers traveling around with my grandparents in their big motor home. They took me to Santa's Village, Disney World, Storyland. One memory that always stuck in my mind was during one of our trips to Pennsylvania. There was a square dance going on somewhere near an Amish settlement and a bunch of people were out on the floor dancing. I had just barely learned to walk but I ran out there to dance along with them when one of the men in charge of the event instructed me to get off the dance floor. The dance was for adults only. I suddenly felt my grandfather's arms go around me and sweep me up. But instead of carrying me off the floor, he argued with the man about denying my inclusion. I got to square dance that night.

Everyone always referred to me as my grandfather's "pet". He had grandsons but I was determined to be a little tomboy so that I could follow in what I deemed to be his perfect footsteps. Whatever he was good at, I wanted to be good at. Whatever he did, I wanted to do. Whatever he liked, I liked. And so I would climb up onto the bed with him and eat sardines out a little tin can and laugh along with him at the Candid Camera show.

On weekend nights, he would always go off to the auction. My grandmother and I would watch the Carol Burnett show while I eagerly waited for him to return. My heart would start pounding the moment I heard that screen door squeaking open because I always knew that he had brought me home presents.

When I got a little older, I would go play golf with him, despite the unhappy looks we got from the other men on the golf league who didn't want a little girl out there in their game. Nights after supper, we would go down into his workshop in the basement and refinish old furniture or build brand new pieces. And on sunny afternoons I would throw on my ball cap and jump into his van so we could go down to the river and fish. Saturdays were our yard-saling days, and Sundays our flea market days.

He was the person who had the answers to any question I could possibly ask. He has been a soldier, a mechanic, a singer, a police officer, an ambulance driver, a carpenter, a fisherman. But most importantly, he had been *my* grandfather. The person who taught me how to hold a hammer and run a jigsaw. How to cast a fishing line out and remove my catch from the hook. How to drive a car, negotiate a bargain, fight for what I believed in.

My strongest memory, though I don't know the reason for it, is of him taking me to the garage where my uncle used to work when I was very little. I can still hear the squeak of him pushing that door open and the smell of the oil on the wide floorboards that permeated the air when you walked in. There was a display case full of tools, penny candy and marbles. I would press my hands against the glass and peer inside to pick out what I wanted. Some days it would be gum. Other days it would be a bagful of colorful marbles. Holding onto that small paper bag as we walked back out to the car was like holding the world in my hands. Maybe this memory is so strong because it represents the way he always made me feel. Like the world *was* in my hands. Like I could do *anything*. I can't imagine what I would have been without him.

He is in my heart. He is in my blood. He is, and always will be, my hero and my most enduring history.

Chapter One: Military

Chapter Two: Crime

Chapter Four: Disease

Chapter Six: Religion

Chapter Seven: Love

Chapter Eight: The Unexplained

Chapter Ten: Murder

Chapter Eleven: Letters

MILITARY

HOMETOWN HERO
HENRY SAUNDERS

The grave of war hero Henry Saunders at Oak Grove Cemetery in Hopkinton.
Photographer: Kelly Sullivan Pezza

In 1861, when seven Southern states decided to withdraw from the nation and establish their own government, it was a decision of enormous proportion. One that would change lives and take lives. And for every man who would die in the oncoming war, hundreds of future generations were wiped away.

When the Confederates put their decision into action on April 12 by attacking Fort Sumter, President Abraham Lincoln issued a call for 75,000 northern men to take part in what was believed would only be a minor skirmish. The terms of duty were to be for three months.

On horseback, recruiters galloped around the Union states, announcing the need for able men and boys between the ages of 16 and 60 to step forward and take an active part in the military campaign against the south. Many residents of Hopkinton answered that call. Among them were 22-year-old Benjamin Franklin Burdick and 18-year-old Henry Freeman Saunders. Leaving their homes, they marched toward Washington DC on October 5, 1861 as members of the 4th Regiment Rhode Island Volunteers.

Their regiment settled at Camp Casey in Washington DC until November 28 when they marched on to Camp California in Virginia. There they remained for the next two weeks.

As plans for the North Carolina Campaign were made, the 4th RI Regiment was selected as one of the troops which would march into Annapolis, Maryland. On January 3, 1862 they brigaded there with the 5th RI Regiment as well as the 8th and 11th CT Regiments.

The course of the war changed quite by accident when two Union soldiers found a copy of the enemy's plans in an abandoned camp. General Robert E. Lee was intending to invade Maryland. Lee felt the invasion would gain his troops fresh supplies and maybe even greater support for their cause.

On September 4, the Confederates crossed the Potomac. In just a matter of days, both armies would be involved in the bloodiest shoot-out in American history.

The Battle of Antietam.
Public domain image: Courtesy of the Lincoln Library.

The beautiful fields that rolled along Antietam Creek would soon be strewn with bodies. Nearby

Dunkard Church, a small white haven of peace, would be riddled with bullets. And the winding dirt road that snaked past it all, would go down in history as *Bloody Lane*.

At 6:00 on the morning of September 17, an explosion of artillery fire came from the woods behind the 40-acre cornfield of the Miller farm. The Battle of Antietam had begun. Soldiers from the north and the south ran out from the dense woodlands, jumped up from their hiding places in the cornfields, swung themselves over wooden fences, and raced across a 125-foot long stone bridge to face combat. Hundreds of cannons roared with fire, echoing over the whiz of musket shots, the shrieking of wounded horses and the screams of dying men.

By the end of the day, the battle had claimed over 4,000 casualties. Residents of Hopkinton would soon receive news that Benjamin Burdick had been killed. While attempting to pull Burdick to safety, Henry Saunders was struck by enemy fire. He died from wounds incurred during his heroic act, at Locust Spring Field Hospital on October 22.

Two hundred and four men from Hopkinton had answered President Lincoln's call for soldiers during the Civil War. Twenty-five of them died for the cause.

Carrying away the wounded after the battle of Antietam.
Public domain image: Courtesy of the Lincoln Library.

THE HELL OF ANDERSONVILLE
ETHAN GREENE

Henry Wirz, the head of Andersonville Prison, is executed.
Photo from Library of Congress Collection.
Image courtesy of Wikipedia.org: public domain photo.

Ethan S. Greene was 34-years-old when he marched bravely into the Civil War as a Union soldier. The son of Mary (Hoxie) and William Bliven Greene, Ethan was born in Hopkinton and eventually became the husband of Aurelia Crandall.

When the call for soldiers went out, Ethan was living in New York. He signed on as a Private in Company C of the 85th New York Volunteer Infantry. But he would never see the freedom he was fighting for. He would instead spend his last days in what has been called the most inhumane prison camp of the Civil War.

During the Battle of Plymouth, North Carolina on April 20, 1864, Ethan's regiment surrendered to the Confederates. Under the close guard of their enemy, they were transported to Andersonville Prison in Sumter, Georgia.

Construction of the prison had been completed on February 24 of that year. The sixteen and a half acres it stood upon included a stockade 1,620 feet long, 779 feet wide and 15 feet high, made of upright pine logs placed close together. Fifty-two guard towers were set up in 30-yard intervals around the stockade, while eight more stood along the outskirts of the prison, packed with all the artillery they needed to keep the prisoners in and everyone else out.

Within the stockade, small posts in the ground connected with a strip of pine, ran along the border, 19 feet from the pine log barrier. This was called *the dead line* and any prisoner who stepped over it was killed on the spot.

On the west side of the prison were the two entrances, called North Gate and South Gate. And 100 feet from there, near the cooking area, was *the dead house.*

John Ransom, a prison-mate of Ethan Greene, kept a diary while he was incarcerated at Andersonville. His words convey the sheer horror of daily life there. *"I wish I had the gift of description that I might describe this place,"* he wrote. But with each day, the horror grew worse. The prison was enlarged by ten acres to hold the more than 35,000 captured soldiers, packing themselves into the stockade like sardines. Those who died in captivity lay among the living, their skin baking in the summer sun. And each morning at 9 a.m., a Confederate drummer would appear at the South Gate banging his instrument to signify that *the dead wagon* would be coming around soon to collect the deceased.

Later in the day, the South Gate would open again to allow the ration wagon inside. Sometimes there were beans for dinner, which maggots and weevils had to be skimmed off of before they could be eaten. Sometimes there was soup, sometimes molasses, other times bug-infested corn bread was the meal of the day. Prisoners broke open their military issued canteens and twisted each half into a plate they could eat off of. Utensils were fashioned out of twisted pieces of tin, or carved sticks.

Before going to sleep, the prisoners who were lucky enough to have had canteens or metal pieces to work with, tied their rustic creations securely to their arms to prevent them from being stolen during the night by less fortunate prisoners. Those without issued items to work with, ate with their hands, and drank soup out of their shoes. *"This is hell on earth,"* David Kennedy, another Andersonville prisoner, wrote in his diary.

Aside from the smell of rotting food and the stench of the dead, which hung heavy in the air, occasional downpours of rain filled the stockade with a stagnant pond. Prisoners used the pond as a toilet, yet it was also where they washed and drank.

While many prisoners were shot for crossing the deadline, many more died of disease. Boney knees, elbows and ribs jutted out of every captive soldier, due to lack of food and clean water. Teeth fell out and gums bled. Some men became immobile due to disintegration of muscle tissue. Clothing hung in shreds upon the pale, withered bodies and at night, the dirty, rain-soaked men would huddle in piles for warmth. The dead were regularly robbed of their clothes, the lice-covered rags eagerly sought by those who were cold and desperate.

Selected prisoners would be allowed to leave the stockade in order to bury the dead. Three hundred yards away were rows of trenches, each to be filled with 100 to 150 bodies. For some, death was a relief.

Ethan Greene only had to survive one month in Andersonville. He died there of sickness on May 24, 1864. Roughly 13,000 Andersonville prisoners expired while in captivity there.

Years later, forty small excavations were found inside the stockade, some nearly eighty feet deep, made by men looking for fresh water, looking for a chance to escape. Andersonville prison commander Henry Wirz was convicted by the federal government of committing war crimes against prison inmates and was hanged on November 10, 1865.

The inmates who survived, brought home with them memories which would never fade. Hearing birds singing just outside of their confines and seeing the branches of trees sway in the distance. The sound of church bells echoing from Savannah and the rays of light penetrating the narrow cracks of the prison walls. The heart-pounding anticipation of waiting for just one moment to escape.

Ransom wrote in his diary that after what he had been through at Andersonville, he would forever appreciate *life*. Ethan Greene was not afforded that chance.

YOU CAN'T GO HOME AGAIN
DAVIS CRANDALL

The grave of war hero, Davis Crandall, at Rockville Cemetery in Rockville.
Photographer: Kelly Sullivan Pezza

They left home to make the world a better place. And spent their nights away dreaming about home. With a tearful kiss on the cheek and a wave of the hand, the mothers and wives of Rhode Island bid adieu to the men they loved. The north would win the war. Eliza Crandall would lose her son.

When the 4th RI Infantry was being formed in Providence in 1861, Davis S. Crandall of Ashaway decided to enlist as a Private in Company D. At 19 years old, he had recently graduated from the Hopkinton Academy in his hometown. He worked alongside his father on the family farm and was a member of the Seventh Day Baptist Church. He loved his family, his animals, and his friends, several of whom accompanied him on his trip to Providence where they would all become soldiers.

A week after enlistment, Davis and the others left for Washington DC where they settled at Camp Sprague. His first letters home expressed his excitement at seeing new places. But the letters that followed showed his dismay at the ways of the world outside Ashaway. He had seen Abraham Lincoln and the White House, but the glory of that paled when added to the experiences of sleeping on the ground, eating hardtack and marching for miles every day. He missed his family, his mother's cooking, and obviously felt an even deeper longing when informed that his brother had a new baby.

Across the miles, the letters passed, his knapsack becoming filled with parcels which he would take out to read over and over. On March 12, as he began writing a letter home from Cape Hatteras, duties forced him to put it aside before he was done. He placed it in his knapsack shortly before his regiment advanced on New Bern. There, he was mortally wounded. His friend and fellow soldier Benjamin Franklin Burdick sent Davis's knapsack home to Eliza. Davis was the first man from Hopkinton to die in the Civil War. Benjamin would soon follow him to the grave.

Along with the hundreds of other men who put freedom above their own lives, Davis Crandall left a legacy of photos and letters. And along with hundreds of other women, that was all Eliza Crandall was left to hold onto.

"Good-bye, Mother. From your baby, Davis........"

A QUAKER'S VOW
SIMEON TUCKER

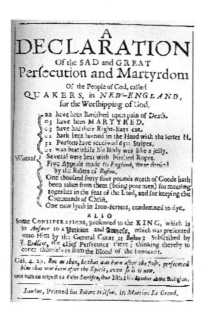

Title page of an old publication concerning the persecution of the Quakers.
Image provided by PDimages.com: public domain image.

It was a war between lands. Between patriotism and religious morals. It was a revolution carving itself both painfully and proudly into history. It was the mid-eighteenth century and America had not yet been given her name. This land, referred to as simply *the colonies,* and the people who lived here, had long been under British rule.

The governing by Britain was tolerated until several impositions by them caused the colonies to revolt, demanding their own rights, free of the British reign over them. A tax on stamps had been imposed, followed by a tax on tea. Refusing to pay such taxes, the colonists destroyed the contents of a British tea ship which had pulled into port here, throwing the tea overboard and costing the British a great deal of money in losses.

The Brits did not take this lack of cooperation well. On April 4, 1775, British troops arrived and a severe battle began in Concord, Massachusetts. Forewarned of their arrival by Paul Revere, the colonists were ready to face the troops. Seventy-three British soldiers were killed compared to forty-nine colonists.

In 1776, the Declaration of Independence was drawn up, stating that the colonists would no longer be under allegiance to England. More death would follow on both sides but the colonists were determined to fight for their rights; all but one particular group of people, a religious sect known as the Quakers.

The Quaker religion had begun in England in the mid-seventeeth century, originally called The Religious Society of Friends. Upon coming to the colonies, the group spread out, eventually purchasing the land we now call New Jersey, which they lost ownership of in 1702. They also purchased the land we now call Pennsylvania but were threatened with being forced out of ownership so merely surrendered.

Little by little, the Quakers gravitated toward Rhode Island, at one time making up half the state's population. The rules of their religion were very strict and all members were expected to abide by them completely. Members were expected to wear only the plainest of clothes, to attend lengthy sermons and respect designated times of silence. They were also expected to abstain from participation in any type of war activity. This included not only refusing to become a soldier, but to help make weapons, prepare for enemy attacks, provide materials for war efforts, or pay war taxes. Failure to abide by this rule was believed to be in direct disregard for God's wishes and was cause for immediate dismissal from the Quaker faith.

Quaker cemetery and Meetinghouse sign.
Photographer: Gregory Pezza

The rule was called *The Peace Testimony* and stated that Quakers had been sent from God to stand witness against violence and bring people from the causes of war to the gospel. For they were *the harmless and innocent people of God,* and they were instructed to never draw an outward weapon upon any man.

By 1777, the Revolutionary War was still causing death in the colonies. Only it wasn't always at British hands. Simeon Tucker was a Quaker farmer who lived in Kingston with his wife Tabitha (Clarke). Tucker had always made it clear to neighbors that he would in no way, shape or form, contribute to war efforts. He refused to pay the war taxes and failed to provide the food and blankets that were requested of him for the soldiers.

One day, Colonel Maxon, also of Kingston, showed up at Tucker's farm with a team of men behind him. They demanded to be given the items they had asked for. Tucker refused. Maxon commanded his men to raise their rifles and level them at Tucker. They did as they were told and Maxon repeated his demand for goods. Tucker staunchly refused again. "Fire!", yelled Maxon. The men shot off their muskets, firing through Tucker's chest and killing him.

One of the men, just sixteen years old, picked up the Quaker farmer's body and carried it into the farmhouse where Tabitha stood in horror. "Here's your husband!" he said, throwing the corpse at her feet.

In 1783, a treaty was signed by the United States and Great Britain, whereby Britain agreed to America's independence. By that time, Simeon's widow had already remarried...to none other than Colonel Maxon.

BROTHERS SEPERATED
JESSE & GILBERT BARBER

1862 illustration of the attack on Fredericksburg, published in Harpers's Weekly.
Courtesy of the Lincoln Library: public domain photo.

The lives of many Hopkinton families were to change in the year 1862. Many wives were to become widows; many children fatherless and many mothers would face the heartbreaking act of having to bury their sons.

The Barbers were one family that would be forever changed by the events of that year, and by the bloodshed, when the boys of the North went to face the Confederates.

Jesse Wilbur Barber was the youngest son of Jared and Sally (Knowles) Barber. A teacher and carpenter, Jesse and his wife MaryAnn had three children. Gilbert Barber, the eldest son of Jared and Sally, worked on the Hopkinton farm where he lived with his wife Darcy and their children.

But in the summer of 1862, they would leave behind the family they loved, to fight for the land they loved. Jesse and Gilbert answered the president's call for soldiers that year. They enrolled together on August 12, and in September they were mustered into the 7th Rhode Island Infantry Regiment. After bidding goodbye to their family, they marched forth to perform their patriotic duty. But only one of the Barber boys would come home.

On November 19, the 7th Regiment set up camp directly across from the town of Fredericksburg, Virginia. After three days, it was decided to move the camp back across the railroad tracks within a dense growth of pine trees. It was there on that hilly ground that the regiment remained until orders came on December 9.

Each soldier was directed to pack three days worth of cooked rations and prepare for a march that would begin at 8:00 the following morning.

However, before the scheduled march could begin, the plans of the 7th Regiment were altered. The 12th Rhode Island Infantry arrived to assist the 7th in their endeavors and so the march was put off until new plans could be set into place.

The next morning at sunrise, a sudden roar of cannons in the not too far distance assured them the time to fight had arrived. At 11:00 a.m., the 7th Regiment marched down Commerce Street until the Confederates were in sight. They stopped beside a brick wall where many of them were minutes away from losing their lives.

Diving toward the muddy ground to escape the gunfire of the South, the Union soldiers fired back until their cartridges were empty. They had little choice but to quickly search the bodies of their own dead and wounded for more ammunition.

Jesse and Gilbert were standing just feet apart when enemy fire struck Jesse's head and he fell to the ground. The battle came to an end at 7:30 that night. In the dark, Gilbert Barber sifted through the dead bodies that lay sprawled across the field for his fallen brother.

The Battle of Fredericksburg claimed the lives of 608 Confederate soldiers and 1,284 Union soldiers. The 7th Rhode Island Regiment lost 199 men. Gilbert Barber returned home without the brother who had left Hopkinton at his side, the memory of Fredericksburg forever etched in his mind.

However the Barber brothers left many descendants here in Hopkinton, an assurance that their blood was not confined to the battlefields of the Civil War.

I REGRET TO HAVE TO INFORM YOU
MERVIN POTTER

A new system of American sea coast defenses was established in 1907. The existing Artillery Corps was divided up, creating a separate Field Artillery and Coast Artillery. The 37th Coast Artillery was stationed at a training camp on Diamond Island in Maine. Here, the soldiers performed their duties while proudly displaying the new American service insignia of two crossed cannons and a shell on their uniform collars.

One young man who had decided to dedicate his life to his country, did not live to wear the insignia of change. One year before the new system went into effect, 21-year-old Mervin Hazard Potter of Peace Dale was completing his training at Fort McKinley, an old Maine fort built during the Spanish American War. There, Mervin was killed. Yet his parents would not receive a letter that he had given his life gloriously in battle. It wasn't a war that took his life. It wasn't an enemy.

May 17, 1906
Dear Mr. Hazard Potter,

Sir, I regret to have to inform you of the death of your son Mervin H. Potter. His death was caused by the accidental discharge of a revolver in the hands of a man with whom he was talking. He and this other man were on guard. They were speaking about revolvers and how to aim them, both having their revolvers in their hands. The matter has been thoroughly investigated by a board of officers and we are satisfied that his death was caused by a most deplorable accident. I extend to you on the part of this company, our sincere sympathy.
Very Respectfully,

L.C. Brown
Captain, Artillery Corps

After being notified of their son's death, Hazard and his wife Jennie had the remains returned to Peace Dale. Mervin's funeral was held at the Congregational Church where his comrades escorted the body to Riverside Cemetery. There, a bugler sent the sound of Taps echoing out across the town.

AN AMERICAN LADY
KADY SOUTHWELL

Kady Cottrell Southwell was born in a British Army camp on the African coast on November 4, 1842. As a child, the only life Kady knew was that of a soldier's family. But then suddenly her mother died, and Mr. Southwell thought it best to send his daughter to live with friends in Providence.

There, Kady had the opportunity to live as most girls of the time did, sewing clothes, cooking meals and tending to the every day household chores. But the young girl didn't fit that mold. When Fort Sumter fell in 1861 and the north and south were preparing to be embroiled in the bloodiest war they had ever known, the soldier's daughter was just nineteen years old. Less than 24 hours after hearing the news, she went to enlist for a three month service with the 1st Rhode Island Infantry.

With her all-male company, Kady trained for battle at a camp in Maryland where she quickly proved to be one of the best marksmen of the group. Training alongside her was Robert Smith Brownell of South Kingstown. The 27-year-old molder had been married for eight years to Agnes Hutchinson, but Agnes had filed for divorce on March 25 of that year. Three weeks later, Robert went to enlist in the militia.

On July 18, the quiet of the afternoon was suddenly shattered by the blast of a shell hitting a roof near Manassas, Virginia. The Rebel army was encamped there and President Abraham Lincoln decided that quick action needed to be taken. His army was composed of 90-day enlistments which were about to run out. He gave his order to attack.

Kady, Robert and their comrades began marching toward Richmond, in perfect columns of four.

40

Through the heat, the dust and the mud, they marched for miles with Kady carrying the company flag.

On July 21, the battle of Bull Run began. General Ambrose Burnside and the Rhode Island troops lead the attack which sent ammunition exploding like fireworks. The cries of the dying filled the air and the blood of the wounded covered the ground. Kady Southwell stood in the center of it all, guarding the flag she had been entrusted with.

In August, the 1st Rhode Island Infantry disbanded. Kady's service to her country had been fulfilled. But somewhere in the course of the madness, she had fallen in love with Robert Brownell and he was going to re-enlist. Unwilling to let him face the war alone, she went with him to sign up for the 5th Rhode Island Infantry.

After a 14-mile march toward the advance on New Bern in 1862, Kady's company came under attack. While guarding the flag once again, she also attended to the suffering soldiers around her. Soon, she discovered that the wounded included Robert. His thigh had been penetrated by a Minnie ball on the battlefield and he was transported to the Soldier's Relief Hospital.

It took Robert several months to recover from his wounds and Kady never left his side. On November 7, 1863, they were married in Providence.

Kady Southwell Brownell, retired from the military life, was granted a veteran's pension of $8.00 a month and left a mark on history that her father would have been proud of.

STARTING A REVOLUTION
THE GASPEE

Sabin's Tavern in Providence where the burning of the Gaspee was planned.
*Originally published in the 1902 book State of Rhode Island and Providence Plantations: A History.

The struggle for American independence was becoming severe. The British had positioned vessels around our waters for the purpose of inspecting all incoming ships for cargo that needed to be taxed according to the trade laws of Great Britain.

The eight-gun schooner, the Gaspee, was stationed at Newport Harbor on the morning of June 9, 1772. Its captain, British Navy Lieutenant William Dudingston, was strongly disliked by Rhode Islanders, due to his high level of suspicion and low regard for the colonists.

That evening, as the Gaspee sailed toward an incoming ship which needed to be inspected, the schooner was lead through an obstacle course that would become a defining moment in American history.

As the Gaspee neared Namquid Point, it ran too close to shore and became grounded. The tide was not scheduled to turn until the following morning to free the vessel, so Captain Dudingston and his crew settled down for the night below decks.

Word of the beached Gaspee spread through town quickly, accompanied by the beat of a drum as a young man made his way down the streets of Newport, announcing the predicament of the British.

John Brown, a merchant from Providence, suddenly got an idea. He gathered his friends Benjamin Page, Turpin Smith, John Mawney, Abraham Whipple, John Hopkins, Ephraim Bowen, Benjamin Dun and Joseph Bucklin together at Sabin's Tavern. In the back room of the bar, the group on men planned what would be the very first attack of the Revolutionary War.

They perfected their plan until 10:00 p.m. when they loaded their guns and began walking towards Fenner's Wharf. Climbing inside the eight longboats they were able to obtain, the men sailed in the direction of the Gaspee. Once they were within sixty yards of the vessel, they stopped rowing. It was nearly 2:00 a.m. and the sleepy Dudingston came up on deck to see who was approaching the schooner.

"I'm the sheriff!" Whipple yelled.

Bucklin told 19-year-old Bowen to hand him a gun. Within seconds, a shot rang out. The bullet passed through the groin of Dudingston and he slumped onto the deck.

The men then boarded the Gaspee, woke the sleeping crew and ordered them into the other boats. Mawney, at just 22-years-old, had been educated in medicine and he took the captain below decks where he cleaned and dressed his bullet wound before transferring him into another boat. Once everyone was safely off the schooner, John Brown and his men set the vessel on fire.

Destroying a ship belonging to King George was a crime punishable by death. The king ordered that the criminals be found and brought to England to stand trial. A hefty reward was offered to anyone supplying information that lead to the identity of the culprits.

No information was ever given. The identification of Brown and his crew were kept secret by the townspeople who knew them. And the reward went forever unclaimed.

CRIME

POLICE RECORDS OF YESTERDAY
ROBBERIES & AXE ASSAULTS

Hope Valley Post Office.
From the collection of the author: public domain photo.

Train robberies and money counterfeiting, selling illegal liquor and having more than one wife; these were the types of crimes that local law enforcement had to deal with a century ago.

At the very first Hopkinton town council meeting, just two police officers were elected to service the town. There was nothing in the budget allotted for a police department, so the officers served warrants and intervened in disturbances when they were called, and at the end of each month, the two men would be compensated accordingly.

By 1885, the police force grew to include a few more men. A total of $400 was paid out to the officers each year. But by the 1890's, the number fell to just four men, each paid ten dollars a month for their services. At the turn of the century, the force once again was comprised of merely two officers.

At the beginning of the 20th century, local crime seemed to center around alcohol related offenses and robberies. On February 12, 1900, the Hope Valley Post Office and the railroad ticket office were broken into. An investigation showed that entry to the post office was gained by several people leaning against the door. Because the safe had been broken several years before, the thieves easily obtained the thirty-three dollars worth of stamps and twelve dollars worth of silver that was inside.

The safe in the railroad office had been drilled open and its outer walls blown off. Two heavy coats soaked with water and left behind were discovered and thought to have been used by the robbers to muffle the sound of the explosion. Old freight receipts were taken from the safe, as well as fifty-seven cents from the cash drawer. Police also discovered that a basket of eggs which had been atop one of the shelves was missing and egg shells were strewn across the floor.

A nearby wagon shop had been broken into that same night, as well as the railroad tool shed. Items missing from the wagon shop included a chisel. From the tool shed, a bar and sledge had been taken. It was believed that these items were used to perform the robbery. Newspapers of the time reported that police had no suspects in the crime.

Four months after this, a murderous assault took place at Corey Lumberyard in Richmond. Two French-Canadian employees had gotten into a scuffle that morning. One of those men, a Mr. Sandeman, had been drinking heavily that day and the two found themselves engaged in yet another quarrel by nightfall.

Sandeman obtained a shotgun and fired through the other man's chest, face and hand. Several other employees tackled Sandeman and got the gun away from him but he picked up an axe and threatened to kill anyone who interfered. They tackled the man again and got the axe away but Sandeman managed to escape.

He was eventually found four miles from the lumberyard and hauled to Hope Valley by police, where he was locked up and held on $700 bail.

LETTERS FROM THE JAILHOUSE
A YOUNG GIRL'S TALES

Bars on the windows of the jailhouse helped keep criminals in.
Photographer: Alecia Keegan

The former Washington County Jail, which stands on Kingston Hill and is now the site of the Pettaquamscutt Historical Society, is where local criminals of the 19th century were detained until being brought to trial.

During the 1880's, the keeper of the jail was Edward Tucker. He, his wife, and his teenage daughter Georgie Anna lived lives more interesting than most, always in the midst of the criminals locked up downstairs.

The following letters, written to relatives by a young woman who lived with the jail keeper's family and worked in the jail, show what life was like for a teenage girl with a unique job:

The old Washington County Jail in Kingston where the author of the letters lived with the jail-keepers family on the second floor.
Photographer: Kelly Sullivan Pezza

June 1882

"You must shut your eyes when you go passed them bars. I am very sorry I poked my head over. I wish I had stayed back. I dreamt one night they carried me down there and said I could stay. I asked them for what. They undertook to tell me. I said I would not stay down in there and I started up, and I woke up."

July 1882

"We have got someone in jail now. His name is John Baptiste. He would not support his wife and children, and everything she got he would eat up from them. The town helps them. He is a real stout looking man, only he walks lame. I expect he likes to stay in jail because he was in here last spring. Georgie said she thought it was because he gets enough to eat and wear, and I don't believe he cares one bit for his folks at home... I hear John thumping in the jail. I am really afraid. Last night, someone brought a man here and he seems like a drunken man. He hollered as loud as he could after he was put in jail. It is awful that anyone would get drunk.

His name is John Kerrens. He was drunk. He thumps all the time. Now I hope he is not going to have the delirium tremens while in here."

September 1882
"One of them in jail had a fit, John Perry. It kind of frightened me. I ran into the barn and told Mr. Tucker and Georgie got the lantern and the keys, and it was quite a while before he came out of it. It must be dreadful to stay in there so long. It would almost kill me if I thought I had to go in there to stay."

October 1882
"I think they in jail must be glad, for the court is next week and they must be tried. But they do swear dreadfully. We got another one here in jail. He is a soldier. There was a young girl here today to see him. She was quite pretty. Some man has come here tonight to give bonds for him. Poor young man. I almost pity him. He looks so sad and today I thought I saw him crying. Oh, do you think he feels sorrow as those who drink? There are others that feel it that would not touch liquor."

January 1883
"Mother and Bella were here today. I took them in jail and then I come out and shut the door on them. I only kept them in just a minute."

February 1883
"We have got a man in jail. I do not know what is the matter with him. They are trying to make out if he is crazy. He seems real funny. He wanted a rope. Mr. Tucker would not let him have one. Then he thought he would climb up on the gate and fall off and break his neck. Mr. Tucker told him that was of no use, for he

should hear him. He told Mr. Tucker the next day that he had given up killing himself.

April 1883

"I hear someone at the door. I think it is a tramp. Yes, it is. It has come in and gone in jail. I have been down and got their supper. There were two of them."

September 1883

"We have four in jail now. One I don't think is more than fifteen years old. I suppose you would like to know how many diners I have got today. Five. One is making us a little visit for stoning the cars. He hollers at us when we go by the jail. Georgie told her father but he said all we can do is to pay no attention to them."

COUNTY'S LAST EXECUTION
THOMAS MOUNT

Plaque designating the old Washington County Jail a nationally recognized historic structure.
Photographer: Kelly Sullivan Pezza

Thomas Mount was born in New Jersey in 1764. His parents never married and his life was one of instability as well as unpredictability.

At the age of eleven, he ran away from home, boarded a ship and spent his childhood upon the sea until he was old enough to enlist in the Army. Soon after becoming a Continental soldier, Mount discovered that he was more dedicated to the causes of the British than those of the colonists. Abandoning his post, he jumped aboard another ship and continued a life of seafaring until he grew bored of staring out at the ocean's waves. Unable to find the excitement he craved, he thought back to what used to excite him as a child. The memory that glimmered in his mind was that of robbing orchards. He had been notorious as a child thief and a life of crime seemed to be calling to him again. While docked at Newport, he planned out a crime which sounded amusing to him and enlisted the help of two other men, William Stanton and James Williams, to carry it out.

The trio broke into a Newport mill where Mount was sure they could find crowbars. The crowbars were needed for the master plan, which was to break into the store attached to Joseph Potter's house and rob it of money and merchandise. But before robbing the store, they next broke into a grain mill and emptied out sacks of grain so that they would have something to carry the loot out in. They pulled the whole thing off, went to Stanton's house where they divided up the $800 worth of money, cotton, silks and fabrics they had scored and went their separate ways.

However, Williams was caught. In exchange for turning the others in, no charges were brought against him. Mount only made it as far as Voluntown, Connecticut before he was arrested. Most of the stolen goods were later found stashed in barns in Stonington and Groton. At the Kingston Court House, Mount and Stanton were brought to trial on charges of breaking into the mill, found guilty and sentenced to receive a public whipping of twenty lashes. But then Mount was ordered to stand trial for the separate charge of robbing the store. His sentence was a bit more severe. He was to be hanged by the neck until dead.

While awaiting his death sentence, Mount was held in Washington County Jail. Locked up, the 27-year-old wrote a poem which read, *"Thomas Mount is my name and to my shame I cannot deny. In New Jersey I was born, and in Little Rest now I must die."*

The Pettaquamscutt Historical Society in Kingston, formerly the Washington County Jail.
Photographer: Kelly Sullivan Pezza

Row of jail cells at the old Washington County Jail. Thomas Mount was locked in the cell at the far end of the wall.
Photographer: Kelly Sullivan Pezza

      Confessions began to spill out of Mount from his cell. He claimed to have committed nearly a hundred robberies in his young life, most of which he got away with. For those in which he had been caught and found guilty of, he had done time in Connecticut,

Massachusetts, Pennsylvania and Virginia, and had managed to break out of every jail he had ever been held in.

In light of this information, a dozen extra guards were hired to keep watch over Mount while he was incarcerated in Kingston. The armed men even followed him out to the west side of the jailhouse on May 27, 1791 as he walked to his execution.

He was buried behind a stone wall on the jailhouse property, the last person ever executed in Washington County.

IMPRISONED IN MINE
WELLS BAGGS

Old postcard of Newgate Prison in 1908, Granby, CT. Public domain image.

Each drop of water that falls to the ground echoes through the dark cavern. Where the screams and anguish of men once resonated off the rocky walls, an eerie silence is left, interrupted only by this rhythmic watery patter.

Old Newgate Prison in East Granby, Connecticut was founded as a copper mine in 1707. By 1773, the copper business had become very unprofitable and the mine was transformed into a prison for Revolutionary War prisoners. Even after the war ended, its use as a prison continued.

The fortress stands behind a massive granite wall. The passing of the centuries has crumbled much of the above-ground structure, but what remains is haunting. Pieces of weathered wood jut out of granite, evidence of long lost partitions. Windows, with their steel bars still intact, look out over a sprawling valley which once must have been thought of as *freedom*. One bar, neatly sawed halfway through, is evidence of one man's aborted attempt to escape. But it was the well shaft, 38 feet deep and where ore was once hoisted up from the mine, which was the most popular means of escape for prisoners.

A myriad of pathways upon the prison grounds leads past the ruins of the chapel, the hospital, and the grain mill where some of the prisoners worked.

Others who were incarcerated toiled in the nail shop, which was the scene of a riot breaking out in 1823 after several prisoners made keys out of their clothing buttons and unlocked their chains. That was the year Wells Crandall Baggs of Richmond became a prisoner at Newgate. Arrested for forgery in New London on February 12 of that year, he was sentenced to four years imprisonment.

Today, heavy chains still hang from the prison's ceilings. On the floors, chains and shackles are bolted to massive pieces of granite. Wooden bunks stick out from the walls of the cells like empty shelves. The sick prisoners lived and died here. Those who were in good health, were imprisoned in the structure's depths.

The stairs which lead down into the former mine descend 65 feet underground. With each step, the temperature seems to drop a dozen degrees. The smell of musty wetness rises off the large rocky ledges that surround the length of the mine's tunnel. Through the darkness, copper-tinted boulders glisten with water. At the end of the tunnel is the solitary confinement cell. Literally a small, dark cave, it reeks with the damp fear of those who were once chained there, so far from the light of day.

Along with the prison's toppling structures and crumbling walls, their presence seems to remain. Their names do, crudely carved into one of the prison's old wooden doors.

HELL'S HALF ACRE
PROSTITUTES & STAGECOACHES

Washington County is filled with little towns and hamlets with names like *Peace* Dale and *Hope* Valley...all bringing to mind a picture of innocent times past. Yet the past wasn't all that innocent. At the intersection of Widow Sweet's Road and Congdon Mill Road in West Greenwich is a little tract of land once known as Hell's Half Acre.

During the 1880's, Rhode Island began to have trouble with what people referred to as abandoned women. These women, in an effort to support themselves, gave a whole new meaning to the term working girl. City officials wanted the women to vacate the bawdy houses they lived in and cease giving the county an aura of disrepute.

The New London Turnpike was strewn with saloons and inns that catered to weary travelers. A gentleman could change horses, grab a meal, enjoy a drink, play a game of cards or rent a room for the night. As this was the main throughway, hundreds of carriages passed daily. Inside some of the inns, the women of ill repute sat at the bar dressed in the finest silks and linens. But now and then, they would venture outside to stand in front of the establishment and wave carriage drivers over with a smile.

Sometimes the girls would all pile into a carriage and drive around to nearby mills where they would invite the male workers to come spend their money on drinks, dice and a little female company.

The inns at the West Greenwich intersection were boisterous and well known to local disapproving residents, such as a local minister who visited the establishments in an effort to save the lost women. Finally realizing it was of no use, he christened the corner "Hell's Half Acre".

THE EVILS OF ALCOHOL
NO MORE DRUNKS THAN USUAL

Everyone knows that over-indulgence in spirituous liquors can lead to no good. But towards the end of the 19th century, imbibing in drink was looked upon as the ultimate in horrific behavior.

Locals who partook of such refreshments were considered by their tea-totaling neighbors to be sinners, and the houses where such refreshments were served were deemed embarrassments to society.

In the 1870's temperance groups sprouted up all over Rhode Island for the purpose of educating people on the perils of alcohol. Many followed the temperance movement religiously. Others simply let the good times roll. Following, are some items that appeared in the Wood River Advertiser during the 1870's:

There were several glorious drunks in and about our villages on the Fourth.

The last Saturday in June was duly observed at Beach Pond by fighting, drinking and racing horses.

Some of the Connecticut villages which voted 'no license' recently, seem to have as much rum as usual.

William Collins of Westerly caused quite a stir a few evenings since, having imbibed a little too freely of the unlicensed and challenging everybody to fight him. His friends succeeded in getting him home.

Thanksgiving to Christmas passed off quietly. No more drunks than usual.

Last Monday evening, three men reeling drunk went passed enroute to Rockville. One of them seemed to have more than he could carry as he fell several times.

Hiram Greene, well known in this vicinity, was shot while attempting to enter the house of Nathan Crumb of North Stonington last Friday night. He was buried in the Wood River Cemetery on Sunday. The shooting caused quite a stir. The Solemnity of an occasion so terrible as to lead every sober, conscientious man to ask himself 'What am I doing to rescue my brother man from the curse of rum?'

Last Wednesday night, a man was found lying aside the road drunk and sick. Restoratives were applied and, after a while, he was able to go home. It is rumored that he procured his drink at a house on the hill on the Hopkinton side of the river.

It's made to sound as if one is unable to pass through Cross Mills without getting drunk.

The principle excitement for the week has been the prosecution and trial of parties on the Westerly side of the river, for the illegal sale of intoxicating liquor. The persons were Michael and Charles Keegan (13 indictments), T.A. Carpenter (7 indictments), Simon Sullivan and his clerk (7 or 8 indictments), E.G. Champlin & Co., A.B. Collins and G.H. Knowles (druggists), Larkin & Co. and J. Crandall. Keegan, Carpenter and Sullivan were found guilty on nearly all complaints. E.G. Champlin & Co. were found not guilty.

Last Saturday night, a man was found drunk and asleep near the depot. He was kindly cared for by some boys who put him under a dry goods case, covered it with stones and burdock leaves and left him to sleep off his drunkenness.

At the funeral of Francis Sheffield, a half rum-crazed Irishman took Captain George Bliven's carriage and horses from in front of the house and drove off.

A New London woman is credited with drinking a half barrel of ale in eight days.

INTOXICATION
THE TEMPERANCE MOVEMENT

Old illustration depicting the Temperance Movement.
Courtesy of Wikipedia.org: public domain photo.

It was a time of speak-easies and bootleggers, rum runners and a wide Christian belief that the devil was working his evil magic through the use of alcoholic beverages. It was a time of freedom for women who lopped off both their long hair and their long skirts to become flappers, and for men who were being afforded more financial opportunities than ever before.

But in 1918, for those who made their living selling liquor, and those who delighted in the effects of it, it was suddenly a time of difficulty that would define an era – an era known as Prohibition.

For the people of Washington County, the prohibition of alcohol began long before the law was enacted. The first temperance movement in the area began in the 1830's in Ashaway. Led by Lester and Isaac Crandall, well-known tea-totalers, a presentation was given to the town on the evils of drinking. Jacob Babcock, Jairus Crandall and Benjamin Potter made a temperance pact and the section of town they resided in became known as Temperance Valley.

Fifty years later, women marched from their churches to their local saloons to preach against the evil going on inside. On November 10, 1882, Mrs. William Dyer of Hope Valley formed the Richmond and Hopkinton Women's Christian Temperance Union.

Many people felt that liquor was the underlying cause of crime, poverty and violence. In 1900, Charles Fuller and the State of Rhode Island filed suit against Rudolph Schaub of Hopkinton, for appearing drunk on Elm Street. Three witnesses testified that Schaub was not drunk, while two others swore that he was. Schaub was found guilty and ordered to pay a fine of one dollar.

Most Hopkinton residents felt that Richmond was not doing enough to stop liquor consumption. They claimed liquor continued to be easily obtainable there and that Hopkinton residents were being lured over the town line.

The people of Richmond felt the opposite way and the two towns battled. The Hope Valley Advertiser reported that the illegal liquor business allegedly being carried out in Richmond *"will make history"*. That town's attorney, John Kenyon, stated that Richmond residents were the ones who were getting sick and tired of having *"the drunkards of Hopkinton come over into Richmond, causing disturbances and staggering around the streets."*

Feds dump out illegal alcohol during the Prohibition Era.
From the collection of the Chicago Daily News at the Chicago
Historical Society.
Courtesy of Wikipedia.org: public domain photo.

In 1918, the 18th Amendment to the Constitution was passed, making it illegal to manufacture, sell or transport alcohol. But in 1933, that amendment was repealed. It was believed that banning drink was costing too many people jobs, and that while the prohibition of alcohol was supposed to deter crime, it was perhaps creating it.

Today there is no need for secret knocks on back doors, or the exchange of crates in quiet alleys. Richmond residents cross over into Hopkinton for their spirits and vice versa. And others are content with just a simple cup of tea.

COUNTERFEITING
SAMUEL CASEY

Our local towns were once made up of sprawling farms and large rural estates. Orchards, groves and cornfields were planted, kept up and passed down through the generations. But what allowed some residents to prosper while others continued to struggle? Was it counterfeit money that some local legacies were built upon?

Samuel Casey was a silversmith who lived in Exeter with his wife Martha and their six children. Known as *Silver Sam*, he had a reputation for being one of the most proficient craftsmen in the area.

In 1746, the 40-year-old Casey suffered a major business loss when the fire in the forge of his shop ignited the interior of the chimney. Leaving the burned ruins of his livelihood behind, he removed with his family to Kingston and built a new shop there. Over time, he acquired new friends and employees, and with each person who joined his inner circle, a threat grew greater...the threat that one of them would expose Samuel for something highly illegal.

Fellow silversmith William Reynolds and Hopkinton resident William Coon counted themselves among Casey's close associates. For quite a while, the three men had been meeting at Reynolds house in Richmond to melt down silver and gold on the equipment Reynolds possessed. But they were not making jewelry or house wares. They were turning out counterfeit coins and bank notes.

With an array of chemicals and dyes, the men traced impressions on blank notes and molded elements into hundreds of coins. Then, in 1770, everything went awry. That year, a local innkeeper was arrested for having counterfeit cash in his possession. The innkeeper told authorities where he had obtained the money and soon the trail lead straight to Samuel Casey. During the search of his house, quite a bit of evidence was found against him. Enough to haul him and Reynolds into Kings County Superior Court.

A witness at the trial told the court that Casey had once confessed that his counterfeit money had exchanged hands during several local business transactions, specifically the purchase of a farm in Hopkinton by Benjamin Barber.

When the verdict came in, Casey was sentenced to death by hanging. But he never made it to the noose. While he was being held in jail awaiting his fate, a gang of men ambushed the jailhouse. With their faces painted black, they wielded axes and crowbars, smashing apart Casey's cell and freeing Silver Sam. The eleven men who made up the gang were eventually caught and arrested. Among them was Nathan Barber, the son of the man who had bought the Hopkinton farm. But Casey got away.

During his long absence, his wife petitioned the state of Rhode Island to grant her husband a pardon. Her request was honored, making it possible for Casey to return home without further persecution. But Silver Sam never came back. Where and how he died may never be known. Perhaps he ventured on to change his life for the better. Or perhaps he simply took his counterfeiting business elsewhere. But the results of his creative forgery may still stand all around us.

THE GYPSIES ARE COMING
GYPSIES, TRAMPS & THIEVES

Mr. O.A. Clarke offered a large reward for assistance in finding out who stole his corn.
Image courtesy of Wikipedia.org: public domain photo.

Gypsies, tramps and thieves…usually the stuff of far out tales. But Rhode Island once abounded with such people. Gypsy caravans often traveled through Washington and Kent counties, setting up camp in the sprawling field where Canob Park now stands, as well as the fields that were near Wood River Cemetery. With no routes or permanent employment, they often had to steal to survive. The following items appeared in the Wood River advertiser during the late 19th century:

*The town of Hopkinton bills ordered to be paid by the town treasurer include: to J.D. Witter, $5.50, for the entertainment of eight tramps.

*Sixty-three tramps found food and shelter during the month of January at the East Greenwich Asylum.

*Look out for a tramp swindler who is trying to sell a recipe for making a pound of butter from a pint of milk.

*Last Sunday, eleven-year-old John Bliven of Exeter was accosted by a tramp who, after enticing him over a wall and into a field, demanded what money he had. The boy said he had no money. He was then ordered to pull off his boots. The boy hesitated to comply until he was threatened with a club. After taking off his boots, he was ordered to proceed on his way, and told that if he made any noise he would be killed. Alarm was then given and pursuit was made without success. The boots were left on the spot where they were taken.

*One night last week, the barn of Joseph Tabor of Rockville was entered, and three or four bushels of meal and corn stolen. On Saturday, a sheep was taken from the flock of Ira D. Palmer and butchered on the spot and the carcass carried off. That same night, a quantity of oats and meal was taken from the barn of the Rockville Company. At Moscow, a lot of hens belonging to a poor widow were taken from their roost. It is supposed that a gang of thieves, not far off, get their living by depredations on those who subsist by honest labor.

*A band of gypsies encamped near Wood River Church last Friday and stayed until Tuesday when they took their line of march westward.

*A buggy and harness was found in the woods last Saturday between Pawtucket and Providence. It is probably stolen property.

*Some person, probably having an axe to grind, stole a grindstone from in front of T.B. Segar's store. By applying at the store, they can have the shaft, crank, friction rolls and other appurtenances belonging with the stone.

*Sunday evening of last week, James C. Eldred and Annanias Robinson of Usquepaug were returning from Wyoming when, near the turn in the road just south of H.P. Clarke's, a person caught their horse by the bridle and stopped them. With a pistol in his hand, he demanded of them to hand over their money. Mr. Eldred gave his horse a sharp cut with the whip, when he jumped and threw the would-be robber to the ground. The sleigh passed over him before the sleigh could be stopped. Mr. Eldred kept on his way home without further molestation.

*A bold and desperate attempt at highway robbery was made Tuesday morning of last week in the village of Wickford. As Horatio Reynolds was proceeding homeward from his store, a ruffian ran up behind him, seized him by the arms and demanded his money or his life, at the same time throwing him down and searching for his money. His cries for help brought a man to his assistance, who was shot at by the would-be robber who then fled. Mr. Reynolds was attacked in the same manner a few years ago.

*If the person who steals our wood will leave their name at this office, we will save them the trouble by having the next load hauled to their wood pile.

*While Mr. Charles Randall and family, of Voluntown, were away from home on Sunday, thieves entered their house and gave it a general ransacking. They carried off about six dollars, half a dozen pies, and other eatables. The thieves were tracked as far as Rockville.

*Two men from East Providence drove into this place last Thursday, peddling oysters. The next day one of them broke into the house of Silas Beverly and stole a quantity of wearing apparel. The theft was discovered by his trying to sell the articles, which were recognized by a lady friend of Mrs. Beverly. He was pursued and the goods recovered by his leaving them in the road and taking to his heels. He next stopped at Isaac Barber's on Skunk Hill Road. After talking for a spell, he started on, carrying with him Mr. Barber's axe. He stopped at several places, asked for cider and tried to trade axes. At Rockville School, he stole two caps from the entry. He sold the axe to a man in the village for forty cents, stating that he was tired of carrying it as he could not get any wood to chop. Mr. Barber came to Rockville and recovered his axe. The young man who bought it, with eight other men, started in pursuit of the thief and overtook him near Grassy Pond Schoolhouse. They compelled him to refund the money and a curry comb and brush he had taken from the barn at the Rockville Manufacturing Company.

*Five dollars reward will be given for evidence that will lead to the conviction of the thief or thieves that destroyed five hives of bees and took the honey there from on the night of July 20; Contact Moses B. Lewis, Hopkinton.

Mr. Greene had no ill will toward the person who stole Bibles from his store.
Courtesy of the Gladys Segar Collection at Langworthy Public Library.

*Twenty-five dollar reward. Mr. Clarke stated that the neighborhood of Rockville is very much troubled with thieves and by offering the reward, he expects to get the required evidence against the parties, although he is well satisfied where his corn went to and only requires a few missing links to the chain of circumstances. It is also suggested that it is no use to steal tools, as the state prison will furnish all that is desired when they arrive, which they certainly will if their depredations are not stopped. The twenty-five dollar reward will be paid for sufficient evidence to convict the following: Five dollars for the person that entered my cornfield on the nights of the 2nd and 3rd of October and carried away several bushels of corn. Five dollars for the person that broke into my blacksmith shop and left as I was about to enter on September 20th before midnight. Ten dollars for the recovery of shingles stolen from near my new house on the 1st of July. And one dollar each to the five suspicious persons if they can prove *they were not on my premises the above dates; Contact O.A. Clarke.*

A pan of biscuits, just taken from the oven by Mrs. S.C. Carr of Ashaway and left for a few minutes to cool, was appropriated by an unknown individual.

Two Bibles were stolen from the counter of G.E. Greene's store last week. Mr. Greene says if the purloiners will make a proper use of them, he will ask no questions.

Thieves helped themselves to clothes belonging to Mrs. F.M. Robinson, hanging on a line at Ashaway.

JUVENILE INCARCERATION
SENTENCED TO SOCKANOSSET

There was a time when crime was simply crime. It didn't matter if the criminal was 13 or 30, the punishment was still the same. Under the English rules of the 17th and 18th centuries, children who committed unlawful acts were imprisoned or hanged just as adults were. There were no juvenile counselors or training programs to get a young person's life back on track. Children's problems were their own problems, not the government's.

It was not until the 1800's that it became clear another approach had to be taken. Children with troubled lives often followed a path that led to criminal behavior. Locking them up with adults was not the answer. For there in jail, the children only gained more knowledge of delinquency from the experienced criminals. While the older generation was basically deemed a lost cause as far as the legal system was concerned, many people began to believe that children could be rehabilitated.

In 1824, the very first American institution for delinquent children opened in New York. It was called the House of Refuge. Many other states jumped on the bandwagon and opened their own institutions for wayward children. The state of Rhode Island purchased two large farms for the purpose of establishing the Sockanosset School for Boys. The William Howard farm and the abutting Stukely farm contained 667 acres upon which several structures were built between 1881 and 1895.

Five dormitories were built to house the troubled boys. Referred to as cottages, each dorm housed boys of specific age groups. Sockanosset quickly became well known as the destination for young Rhode Island males who were unwilling to follow the law. By 1900, the school contained over 300 boys who had been placed there by the courts to serve out a two-year work instruction program.

Sockanosset maintained several different departments of study geared toward offering each inmate the knowledge of a specific trade. It was hoped that this type of education would enable the boys to obtain work once they were released, and allow them to go on and live honest, prosperous lives.

The carpentry department taught boys building skills by having them make all the structural repairs in the school. The inmates assigned to the engineering department tended to the school's boilers and pumps. Those in the shoe department were responsible for the repair of all inmates' shoes, while those studying tailoring were given the tasks of mending clothing and doing laundry.

A printing department taught boys the skill of journalism and a school newspaper, *The Howard Times*, was put out regularly. Future blacksmiths, masons and machine workers were also prepared for life on the outside.

In addition to employment training, regular schooling took place for three hours per day, five days a week. Studies included reading, writing, arithmetic, spelling, physiology and history. Each summer, the boys were awarded a two-week vacation.

The school maintained a large garden and the boys were expected to sow and reap their own produce, as well as prepare their own meals.

As more modern ways of treating juvenile delinquency have evolved, and newer structures have been erected for that purpose, the past falls into history. The decrepit buildings long stood against the horizon like upright skeletons. The rows of large windows, like empty eye sockets, seemingly able to stare out at the world around them. But rumors persisted that the dead buildings were not exactly still. Was the school an institution of learning that helped young boys eventually live better lives than the ones they were heading for? Or was it a dungeon, rampant with abuse that forever scarred the bodies and the souls of the young? Many people believe the latter to be true, and that the restless spirits of those who died while incarcerated there are still screaming out for mercy.

WARNINGS OUT
THE PLIGHT OF PAUPERS

Almost everyone, at some point in their lives, has fallen upon hard times. An illness may keep you in bed and unable to work, lack of available jobs may find you pinching pennies. People faced the same hardships centuries ago, only there was no workman's compensation or unemployment benefits to help them get on their feet again. Back then, if you could not maintain your livelihood, you were literally driven out of town.

During the 18th and 19th centuries, every adult "belonged" to a specific town. The town one originally belonged to was the one in which he or she was born. However, if one moved to another location and maintained property there for a period of five years, that became their new town of belonging. A married woman took on her husband's town as her own, unless she owned property and he didn't.

Each town had an Overseer of the Poor, whose job it was to set up employment or residential situations for paupers. Unfortunately many of the poor were elderly or sick and unable to perform physical work. The town financially supported its own needy residents at the local poorhouse if the resident had no family members to help support him or her. Those who refused to financially support a poor family member could be fined.

Paupers who found themselves in towns which they did not legally belong to, were given a "warning out". This meant they were brought before the town council and asked to explain what they were doing there. After determining in which town the pauper legally belonged, he or she would be placed in a wagon and deposited there. Those who owned no land and therefore belonged nowhere, were transported to the state almshouse.

There were extremely heavy fines for anyone caught sheltering a person who had been warned out. Fines were also imposed on anyone who knowingly brought a poor non-resident into town.

On January 25, 1759, the Hopkinton Town Council informed a transient named Latham Clarke that he must either depart from the town immediately, or appear before the council at a future date to explain what right he felt he had to reside in Hopkinton.

On May 14, 1759, Clarke stood before the council and declared that he came from Shrewsbury, New Jersey *"about fours years past from last Christmas."* He stated that he had owned a piece of land in Shrewsbury with a house on it but had sold it for thirty pounds. Since that time, he said, he had obtained no new legal residency. Under New Jersey law, any legal resident of a town who was absent from that town for more than one year and one day, lost their settlement rights.

The town council decided to review the situation and on July 30, 1759 brought Clarke before them again to determine where he had been born. Town council records state that *"according to the best information that ever he hath had, he was born in Rhode Island in the town of Newport, in a house that was formerly Governor Cranston's."* The council decided, since Clarke was liable to become chargeable on the town, that the Town Sergeant would carry him over to Newport and deliver him to the Overseer of the Poor there. Nathan Burdick was paid twenty pounds out of Hopkinton funds to transport Clarke back to where he belonged.

On January 8, 1868, Hopkinton's Overseer of the Poor informed the town council that *"Samuel Titus, a lunatic, now resides in said town of Hopkinton, not having therein gained a legal settlement. Wherefore I pray said council to order his removal to the Butler Hospital for the Insane or take such action in the case as may be deemed proper."*

Old town council records from any given Rhode Island town provide details of all people who had been warned out. Women with illegitimate children, widowed mothers, mentally ill men and physically sick elders were shooed out right along with run-of-the-mill bums. During the 18th century alone, over 2,000 people were warned out of Rhode Island towns.

INDIAN BURIAL GROUNDS
THE GRAVE DIGGERS

In the summer of 1859, a new project was about to begin in Charlestown. A group of local men would be organized to undertake the project and report their findings. Joshua P. Card, John Congdon, Charles Cross, Asa Noyes, George F. Babcock, Christopher P. Card, Oliver Fisk, Samuel Noka and Benoni Henry made up the group. Their mission? To excavate the gravesites of local Indians so that it could be ascertained in what manner the Native Americans buried their dead.

The nine men ventured out to the Narragansett Indian Royal Burying Ground about one mile northeast of Cross Mills. With their excavating tools in hand, they climbed up the small elevation which held the bodies of local sachems and their families. Part of their duties were to look for and collect any funerary objects in the graves, as legend had it that Indians buried their dead with an array of different items. So in the name of science, the final resting places of those interred at the Royal Burying Ground were disturbed.

While opening the first grave, the men found that two large flat stones had been placed several feet above the body. The remains were encased in a single log, split in four pieces to create the top, bottom and sides of a crude coffin. The coffin was held together by heavy iron chains encircling it. At one end of the grave, the group discovered a brass kettle, at the other end a kettle made of iron.

Once the project was completed, the men returned to the village of Cross Mills with dozens of artifacts they had removed from the graves. The collection in most part was sent to Brown University in Providence, to be studied.

Members of the Narragansett Indian tribe were not about to simply accept the fact that the sacred slumber of their loved ones had been destroyed for the purpose of scientific research. Joshua Noka, Gideon Ammons and Henry Hazard brought a lawsuit against the nine men, for disturbing the graves and robbing them of burial relics. The group was rounded up and brought to the courthouse in Kingston where they were arraigned by Judge Joseph H. Griffin. In the end they were acquitted and exonerated of any blame.

Four years later, 75-year-old Dr. Usher Parsons of Providence, visited the Royal Burying Ground for the purpose of adding to his collection of scientific curiosities. Parsons had spent many years as a Navy surgeon and had honorary degrees from Harvard, Dartmouth and Brown universities. A past vice president of the American Medical Association, he had also worked as a professor of anatomy and had a particular fascination with the history of the Narragansett Indians. While at the cemetery, he excavated a grave from which he took the thigh bone of an adult male skeleton. His later studies of the bone concluded that the burial had probably taken place around the year 1660.

The next grave he opened appeared to contain the body of an Indian princess. Of certain interest to him was that the remains included hair of a tubercular structure. The conclusion of this dig was that the male body belonged to that of Indian Sachem Ninigret and the female body to his daughter Weunquest, whom he left rulership to when he died in 1676.

All remains and artifacts collected from Parson's excavation and that of 1859 were housed at Brown University until the Peabody Museum of Archeology at Harvard took custody of them in 1923. The collection contained the thigh bone, an adult female skull, a brass container, a silver container with handles and a link chain, kettle fragments, two pieces of a silver chain, a leather sole and pieces of a brass sole, fragments of glass, remnants of a knife, two circular pins, an oval metal ring, and a glass container with liquid inside it.

In September of 1912, another group trudged up the hill at the Royal Burying Ground, with excavating tools and plans to further science by exhuming the dead. Dr. Harris Hawthorne Wilder, of Smith College in Northhampton, Massachusetts, brought along his wife Dr. Inez Whipple Wilder and two assistants to help him with the exhumations, collection and recording of artifacts. Wilder had obtained permission for the dig from the owners of the land, the heirs of James S. Kenyon.

While planning the project, Dr. Wilder had drawn a map of the cemetery and marked ten of the plots as excavation areas. All ten graves were opened and two were found to be empty with signs of having been previously dug up. Atop one of the empty graves was a stone baring the epitaph *"Ninigret, George, son of Charles, King of the Natives and his wife Hannah 1731 – 12-22-1732."*

The Wilders recorded each item discovered in the graves. These included pieces of cloth, metal and wood coffin fragments, shroud pins and skeletons. The artifacts they collected, including the human remains of eight bodies, were taken to the Smith College laboratory and exhibited in the college's Anthropological and Zoological Museum as *"Skeletons of People from the Narragansett Reservation"*. In 1966, the college loaned the remains and artifacts to the University of Massachusetts where they were added to the school's anthropology department collection.

In 1990, a federal law was passed called The Native American Graves Protection & Repatriation Act. Under the law, all museums and federal agencies were ordered to return all Native American human remains, funerary objects and other sacred artifacts to the federally recognized Indian tribes they belonged to. Since the law went into effect, thousands of remains and artifacts have been returned to tribal descendents.

Although the majority of universities and museums are adhering to the law, it has not completely stopped the disruption of burial sites, Indian or otherwise. Gravestones are removed and entire family burial grounds are regularly obliterated when modern industry calls for bigger parking lots or the need for more roads. Disruption is usually no longer for scientific study but for the convenience of building or embellishment. It is a sad notation to what we are willing to forsake, whether it be in the name of science or modernization. Burial grounds are all sacred places, regardless of race, religion or stature. And those who sleep there should forever go undisturbed.

"B" IS FOR BLASPHEMY
BRANDED FOR LIFE

Criminals were often given a public whipping before being branded with a hot iron.
Image provided by PDImages.com: public domain image.

Today it is fairly easy for a former criminal to conceal the events of his past from new acquaintances. Court files, police records and other legal documentation are about the only means of gaining information concerning a jaded history.

But centuries ago, one needed to only look at a person to discover what crimes they had been accused and found guilty of. Criminals bore their punishment upon their bodies for the rest of their lives.

Under English law, a number of devices were used to punish those who had legally erred. Each town maintained a wooden pillory where punishments were carried out by clamping down one's head and hands. While confined there, the criminal could expect to undergo any number of painful inflictions.

Ear cropping was a popular form of attempting to teach a lawbreaker a lesson. As crimes of the time included such minor things as being in debt, it wasn't unusual for a town to contain several residents with pieces of their ears missing.

Another method of punishment was performed with a branding iron. After being heated over hot coals, the iron was pressed into the flesh of the criminal, a specific letter forever identifying the wrong he had done.

Although the branding irons pictured were for use on animals, the same type was used for branding humans.
Photo courtesy of Wikipedia.org: public domain photo.

For committing blasphemy, one was branded on the tongue with the letter B.

Hog theft earned the thief an H burned onto the forehead. A man slaughterer received an M on the forehead and forgers got an F.

Rogues were branded on the shoulder with the letter R, and burglars with a B on the right hand.
Those convicted of seditious libel received an S and L on the left cheek and thieves were released with a T burned onto the left hand.

A criminal who was sentenced to death could always plead for the benefit of clergy. This would usually spare them the noose but get them the letter of their crime branded high on one or both cheeks.

On March 16, 1792, 41-year-old Stephen Pettis of Hopkinton was brought to Newport to have his forgery sentence carried out. After standing at the pillory for one hour, both of his ears were cropped and he was branded by a hot iron on both cheeks with the letter F.

In 1771, William Carlisle of Kingston was convicted of counterfeiting and sentenced to stand at the Pillory in Little Rest for one hour. He also had both ears cropped, and the letter designating his crime burned onto both sides of his face.

In 1822, the use of the branding iron as a way to punish criminals was abolished. Unfortunately that decision came too late for the hundreds of men and women who had been maimed and disfigured for life.

PIRATES OF THE ATLANTIC
WILLIAM KIDD

Captain William Kidd.
Image courtesy of Wikipedia.org: public domain image.

In the movies, they sail the high seas, plundering and pillaging. With a jolly roger flying high and chests of loot below decks, pirates were a source of fear, both for Hollywood and in the real world.

In the early days, Rhode Island was a haven for the swashbuckling bandits, and some say their secrets are still here...entombed in the soil of the centuries.

In 1695, William Kidd was commissioned by New York merchants to patrol the east coast for pirates. This allowed Kidd to attack and seize any vessel carrying those who murdered and stole their way across the Atlantic. The 50-year-old Scottish born privateer was so well respected in his work that he was later sent to protect Indian Ocean passages from scoundrels.

But once in Madagascar, Kidd lost his respectable standards. Instead of attacking the pirates there, he found himself enthralled by them and the lives they led. Before long, he was on their side, robbing every ship he had been sent to protect.

When the British government found out about Kidd's new alliance, a warrant for his arrest was issued and he was ordered to return to Britain. Knowing he would be hanged for his actions, Kidd decided to bury his loot and go into hiding. Aboard a small vessel laden with gold, silver, jewels and ivory, Kidd sailed for the shores of the east coast. He docked his boat at Conanicut Island in Jamestown and paid a visit to Thomas Paine.

Paine had also been a privateer who had switched loyalties during his pirate-fighting days. He and Kidd had once been good friends but Paine had since mended his ways and wanted nothing to do with the lifestyle he once advocated. Because of this, he refused Kidd's pleas to hide treasure on his property.

With a new plan in mind, Kidd moved on to Gardiner's Island in New York and quickly buried his loot deep in the sand. Confident that it would be safe until he returned, he went on to Boston. There in Massachusetts, the legend of Captain Kidd would near its end. Officials were waiting.

The infamous pirate was arrested and placed aboard a ship to be taken back to England. Kidd confessed to having hidden his treasure on Gardiner's Island and a group of men were sent there to recover it. Two million dollars worth of diamonds, rubies, gold and silver were excavated.

Kidd was brought to trial and found guilty of murder and piracy. He was sentenced to be hanged and on May 23, 1701, his execution was carried out on a London dock.

Yet Kidd's death did not bring a close to the pirate tales of our area. The work of these olden-day terrorists went on for several more years. Early logs of those sentenced to death on the eastern shore are testimony to the many men who followed William Kidd to the noose.

On July 19, 1723, 26 pirates were executed on Goat Island in Newport, nearly all of them under the age of 30.

Long after Kidd's death, several maps believed to be drawn by him were discovered. Supposedly the maps pinpoint the hiding places of treasure chests around the Indian Ocean.

Considering that so many pirates returned to our shores after their thievery, there is certainly the chance that treasure was buried in the Ocean State, treasure which no maps were left to designate. Yes, somewhere beneath the ground may be riches, much closer to us than the aged pirate legends of the past.

EXECUTED BY ACCIDENT
SACCO & VANZETTI

Sacco and Vanzetti in handcuffs before their trial.
Courtesy of Wikipedia.org: public domain photo.

Convicted robber Celestino Madeiros made a confession from his Dedham, Massachusetts jail cell. Admittedly guilty of the crime he was incarcerated for, he was now claiming that he had also been involved in a murder/robbery.

The robbery, he explained, was planned out by him and several other men at a Providence bar. Sufficient details that backed up his claim were volunteered. But the confession went unaccepted by authorities. And two other men would die for the crime.

Nicola Sacco was born in Italy on April 22, 1891. At the age of 17, he immigrated to the United States. Bartolomeo Vanzetti was also born in Italy on June 11, 1888, and sailed to American the same year as Sacco. The two men met in 1917 while attending an anti-political meeting in Boston. Over the next couple of years, the two became good friends and heavy supporters of anarchist beliefs and organizations.

Vanzetti was employed as a fish salesman in Plymouth, Massachusetts. Sacco worked at a shoe factory in Stoughton. Aside from the radical behaviors of the groups they supported, the two men lived simple existences, which would never have left a mark on history. But an occurrence on April 15, 1920, just one week before Sacco's 29th birthday, would not only change their lives, but turn them into legends.

At 3:00 p.m. on that spring day, Frederick Parmenter, a payroll clerk for the Slater & Morrill Shoe Company of South Braintree, Massachusetts was transporting a payroll of over $15,000 down Main Street. He was accompanied by a guard, Alessandro Beradelli. Suddenly shots rang out, the two men fell to the ground and the box of money was grabbed by two other men who fled toward a waiting Buick.

Suspicion centered on likely culprits, the Morelli gang of Providence. The group was well known to authorities for their history of robberies. But then the suspicions of investigators and police shifted. In the recent past, the behavior of the local anarchy followers had intensified. Bombs had been detonated by them, suicides carried out. It became the common belief that the murder/robbery had been executed by anarchist members. Sacco and Vanzetti were well-known supporters.

Authorities approached the two men on May 5, 1920 and questioned them about their anti-political involvement. Fearing deportation, they lied about their relationship to such establishments. Neither man had a criminal record, yet there was evidence they had taken part in anti-war movements, labor strikes and rallied the rights of the foreign born.

Knowing they lied, authorities arrested them, using their untruthful statements to automatically make them suspects in the murder.

The two men went on trial in the summer of 1921. The defense produced just as much evidence as the prosecution.

Witnesses to the crime changed their testimonies and contradicted their statements over and over, to the dismay of both sides. All agreed there were two men standing on Main Street who suddenly pulled out guns and committed murder. Some said it was definitely Sacco and Vanzetti. Others said the two men they saw that day weren't in the courtroom. Some described the gunmen as heavy, others as sickly. Some mentioned they had dark hair, while others claimed the hair color was light.

The testimony of witnesses only helped to add confusion to both sides of the courtroom. And, to the detriment of the two men on trial, they often gave confusing statements of their own, as neither spoke or understood English perfectly. Not a single Italian sat on the jury and many people felt that prejudice against the foreign born would highly affect the outcome of the trial.

Sacco and Vanzetti's attorney, Fred Moore, told the press that the trial was based on tearing down the Italian anarchist movement, not on his clients' involvement in a murder.

There were questions concerning the police who arrived at the scene, tampering with evidence. A cap found nearby, which witnesses claimed had been worn by one of the shooters, was said by the prosecution to contain strands of Sacco's hair. Yet when Sacco was asked to try the cap on in front of the jury, it didn't fit.

Sacco claimed that at the time of the murder, he was in Boston attempting to obtain a passport to go home to Italy and visit his family. Several witnesses testified they had seen him in Boston at that time.

Vanzetti said he had been in Plymouth at the time the crime was committed, selling his fish to customers. Many people said they had witnessed him working that day. Yet in weighing the evidence during the 6-week trial, the jury found the scales tilted toward the prosecution and the two men were found to be guilty of murder in the first degree.

Appeals for a new trial went on for the next six years. All were denied by Judge Webster Thayer. Eight times, the attorney for Sacco and Vanzetti felt he had found evidence that would clear his clients and each time, the motion to be heard again was turned down. One piece of new evidence was a confession by another man that he, not Sacco and Vanzetti, had committed the crime. Celestino Madeiros claimed that he and six other men pulled off the murder and robbery that fateful day. He described how he and four of the men waited in a nearby Buick, while the other two did the shooting.

It was proven that Joe Morelli, the leader of the Morelli gang to which Madeiros belonged, carried a Colt revolver, the type of gun used to kill the payroll clerk and his guard. It was also proven that Morelli's brother Mike drove the same type of Buick that witnesses saw at the scene of the crime. But that evidence was never allowed to be heard by a jury and Vanzetti and Sacco's final fate was determined on April 9, 1927.

On that day, Judge Thayer announced that the two men would both receive, "the punishment of death by the passage of a current of electricity through the body." Protests broke out around the world. From Paris to London, thousands gathered to fight what they believed to be prejudicial injustice. In a protest rally held in Peabody, Massachusetts on May 22, 7,000 people were warned and removed by police. Of those protesters, 154 were arrested, including famous poet Edna St. Vincent Millay and esteemed author John Dos Passos.

The attempts to hold new trials, the hopes of admitting new evidence, the rallies for justice all failed. On the morning of August 23, 1927, Sacco was lead to the electric chair. At 12:19 he was pronounced dead. Vanzetti immediately followed, his life over at 12:26.

Just before his execution, Sacco said, "Goodbye wife and children. Farewell Mother." Vanzetti continued to proclaim his innocence and insisted that the court knew he was innocent. "I have never stolen or killed, or spilt blood in all my life," he replied. He said that he hoped all people would learn something from what was about to happen, "so that our deaths will not have been in vain."

An early electric chair.
Part of collection at PDImages.com.
Courtesy of Wikipedia.org: public domain photo.

TRAGEDIES

A DROWNING WHILE DUCK HUNTING
EDWARD BENNETT & CHARLES SPENCER

East Greenwich Bay where Edward Bennett and Charles Spencer were killed.
Photographer: Kelly Sullivan Pezza

The waters of East Greenwich Bay rustle about with a quiet fortitude. Yet in the depth of its tranquil beauty, the bay holds memories of sadness.

On Saturday, March 18, 1894, the weather was expected to be perfect for duck hunting. Edward H. Bennett and his cousin Charles P. Spencer rose early that morning, bundled up in warm clothing and arrived at Crompton's Wharf just before 3 a.m. Once in their boat, they started for a small creek near Buttonwood's Shore, having no idea what fate held in store for them that chilly winter day.

Professor Bussey of the East Greenwich Academy was also out duck hunting on the bay that morning. A few minutes past four o'clock, the sound of

95

water lapping up against the side of his boat was suddenly interrupted by another sound, that of a young man screaming.

Bussey looked out toward Chippewanoxette Island where the sound seemed to be coming from but he saw nothing. Rowing his boat in that direction, he searched for the source of the scream but there was nothing to be found and nothing more to be heard.

At 5:30, Bussey decided he had had enough hunting for the day and began to head back to the shore. As he sailed toward the wharf, he noticed four decoy ducks anchored near a red buoy. Figuring someone had forgotten them, he pulled the decoys into his boat and continued on his way. Once at the wharf, he informed Captain John Saunders that someone had left their decoys in the water and that if the owners came back looking for them, they could contact him.

Jared Burdick and Charles Hatch were two other local men who decided to spend that day duck hunting on the bay. For them, the afternoon was pretty uneventful until shortly after 1 p.m. Three hundred yards east of Chippewanoxette Island, they discovered a boat floating upside down in the water. After taking a quick look around for any ejected occupants, they rowed back to the wharf and put together a search party. Those in the party rowed around for several hours and, shortly before sunset, Henry Burdick found three more decoys and a boat oar near the shore of Greene's River.

As darkness falls early in the wintry months of Rhode Island, the search had to be called off until morning. But no sooner had the sun risen again when dozens of men in boats of every size, shape and color dotted the bay looking for any victims there may be.

Two minutes before noontime, one of the searchers gave a shout. About 100 yards east of Chippewanoxette Island, the body of Edward Bennett was floating face down in about four feet of water. He had stripped himself down to his pants, shirt and socks in what must have been a desperate attempt to swim. His two heavy coats, cap and coveralls were found in the water nearby. The time on his wristwatch read 4:07.

The high tide put an end to that day's search and the boats left the water until the following morning. Seine hauls were thrown out and trawling lines were rigged but nothing more was discovered.

It was not until 12:45 on Tuesday afternoon that the body of Charles Spencer was found floating a mere 150 yards from where his cousin had been discovered. His watch also read 4:07.

The schools in East Greenwich closed down so that students could attend the boy's funerals. Spencer, age 16, was the only son of Paul and Susan Spencer. He had been living with Bennett's family while he attended East Greenwich Academy. During summers, when classes weren't in session, he worked as a carriage driver.

Bennett, age 22, was the only son of Delonde and Sarah Bennett. His father had passed away when he was a child and his mother had remarried to Clarence V. Babcock, with whom he lived. He had been a student at East Greenwich Academy and played on the school's football and baseball teams. He worked as a carpenter and had been a member of the Columbia Fire Company and 2nd sergeant in the Kentish Guards. The day before his death, he had gone to Providence to attend a birthday party at the home of his girlfriend, Grace M. Paine. The two were engaged to be married.

DISAPPEARENCE AND DEATH
JOHN ADAMS

John Fanning Adams was the owner of a harness shop in Kingston during the late 19th century. His wife Ann had passed away in 1873 at the age of 44, leaving him alone with six children.

In 1882, the 53-year-old man was living with his daughter Mary and her husband Isaac D. Russell, a stone cutter; his daughter Ida and her husband John B. Wilcox, a carpenter; and his grandchildren. That year, a few weeks before the anniversary of his wife's death, Adams made a decision that shocked the entire town. On the cold morning of December 4, he left his home and family and never returned.

By early evening, a search party was sent out to look for him. As darkness began to fall, the searchers went home and reassembled again at daybreak.

The next morning, 33-year-old carpenter George Briggs located Adams not far from his home. The shop-owner appeared to be leaning quietly up against a tree. Briggs approached him and began to say something when he suddenly noticed a noose encircling the man's neck. John Adams was dead.

A note was found at the house, left for his daughter but written to his brother Samuel. In quickly written, hard-to-decipher sentences, the note stated that Adams felt he should have done this a long time ago and that he hoped Samuel would look after his children and give them good advice.

The following letter, found recently in the attic of a Charlestown home, was written by a Kingston resident, recalling the chilling details of the sad event.

"Monday, December 4, 1882...There has been a terrible accident happened here today. Mr. Adams, George Adams' uncle, has disappeared. He said he was

going to the river to set a trap. People have looked all day for him and have not found him. He dressed up in nearly rags. I do not know as they were rags but they were worse than he general wore. They have given up looking for him tonight. He left a letter directed to his daughter Mary to give to his brother Samuel. He told him that he had left enough to pay his debts. Ate his breakfast this morning.

Tuesday…They have found Mr. Adams this morning. It was only a little ways from where he lived. After he told Mary he was going to set a trap, he came back to the house and said 'Mary, I am going now. Goodbye.' And she never made him any answer and she did not think anything of it until his son-in-law John Wilcocks went to look for him. He has a harness shop on the hill here. I have seen him pass nearly every day."

WRECK IN RICHMOND
THE STEAMBOAT TRAIN

Train Depot at Hope Valley.
From the collection of the author: public domain photo.

Trees were cleared and the ground was broken. Heavy rails and sleepers made of pine, granite, oak and iron were laid out along the three-mile stretch from Quincy, Massachusetts to the Neponset River. It was 1826 and the first railroad in America would soon be a reality.

With wares from every state in the country needing to reach the ships that would take them to their marketing places, the necessity of railroads was becoming obvious. In 1837, Rhode Island installed its own rails, providing transportation for both passengers and merchandise from Providence to Boston.

Thirty-five years later, plans were carried out to construct a branch railroad that would connect Hope Valley with the depot of Wood River Junction, then called Richmond Switch. Tracks were laid the 5 ½-mile distance and the train whistle became a familiar sound to farmers' ears.

Everything from immigrants coming to town to begin new lives, to goods from local mills leaving town to be sold, was carried upon this railroad to its ultimate destination. However, for some, the railroad would carry them to their death, leaving survivors to have nightmares about one dark morning when the sound of screaming echoed out across Richmond.

At quarter of three on the morning of April 19, 1873, the Steamboat Train, which regularly ran through Richmond, sat idle beside the Stonington boat landing. Bound for Providence and chock full of freight, baggage and tired passengers, the train's crew had been impatiently awaiting the arrival of a New York boat which was scheduled to be there at 2:15.

The train's conductor, Orrin Gardiner, wasn't happy about the delay and once the boat arrived and transitions were made, he was eager to continue his trip toward Richmond Switch. Yet, just as the train entered Stonington Junction, the Shore Line Express mail train was arriving. An unhappy Gardiner was informed that once again he would have to wait, as the other train had to finish its business there. Gardiner explained that he was already late and the conductor of the Shore Line finally agreed to let Gardiner leave first.

At 3:13 a.m., the Steamboat Train was at last on its way, comprised of three freight cars, five passenger coaches, a locomotive and a coal tender. The passengers included 91 ticket-holders, nine crew members and six railroad hands, all oblivious to what was going to happen to them in just a matter of minutes.

Heavy rains had pelted Richmond for several days that week, flooding farmlands, raising rivers and testing the strength of man-made structures. The Meadow Brook, which flowed beneath the rails at Richmond Switch, had previously been dammed to provide water power to the wheel at E.R. Ennis' gristmill. That morning, the forty acres of dammed up water rose so high, it spilled over the dam, crashed through the railroad bridge and carried it away down the river. None of the passengers on the Steamboat Train had any idea that they were speeding toward a 40-foot gap of emptiness.

As the train plunged into the abyss, a steel rail from the broken bridge pierced straight through one of its boilers. The locomotive buried itself seven feet into a hill and the coal tender flipped upside down, landing on top of the cab.

Screams echoed out through the darkness as the five passenger coaches slammed into each other, each crashing through the walls of the one before it.

Suddenly, an engine boiler exploded, giving way to towering flames that ignited everything in sight. The brakeman, Walter Monroe, escaped from the inferno and ran up to the track, frantically waving a lantern to warn the oncoming Shore Line Train. But for many passengers of the Steamboat Train, it was already too late. Bodies had been thrown into the eight-foot deep water that surrounded the wreck. Others lay trapped inside the twisted, burning wreckage.

The moment the conductor of the Shore Line saw the light of the lantern, he called for the brakes and his train screeched to a halt. Heroically, he and his crew attempted to save as many lives as they could from the wreck.

Engineer William D. Guile of Providence was killed when he was pinned beneath a boiler. Fireman George Eldred of Wickford was burned to death, along with nine passengers. A train arrived to take more than twenty injured passengers to Rhode Island Hospital. The dead were transported to Swarts Funeral Home in Providence.

Within three days, the bridge was repaired and trains were once again passing through Richmond Switch. But the clothing and personal items that were found washed up on local river banks for months after the wreck, were a horrible reminder of that fateful spring morning.

In 1886, another flood in the area would overpower the makings of men. The tracks that snaked through Hope Valley were twisted beyond repair, causing the need for total replacement.

In 1927, yet another downpour of water washed away sections of the railroad, calling for further repair. The new rails stood strong until it was decided the train was no longer needed. With automobiles and airplanes providing faster and more convenient ways to transport goods and passengers, the rails were pulled up and the depots silenced.

SUICIDE AT THE CHURCH
IRA FLETCHER

The East Greenwich United Methodist Church where Ira Fletcher committed suicide.
Photographer: Kelly Sullivan Pezza

On the night of April 30, 1881, just a little past 8:00, residents of East Greenwich were awakened by the blast of a single gunshot. On the steps of the Methodist Church, a man lay dead.

Witnesses to the shooting ran and summoned Dr. E.G. Carpenter, who came and attended to the man by the glow of a lantern. The body lay upon the top step with his feet dangling over the side. His white waistcoat was stained with blood and a bullet hole showed near his heart. Who the man was and why he had taken his life became the talk of the town for the rest of the evening. Then a gentleman from out of state came to Rhode Island for the purpose of identifying his brother, Ira Fletcher.

Fletcher was born in Skowhegan, Maine in 1820. Employed there as a carpenter, he was engaged to be married to the love of his life until she unexpectedly married another man. Fletcher packed his bags, obtained a job on a ship and headed out to sea where he hoped to get over his heartbreak.

Once back on dry land, he took up residence in New York, fell in love again and finally married. But in 1881, his wife died and he was once more thrown into the depths of despair. He decided to go home to Maine where he had not seen his family for more than forty years.

When he knocked upon the door of his old home, his relatives were shocked to discover that he was still alive. After so many years without any word, they had assumed he was dead. Fletcher, in turn, was shocked at how old they had all become. Those who remained in his memory as children now had gray hair. All of his friends were deceased, and the buildings and landscape of his boyhood days were now unrecognizable.

The church as it was when Ira Fletcher committed suicide.
Public domain photo

Fletcher ventured out to the local cemetery where those he once knew lay buried beneath the dirt. His brother followed him. "All is changed," Fletcher lamented. "All is changed."
He rose to his feet and walked out of the cemetery. Unable to bear that life had gone on without him, he left town once again. Only days later his brother would claim his body.

At the hearing, which was held after the shooting, witness Ammon Rowers testified that Fletcher had been sitting on the church steps for about twenty minutes before he suddenly flung his cane to the ground, pulled a four-barreled revolver out of his coat pocket and announced, "Here goes the last of Ira Fletcher."

Philetus Bennett, a Stonington railroad agent also testified. He stated that he had sold Fletcher a ticket to Wickford Junction a few days before. Fletcher had told him, "I have some money and I am going to go enjoy myself."

Inside the pocket of Fletcher's undershirt, $180 was discovered rolled up in paper and sewed securely in place with black thread. Whatever plans for enjoyment Fletcher had must have been overshadowed by the pain of reality. With all he had ever known and loved gone, Ira Fletcher finally gave up his journey.

ACCIDENT AT THE DAM
JOSIAH LANGWORTHY

The Old Stone Dam in Hopkinton where Josiah Langworthy was killed.
Photographer: Kelly Sullivan Pezza

Fishermen sit beside the Old Stone Dam hoping the rushing waters will offer up their bounty. But most who stand there taking in the splendor of this beautiful spot do not know of the tragedy that occurred there more than 120 years ago.

When the town of Hope Valley was settled by Hezekiah Carpenter, he owned 700 acres of land on both sides of the river. There, he constructed a dam, a sawmill, gristmill and fulling mill.

In 1824, the mill on the Hope Valley side was sold to Gardner Nichols and Russell Thayer. Carding and fulling, as well as the manufacture of tools for woolen machinery were done there.

In 1835 Thayer sold his share of the business to his brothers-in-law, Joseph and Josiah Langworthy. Two years later, the Nichols & Langworthy Mill was enlarged to stand 63 feet long, 52 feet wide and three stories high. By this time, it was running over 4,000 spindles and turning out ten thousand pounds of yarn per week.

The former Nichols& Langworthy Mill.
Photographer: Kelly Sullivan Pezza

Five years before becoming co-owner of the mill, Josiah and his wife Lucy had a son. The boy was named after his father and grew up to work alongside him in the mill. By that time, operations had grown to include the manufacture of cotton machinery, printing presses and even steam yachts. The mill was very successful and things were going well for the Langworthy family. Until one day in the autumn of 1882.

A temporary framework had been set up to hold back the river while a new bulkhead was put into position at the dam. The younger Josiah stepped out onto it. Suddenly one of the timbers broke, sending the 52-year-old man into the waters below. His efforts to swim failed as the force of the water drew him through the dam and into the flume. By the time a group of men was able to pull him out, Josiah had drowned.

Photographer: Kelly Sullivan Pezza

Josiah's funeral procession was over ½ mile long and included over fifty carriages, as an entire town mourned the loss of a respected man.

In 1906, the mill was sold out of the family and an explosion there three years later destroyed much of the structure. However, the sluiceways are still visible, as is the crumbling stonework that men once built dreams upon. And of course the river that once turned the wheels of an industrial revolution remains.

Old photograph of the Nichols& Langworthy Mill.
Reprinted from the History of the Town of Hopkinton, published by the Town of Hopkinton in 1976.

As for one who lost his life there, his story remains as well. Hidden by the splendor of the river, buried deep beneath the sand of the centuries.

BROTHERS UNTIL THE END
FRED & CHARLES GREENE

The grave of Fred and Charles Greene, at Pine Grove Cemetery in Hopkinton.
Photographer: Kelly Sullivan Pezza

Job Clark Greene was born in Richmond in 1826. At the age of 32, he married fellow Richmond resident Phebe Webster and the couple settled down in Locustville. Job became well known in the community as the proprietor of a Hope Valley paint shop and life for the Greene's was, by all accounts, happy.

The following year, Phebe gave birth to a son which she named Frederick Clarke. Five years later, another son, Charles Allen joined the family. The boys welcomed baby sister Abby Fannie in 1866.

For young boys, there was plenty to do in Locustville and the surrounding areas. The local ponds and rivers provided hours of boating and fishing. But in 1877, upon one of those rivers, life for the entire Greene family would undergo a dramatic change. One spring day that year would, in fact, jolt the existence of the whole town.

It was March 3rd and heavy rains had risen local rivers, beckoning young boys to the water. That day, 18-year-old Frederick and 13-year-old Charles met up with their friend Everett Kenyon, to take a boat ride down the river. Headed downstream toward the mooring place, the boys discovered that the current was much stronger than they had anticipated. But before they could turn back, the boat crashed into an exposed tree stump and flipped over, tossing the three of them into the cold water.

Charles quickly grabbed onto the stump to keep himself up, while Frederick and Everett clung to the side of the overturned boat. The boat, however, continued to float down the river, leaving Charles further and further behind.

Seeing his terrified little brother in peril, Frederick told Everett, "I am going to go and help Charlie." He let go of the boat and struggled to swim against the current toward his sibling. "Hold on, Charlie," he called. "I'm coming."

Everett continued to hold onto the boat as it floated further out of sight of the other boys. Finally it collided with some bushes and Everett let go, transferring his grip to a tree branch. Struggling to hold on and straining to catch some sight of his friends, the young boy did the only thing he was capable of. He tightened his hold on the branch and screamed for help.

Nearby residents who heard Everett's screams rushed to the river and pulled him out. But there was no sign of the Greene brothers. Searchers spent the rest of the day calling for them around the banks of the water and, finally, raking the river bed.
At sunset, the search was called off until morning.

At 11:00 a.m. the following day, the boys were found. As the bodies were pulled to the surface of the water, the residents who had gathered around the river saw a sight they would never forget. Frederick and Charles were clasped together so tightly, they had to be pulled apart to get them onto the raft. While Frederick's grip on Charlie was loosened, heavy rains pelted down upon the river, the hysterical onlookers and the bodies of the two brothers.

On the day of the double funeral, local mills and schools closed down so that everyone would have the opportunity to pay their respects. So many residents attended the service that there was not room to accommodate them all. One of the mourners wrote a poem which appeared in the local newspaper a few days later; *God knew all about it, how noble, how gentle Fred was, how brave – how brilliant his possible future, how he died a brother to save.*

Job and Phebe were left to mourn the loss of their sons for the rest of their lives. However, alongside their pain was the knowledge of a love stronger than most can imagine, a love that caused their oldest boy to hold onto his little brother through both life and death.

THE SADDEST GOODBYES
EVERETT KENYON

Everett Rogers Kenyon was born on May 15, 1858 in Hopkinton. His father Augustus and his mother Fidelia (Burdick) supported the family with the bounty of their farm.

At the age of forty, Everett married Attalissa Ingram and the two went on to begin their own family. But Attalissa passed away in Canonchet on April 29, 1917 at the age of 54, leaving her husband to raise their two young daughters alone. This was a duty that Everett took seriously, and one that consumed his thoughts when he discovered he would not be able to see them into adulthood.

Soon after his wife's death, Everett had become ill. On July 15, 1917, he penned a letter to the keeper of the Hopkinton town asylum, which read, *"I suppose you have engaged the bed for me at the hospital, for I know they can not keep it for me only about the necessary time for me to get ready and get there. In regards to the children's aunt, she has no property in her own name. They have not been well to do a great while, but Mr. Clark is getting a very fair salary now and they are substantial people. They have kindly offered to take care of our girls and it is understood that they will be educated. I really do not know how to ask them for more. When my companion was living, they sent us an occasional present to help along. I now have in safe-keeping the last present they sent at Christmas time. ($10.00). Am saving it to help to fit out the children with suitable clothing for the trip. This is all they have to rely upon for this purpose. Neither do I know how to ask the town for help. I have asked the Lord a thousand times – Why is it so? But I only get the quiet answer. Sometime you will understand. Mr. Witter assures me that if I leave here first, the children will be* *cared for, so I shall trust. The girls have come to you for the papers that they may be prepared at once. P.S. I would rather that the girls would know nothing about the matter of transportation at present."*

On August 5th of that year, the girls' aunt posted a letter to the asylum, concerning the welfare of the children and their upcoming journey to her home in Kansas. She wrote, *"Your letter just read. Will say this in regard to the girls. When they come to Kansas, the good people of the town of Hopkinton, RI will be relieved from any further obligations. And if it should ever be necessary they should need help again, Kansas can and will care for them. We expect to care for the girls the best we can and help them to help themselves. I wish to thank the good people there for their kindness and help in caring for the family. Theirs is certainly a sad case. I feel so sorry for Everett. It will be very hard for the girls to leave their father to die alone. May God help us all to do our part."*

Everett Kenyon passed away one month later at the Hopkinton Town Asylum. The 59-year-old doting father was laid to rest at Oak Grove Cemetery in Ashaway.

Sixteen-year-old Maude Kenyon and fifteen-year-old Leona Kenyon went to live with their 58-year-old uncle Charles A. Clark, a mail carrier, and his wife Louisa A. in Republic, Kansas.

THE PARTY'S OVER
BLANCHE COLSTON

After immigrating to America in the latter part of the nineteenth century, Swedish couple Charles and Sophie Colston settled in New York. When their family, which eventually grew to include three daughters and a son, decided that it was time to relocate, they chose a home in Peace Dale as their new residence.

The peaceful countryside and beautiful sea offered them a bounty of fun-filled summer days with friends and loved ones. But one particular outing blacked out the sun and turned a dreamy summer into an unimaginable nightmare.

The Colston family, along with nearly twenty others had decided to spend the afternoon picnicking at Ram's Island. One of the revelers was the Colston's youngest daughter, 17-year-old Blanche. Beautiful and full of life, she had the day off from her job in the sewing room of the Peace Dale Mill. With the others, she enjoyed the food and the water, frolicking on the beach and laughing into the wind. But at 1:30, something happened that brought the entire party to a standstill.

Blanche was swimming through the channel of Salt Pond, between Ram's Island and Jonathan's Island, when those swimming alongside her saw the young girl slip beneath the water. When she failed to come back up, they began to scream in panic.

Blanche's cousin, Ethel Smith, who was fully dressed on shore, ran to the water and dove in. Hysterically she tried to swim toward the area where Blanche had descended, but she ran out of breath and was unable to make it that far.

Another party member, William Eccleston, quickly jumped into the water with Blanche's uncle

Herbert Smith. Smith had long worked for the Quonachotaug Life Saving Station and was highly trained at locating and rescuing swimmers in peril. In just three minutes, he found his niece. After dragging her to the shore, he began pumping the water from her lungs. With the assistance of two other party members, he performed artificial respiration after drawing nearly three quarts of water out of the girl's body. But it was of no use.

At 4:00, Blanche Colston returned to Peace Dale. Not as a carefree teenager, but as a lifeless body. Doctors believed that a cramp or a sudden heart disturbance had been the cause of the drowning, as Blanche had been an experienced swimmer. Her funeral was held two days later at the Church of the Ascension, and an entire town said goodbye to one who had been in the flower of her youth.

THE JOKE THAT BACKFIRED
BENJAMIN JORDAN

It was supposed to be a joke. William Lewis was supposed to be frightened for a moment and then Benjamin Jordan was supposed to laugh and it would all be over. But by the time the joke was finished, William was dead and Benjamin was headed to jail.

It was a Thursday evening no different from any other in Biscuit City, not far from Shannock. Benjamin Jordan had ventured out to the Lewis house to visit the elderly Mrs. Lewis, who had been ill. He and 27-year-old William were co-workers at Kenyon Mill, although William was taking time off to care for his mother.

Earlier that day, William had gone out hunting for the weasels that were making meals out of his mother's chickens. When he returned to the house to fix dinner, he left his double-barrelled shotgun outside the front door.

When Benjamin approached the house, he saw the gun and picked it up. Quietly, he looked through the window and saw William sitting at the kitchen table eating his meal. Wouldn't it be funny, he thought, if he threw a little scare into his brother-in-law. He slowly lifted the gun and placed the barrels just below the window frame. Aiming directly at William's head, he yelled, "Look out! I'm going to shoot!"

Just as William turned to look in the direction of the window, the gun accidentally went off, sending its contents through William's right eye. His body slumped over and fell to the floor.

Benjamin was taken into police custody and William's remains were turned over to the medical examiner. It was only supposed to be a joke, Benjamin explained. It had been a terrible accident and he was truly sorry. Although officials believed his regret to be sincere, Benjamin Jordan's joke earned him a charge of manslaughter.

HIT & RUN
MICHAEL REYNOLDS

The mill villages of Rhode Island hold centuries of history within the walls of their structures and the quiet of their shadows. Once thriving centers of manufacturing, some hold stories clouded in mystery, wrought with despair.

Michael J. Reynolds was born in Smithfield on November 7, 1857. His parents, Michael and Ann, were Irish immigrants who found a living to be made in the textile mills of America. When Michael was just ten years old, his father died. On his 13th birthday, his mother married again, to Richard B. Pierce.

Michael had begun working at a young age, toiling in the mills of Pawtucket to help maintain a sufficient family income. Whether or not he knew it at the time, this would be his life. Spinning and laboring in the stuffy factory buildings and returning home each night to a cramped millhouse.

By 1875, he was employed as a spinner at a mill in Warwick. Fifteen years later, he was still spinning, but now in New Bedford, Massachusetts. A break in the routine of his life came when he married Mary Elizabeth Hackett. Her father had been killed by a train when she was just eleven years old. Her own life would be cut short as well.

In 1897, Michael married a second time, to Mary A. Morin. Two years later, while Michael was employed at a North Providence mill, their son Michael Bernard Reynolds was born.

By 1908, the family had taken up residence in the village of White Rock in Westerly, and Michael passed down to his son the only thing he knew, spinning yarn and working long days in order to pay the bills and put food on the table.

Twelve years later, living in Plainfield, Connecticut, the father and son worked side by side in the finishing room of the Farnsworth Mill. Once again, life had become routine. But that changed on Christmas Eve of 1923 when Michael's wife complained of not feeling well. Just one half hour before midnight, she took her last breath. Michael had less than two years to live himself. But he would not die in his bed. He would die an unimaginable death, and justice would never be served.

Just after 9:00 at night on May 25, 1925, a passer-by notified police that a man was lying alongside Moosup Road in Plainfield, not far from a boarding house shed. Dr. W.C. McCormick arrived at the scene to find the 68-year-old Michael Reynolds bleeding profusely from the face and head. It was obvious he had been hit by a vehicle, whose driver never even stopped to render aid.

Michael was unable to talk and police could not obtain any clues as to what had happened. While the ambulance sped toward Norwich Hospital, the lifelong textile worker inside it passed away from his injuries.

Perhaps it was for the best that Michael did not live long enough to see what other cruel blows the hand of fate had planned. On New Year's Day of 1944, Providence rooming house owner Eva McCall smelled smoke coming from one of the fourth floor rooms. The occupant of the room had been staying there for the past four months and when she entered the room, the lifeless body of the 45-year-old man was lying upon the bed.

Michael Bernard Reynolds bared the gruesome effects of third degree burns. His rocking chair, clothes and bed linens were also badly scorched. Fire department personnel believed that a fire had started in the room which he had succeeded in extinguishing before dying of his wounds. He had never married or had children, and so the final member of Michael J. Reynolds family was laid to rest.

To this day, the mystery of the elder Michael's death remains unsolved. An innocent hard-working man was simply buried. And a killer simply drove away.

TO FETCH A PAIL OF WATER
THE DANGER OF WELLS

Type of well built in past centuries.
Photographer: Kelly Sullivan Pezza

The bare essentials of life today are just what they were a hundred years ago. Food, shelter and water. That's really all we need for survival. Today, however, it is much easier to obtain these things. We no longer have to spend our days plowing and sowing gardens, milking cows or butchering animals. We simply look through real estate magazines to find our shelters and tapping into the water supply is as easy as twisting a faucet.

In centuries past, farm injuries were numerous. Homes usually left something to be desired, and even going for water could be life-threatening. Most old wells were dug by hand, with a pick and shovel, to a depth of twenty to one hundred feet below ground. The bottoms were lined with stone as were the tops, which were often circular walls rising several feet above the surface of the ground.

To draw water, one had to lean over the well and crank up a wooden bucket. The bucket was tied onto a rope which was secured to a beam that crossed the top of the well. Full water buckets were very heavy and required a certain amount of physical strength to crank them up. In performing this task, a simple mistake could be fatal.

On the evening of February 4, 1792, Reverend Pitman of Providence began searching for his maid. The fifteen-year-old Hannah Jaquays had gone outside to get a pail of water and, fifteen minutes later, had not yet returned. The search for her quickly produced her body, laying head-first at the bottom of the well.

The deep, open wells were a particular danger to curious children. In August of 1679, Elizabeth Pearce, the young daughter of Ephraim Pearce of Providence, followed her older sister outside and seemingly disappeared. An inquest into her death resulted in a jury deciding that "she accidentally fell into the well and was overwhelmed in water and, by the providence of God, drowned."

Old wells can still be found in most rural areas of the state. Most now are simply gaping holes in the ground, but they still pose a danger. Anyone with an abandoned well on their property should take care to fill in the opening with rocks, to ground level.

A NUCLEAR NIGHTMARE
ROBERT PEABODY

On one particular July 24th, a blue flash of light in a Wood River Junction facility took a man's life and made national news.

In the summer of 1964, Robert Peabody and his wife Anna were living in Shannock and raising nine children, the youngest being just five months old. Robert's job as an auto mechanic at Mystic Motors wasn't providing him with the income he needed. A new business, United Nuclear Corporation, had recently been established in Charlestown, so Robert decided to inquire there about a second job.

He was given a second-shift position as a production worker at the plant, which extracted uranium from nuclear industry scrap. Training was to be on the job, but the 38-year-old man was wise enough to know that the work was dangerous and that he should educate himself on safety procedures. So, in addition to bringing home the company manual to study, he poured over library books about the materials he would be working with.

When Robert arrived at work at 4 p.m. on July 24, he noticed that some of the containers in the building appeared to be mislabeled and he informed his supervisors. Apparently this happened often, as keeping the gummed labels affixed to the bottles was a problem. The solvents inside the containers dissolved the adhesive. Scotch tape was then tried but that didn't work either. Next, rubber bands were employed, but the chemicals in the containers deteriorated them. Finally, pieces of wire were wound around each bottle in an attempt to keep the labels in place.

At 6 p.m. that day, Robert approached the shoulder-high vat in the small tower room carrying a four-foot tall bottle of solution. There are conflicting statements as to whether or not the bottle contained a label, but Robert assumed it to be trichloroethane as he had taken it from the area where that specific solution was kept.

He propped the 11-liter container on the edge of the stainless steel vat which was filled with 41 liters of sodium carbonate solution, and began to pour in the contents of the bottle. But the contents were not that of trichoroethane. The bottle held highly concentrated uranium which had been drained out of a plugged evaporator 30 hours earlier.

Over the motorized grinding of the mixer, Robert heard a splashing sound. Suddenly, a blinding bluish white light flashed brilliantly and knocked him to the floor. The bottle spilled its remaining liquid on him and the contents of the vat exploded 12 feet, drenching the ceiling. As the uranium atoms split, setting off a chain reaction, the nuclear criticality alarm began to blare its deafening warning. Robert Peabody had just been exposed to 1,000 times the lethal dose of radiation.

Immediately he jumped to his feet, ripping off his contaminated clothes as he raced down three flights of stairs. By the time he made it to the emergency shack, 450 yards west of the building, he had already begun to lose control of his bodily functions. Wracked with stomach cramps and a blinding headache, he began to vomit. He shook violently as he ran from the shack into nearby woods where his co-workers held him down, wrapped him in blankets and waited for the ambulance to arrive.

John Shibilio of Hopkinton was the 24-year-old ambulance driver who took Robert to the hospital. He is believed to be the last surviving witness to the events of that night.

"When I arrived, I found a man laying down in the woods, wrapped in an Army blanket," he recalled. "He was completely nude and had second degree burns over pretty much all of his body."

Shibilio said that Robert was conscious and talked in the ambulance throughout the ride to the hospital. "He didn't talk about the accident," Shibilio said. "He was concerned about his wife and children. He wanted to make sure they had been notified."

The ambulance took Robert to The Westerly Hospital. We only got as far as the parking lot," Shibilio said. "There was a policeman and a doctor waiting there. They wouldn't even let us get out of the ambulance."

Robert was then taken to Rhode Island Hospital, where he arrived at 7:25 p.m. "We were all measured for radiation there," Shibilio said. "The needles went up so they took our clothes and gave us johnnies to wear."

Shibilio and the other ambulance personnel were then sent to the Nuclear Medicine Facility at the University of Rhode Island where they spent several hours showering and being remeasured for radiation exposure.

At the hospital, Robert's body was scrubbed clean. His hair, now radioactive, had to be shaved off. And despite his protests, his wedding ring had to be cut off due to the acute swelling of his limbs. Soon, his wife Anna was at his bedside.

"Somebody put the bottle in the wrong place," he told her. He explained that he had taken the bottle from among other bottles of TCE and therefore had assumed that bottle also contained that solution. Anna sat on the side of the bed holding her husband's hand until one of the doctors told her that, in order to prevent herself from becoming irradiated, she should stand at the foot of the bed.

In the early evening hours of July 26, Robert began to thrash about violently as his body went into shock. Doctors and nurses restrained him before he slipped into a coma. At 7:20 p.m., Robert Peabody died.

He was sent back to his family as ashes within a cardboard box. Or at least that's what the family was told. Anna placed the box in her closet, never believing it was actually her husband's remains inside. She brought eight lawsuits, totaling $1,200,000, against the United Nuclear Corporation, Rhode Island Hospital, the United States government and the Insurance Company of North America.

Throughout it all, the UNC claimed no responsibility in the death and finally on July 19, 1968, unable to pay her legal bills, Anna agreed to a settlement out of court. Part of the agreement was that she not disclose the amount to the public. Documentation shows that it was meager amount, which was depleted to $22,631 after her lawyers were paid.

Leo Goodman, a nuclear industry investigator said at the time that he believed it was "absolutely unforgivable management practices that lead to Peabody's death and there should have been criminal penalties for the failure to comply with the simplest of safety requirements in the nuclear industry." Goodman also suspected that the UNC had tampered with physical evidence in order to conceal their guilt.

An investigation showed that logbooks at the plant, which were supposed to be implemented in order to alert incoming shifts of plans or problems, were not being used. One of the supervisors at the plant had no prior experience in nuclear materials prior to becoming employed at the plant four months earlier. And, according to the official report of the Atomic Energy Commission, "the tags did not always bear the information required for identifying the contents of bottles."

The AEC eventually charged UNC with 14 violations of nuclear safety and licensing regulations, but no fines were ever imposed.

Although Robert had stated from his hospital bed that the bottle he had been using was not labeled and that it had not been in a protected area, his statements were never included in the AEC's report of the accident.

And while United Nuclear continued to maintain that they were free of fault, they continued to wrack up non-compliances and safety infractions.

Following the accident, they were cited for failure to file reports of airborne and liquid radioactive waste resulting from the accident, within the prescribed time. And when the reports were eventually completed, they did not adequately determine whether or not there was any airborne radiation.

UNC was cited for failure to test the nuclear alarm system and emergency radiation meters as required. They were cited for failure to thoroughly clean up a radioactive liquid which had been spilled on the roof of the building. Regulations were also violated when it was discovered that radioactive wastes were being disposed of by dumping them into the ground at the rear of the plant. The citations continued for years.

In 1973, an inspection at UNC showed there had been several airborne exposures; that a pressurized pipe had exploded and sprayed a uranium solution over a 20-foot radius; and that a container holding enriched uranium had accidentally been spilled. That same year, they were cited by the AEC for failure to adequately evaluate hazards, evaluate bio-essay results and document evaluations of airborne exposure.

From 1975 through 1978, the plant was cited for failure to conduct continuing safety sessions. There was, in fact, no designated plan of action in the event of emergency evacuation, radiation criticality or terrorist attacks.

In 1977 and 1978, inspections showed that radiation was being released into the air of one of the work areas and that, even though air monitors were registering excessive radiation, no evacuation of employees was carried out.

In 1978, the Nuclear Regulatory Committee cited the plant when it discovered that the exhaust hoods over four trays of acid dissolving scrap were drawing off contaminated air because of worn out filters. Inspectors also discovered uranium dripping directly onto the floor of the plant.

A 1979 inspection showed that five steel drums containing radioactive material and labels warning that the drums be kept at least 20 feet apart, were set a mere 15 inches away from each other. That year, the plant was cited for failure to search workers leaving the premises for concealed metal and failure to detect pieces of fuel scrap sent to another nuclear facility.

Victor Stello, Director of Inspections at the time, stated that many of the plant's violations had been "repeat" offenses over the course of three years.

Other violations included failure to comply with plant security regulations, falsifying records concerning firearms qualifications of the guards, transport of a container which was supposed to be empty but which contained nuclear fuel scrap, failure to perform adequate searches of shipping containers, and failure to keep records on the movement and disposition of scrap pieces.

There were no more violations or citations after 1979, as the UNC closed down its Wood River Junction facility. The state then began a 10-year decontamination of the 1,100-acre site.

Of the three types of uranium, all are radioactive, but each contains different chemical properties. The least radioactive is U-238, which decays over a period of 4,500 million years. U-235 (the type employed at

United Nuclear) decays over 710 million years. The most radioactive, U-234, decays over a period of 244,000 billion years.

As uranium decays, it produces radon, one of the most deadly carcinogens known to man. Traveling close to the ground, it can move hundreds of miles in a matter of days, depositing solid radioactive fall-out into soil, water and vegetation. When this material is inhaled or ingested, it is likely to produce lung cancer, respiratory illness or fibrosis of the lungs.

The land which the United Nuclear facility set upon is bounded on the south by Cedar Swamp, on the north by Route 112, and on the west by Kings Factory Road. Wetlands compose 300 acres of the property, with the southern section draining into the swamp. Another 125 acres is stream and property buffers. Although the 45 acres where the plant stood is not buildable, another 580 acres is, 350 of which contains rolling, rocky hills covered with oak and hickory forest. In 1995, the NRC declared the site safe.

Anna Peabody died on January 23, 2002, after spending the last twenty years of her life suffering from kidney, ovarian, brain and throat tumors, which may have been caused by radiation exposure while standing at her husband's bedside in the hospital.

Robert Downing Peabody had been an airplane mechanic in the Navy. He had helped develop the first atomic submarine at Electric Boat in 1952. He was known to everyone as a hard-working man, a highly intelligent man. And yet his family was never afforded any resolution or comfort concerning his death. Instead they were forced to go on with their lives, hearing arguments about their tragic loss being just a terrible "accident" caused by Robert's own "negligence."

But this was a man skilled in nuclear technology, a man who took it into his own hands to acquaint himself with the safety procedures his employer failed to train workers in. This was a man with no history of negligence. The only negligence found is that which fills the many inspection reports concerning UNC.

SUFFER THE CHILDREN
CHILD LABOR

The old abandoned Potter Hill Mill in Westerly.
Photographer: Kelly Sullivan Pezza

Ring around the roses
Pocket full of Posies
Etchoo, etchoo
We all fall down...

That was the original way the song went. Composed and sung by children during a time when childhood held little magic.

Aside from singing songs about deadly plagues that were almost sure to claim them, young people in the 19th century did little else to amuse themselves. There simply wasn't time.

A child's ultimate destiny was to survive, help with the family income, marry and have children of their own. It wasn't uncommon for girls to become wives as young as 13, or die in childbirth the next year. It wasn't uncommon for little boys to be killed in farming accidents, or lose arms and legs in dangerous machinery.

Children who attended school were extremely lucky, for most families could not afford to spare an able-bodied worker.

For years, the boys helped their fathers take care of the farm and the girls helped their mothers take care of the house. Then came the industrial revolution. Mill work promised every family a chance at achieving the American dream. But for most of them a nightmare was in store.

Mills advertised for laborers, making their jobs seem like an incredible opportunity. Sawmills, gristmills and textile mills were cropping up everywhere. Many insisted that their employees live in the company-provided mill housing, with the cost of rent being deducted from their paychecks. Others paid their employees in vouchers instead of cash, which could only be redeemed for goods at the mill store.

Poor families were highly sought as employees, for they were trusted to take their work and the "benefits" of it seriously. And families with lots of children were sought after even more. The greater number of people in a family, the more employees for the mill.

In 1855, over half the mill workers in the state of Rhode Island were children aged 5 to 12. Earning about 70 cents a week, little ones were in high demand by mill owners. Their small hands and flexible fingers were perfect for reaching into cramped spaces and mechanical openings to repair broken threads and change bobbins.

Children who were not tall enough to reach certain pieces of machinery had to stand on top of the machine and bend down over it to perform their duties. Few safety measures could be taken when work had to be done this way and it was not a rare occasion when little girls were scalped by their hair getting caught in the whirling machinery, or when little boys went home at night with one less finger than they had that morning.

The majority of child mill workers were illiterate. School was not an option for those whose families depended on the extra income for survival.

Work in the mills began before sunrise and ended at around 7 p.m. The buildings were freezing cold in the winter months and stifling hot in the summer. Children who did not loose life or limb at work were likely to end up with any variety of respiratory illnesses due to the constant inhalation of airborne lint, dirt and dust.

There were peckers and spinners, carders and dyers, dressers and weavers and many of our local families had their own children filling these positions. Royal Lewis received $67.57 in 1812, in exchange for his daughter working at Arnold's Mill for one year. In 1814, Moses Kenyon received $17.62 after his daughter Elizabeth worked in the mill for ten weeks.

In 1833, a law was enacted in Rhode Island which stated that *"no child under 10 years of age shall be employed in any manufacturing establishment in this state. No child under 14 years of age shall be employed except during the vacations of the public school."*

Many people at last realized that while the mills had provided adults with the vision of a better life, they had robbed hundreds of children of any chance at one.

DISEASE

FATAL EPIDEMICS
DIPHTHERIA & SMALLPOX

Sometimes an epidemic would wipe out an entire family within a matter of days.
Photographer: Kelly Sullivan Pezza

In the year 1860, the town of Hopkinton was united in a single fear. A terrible disease was sweeping through town and turning many residents into victims. No one, it seemed, was safe.

Fifty-six-year-old Dr. Henry Aldrich and twenty-seven-year-old Dr. Elisha P. Clark did all they could to accommodate the overwhelming reign of suffering that had fallen over their neighbors but, in truth, they knew no more about the disease than anyone else.

On December 15, 1860, Willet Watson of Hopkinton would have turned three years old. But two days before that, William and Susan Watson watched their child's life be extinguished. Before darkness fell, their remaining child, five-year-old Susan, would also pass away. In the span of 24 hours, this family was reduced to a childless couple, Diphtheria robbing them of their children less than two weeks before the town celebrated Christmas.

The Watsons were among the hundreds crushed by this epidemic. Spouses, siblings and parents were torn from families too numerous to list. Highly contagious, Diphtheria was passed along through coughing and sneezing, which released thousands of droplets into the air. The droplets would then settle into a new host's mouth or nose. Made up of bacteria which produced deadly toxins in the body, Diphtheria showed itself about two days after contamination. Swollen lymph glands, hoarseness of the voice, sore throat, fever, bloody nose and cough preceded the growth of a large, tumor-like appendage over the tonsils.

Swallowing eventually became impossible and breathing difficult. Because this obstruction in the airways led to the diminished availability of oxygen, the skin took on a blue pallor and usually broke out in patches of lesions. Once the disease was in the blood stream, it traveled to the heart and nervous system. The bacteria produced by the disease slowed the pulse until heart failure, paralysis or asphyxiation occurred.

The long suffering endured by those infected was a difficult experience for loved ones to witness, especially when the infected was a child. The epidemics that passed through this area in the 1800's put children most at risk, their bodies not yet strong enough to fight off disease. The odds of losing a child before his or her fifth birthday were very high.

The double grave of young siblings Willet and Susan Watson, in Wood River Cemetery in Richmond, who both died of an epidemic on the same day.
Photographer: Kelly Sullivan Pezza

Small Pox entered Hopkinton in 1796, causing an outcry of fear and concern. In February of that year, the town council held a special meeting to discuss the fact that the disease was present in the home of Abel Tanner. The council voted that George Thurston and Israel Lewis would oversee a quarantine of the house and set up blockades to keep anyone from entering or exiting the property.

A former Small Pox Hospital in Pawtucket.
Originally published in the 1902 book State of Rhode Island and Providence Plantations: A History.

The next week, another special meeting was held. The council decided that inoculations should be made available to residents, and two locations were set up for the purpose, one at Benjamin Langworthy's house and one at Benjamin Barber's. It was also voted that anyone entering or leaving a house in which Small Pox was present, would pay a fine of $20 and face legal punishment. Anyone who had been afflicted with the disease and recovered would be required to show the council a certificate of recovery, signed by a doctor.

Small Pox Trail, named for hospital that once stood on the street, to house the afflicted.
Photographer: Alecia Keegan

Captain Joseph Spicer was one of the lucky few who survived the illness. After being placed in a local log-barricaded Small Pox hospital, he got well and returned home to Hopkinton. But recovery did not mean a lack of suffering. The almost unbearable pain of Small Pox symptoms took a strong person to overcome them. Highly contagious, the disease did not even have to be carried on the moisture of a sneeze or cough to be passed along from person to person. Merely opening one's mouth was enough to send the microscopic bacteria airborne and only a single particle needed to be inhaled to infect.

About ten days after becoming afflicted, Small Pox caused fever, backache and vomiting. Red spots then appeared over every part of the body except for the mouth. Turning to pea-sized blisters, each spot eventually burst, immersing the victim in agonizing pain. The body would at last become so weak, the heart would simply give out.

But those left behind suffered also; those who began the day with a family, and ended it without one.

GROCER'S ITCH & MILK LEG
MEDICAL TERMS OF THE PAST

The grave of Doctor George Sisson, in Pine Grove Cemetery in Hopkinton, who treated the ailments of yesteryear.
Photographer: Kelly Sullivan Pezza

Before modern medical technology, it wasn't uncommon for death certificates to list things such as *toothache* or *fright* as causes of death. Most illnesses of the time were not well understood. Following is a list of long-ago clinical terms:

Dancing Madness: Acute swelling of the brain due to an injury or illness, which causes spasmodic jerking of the face and limbs. This affliction is now called *convulsions*.

Bladder In The Throat: The inhalation of a contagious germ which causes fever, sore throat and weakness, also caused the growth of a thick gray membrane in the throat. This membrane interfered with breathing and was often life-threatening. The disease came to be known as *Diphtheria*.

The Kink: An irritation within the breathing tract which causes the victim to vibrate the throat in order to ease the sensation. The vibration may be persistent enough to interfere with air passing in and out of the lungs. We now call this ailment *persistent cough*.

Jail Fever: A painful, red-spotted rash, high fever, head and limb pain, delirium and an affected nervous system were the symptoms of this disease. It was carried by body louse and rat fleas, which were rampant in confined, dirty places. The affliction later became known as *Typhus*.

Winter Fever: The passing of certain germs through the nose or mouth and into the lungs, caused a rise in body temperature, chills, shallow breathing and general pain. We now refer to this as *pneumonia*.

Bad Blood: A venereal disease which was spread by intimate contact produced painful symptoms such as sores in the groin area. We now call this *Syphilis*.

Barrel Fever: The physical deterioration and mental disintegration caused by the long-term ingestion of alcohol. The illness is now known as *alcoholism*.

Dry Bellyache: Irritation of the intestinal tract, paralysis of the peripheral nerves and blood cell damage are all symptoms of this disease. Its long-term effects included brain damage. Its medical term today is *lead poisoning*.

Brain Fever: Infection in the coverings of the brain and spinal cord, due to the presence of germs, produced a sore throat, fever, chills and a red rash upon the body. Today we call this illness *Meningitis*.

Canine Madness: The bite of an animal which carries deadly organisms in its saliva, causes a severe dryness of the throat and an attack of the nervous system. We now know this as *rabies*.

The Screws: Painful joint stiffness, heart damage and throat infections were symptoms of the illness we now refer to as *rheumatism*.

Putrid Sore Throat: An irritation that goes beyond a normal sore throat to ulcerate the area and spread to the tonsils and pharynx is what we call *tonsillitis*.

Worm Fit: Parasites in contaminated food travel to the intestinal tract of the consumer. The worms survive on the nutrients in the host's body, causing anemia, fatigue, weight loss and abdominal pain. This is presently known as *tapeworm*.

Delirium Tremens: Having hallucinations and being overcome with body tremors was often the result of stopping long-term alcohol or drug consumption. This is what we now call *withdrawal*.

Grocer's Itch: A skin disease marked by itching and discolored eruptions on the skin was caused by handling sugar or flour that was infested with mites. Today this would be called *eczema*.

Scrivener's Palsy: An impairment in muscle power caused by a stiffening of the muscles in the hand. Presently, we call this *writer's cramp*.

Milk Leg: A painful swelling of the leg soon after childbirth was caused by blood coagulating in the vein that runs from the groin to the ankle. Probably caused by the strain of labor, we would refer to this as *thrombosis*.

Nostalgia: Insomnia, decreased appetite and obsessive thoughts caused by a change in lifestyle or a dramatic loss would today be called *depression*.

Gravel: A hard mass of crystals within the kidney was caused by a separation of calcium or phosphate in the urine. The deposits were often painful if they could not be passed out of the body. This affliction is currently called *kidney stones*.

Barber's Itch: This itching of the head and face was caused by mites being spread from person to person via a shaving brush or comb. Today, it is known as *lice*.

Sanguineous Crust: Spots on the body and the bleeding of mucous membranes was caused by blood being forced out of its proper place. The present term for this condition is *scurvy*.

Mad Hatter's Disease: The use of chemical solutions to transform fur into felt was a common process for hatmakers, who were forced to breathe in the toxic fumes. Long-term exposure caused hallucinations, depression and delirium. Today, we call this *mercury poisoning*.

FROM CRADLE TO GRAVE
THE RISKS OF CHILDBIRTH

During the 19th century, women did not have a lot of choices about how to spend their lives. It was expected that a woman marry, have children, take care of the house and eventually pass away.

For many women though, the span in which she would accomplish all those things was very short. While farm and factory accidents were a leading cause of death for men, and epidemics often fatal for children, women knew that each pregnancy could end in her own death.

Babies were born in homes, delivered by doctors, mid-wives or female family members. The pain of childbirth was alleviated by the woman being administered chloroform or cannabis, and attempts were made to shorten the pain by pulling the baby out with forceps.

Conditions were usually unsanitary. Doctors treating diseased patients would often arrive to deliver a baby with the same instruments utilized on the sick. Mid-wives often had traces of daily farm life on their hands when they arrived to bring a child into the world. But little was known of the transfer of contaminants or the consequences of rushing a delivery, and one woman after another died as a result of this.

Mary Priscilla Witter of Hopkinton died in 1889 at the age of 36 after giving birth. It was her fourth child in six years. Immediately following her delivery, Mary began having violent muscle contractions. Brain function began to subside and the woman quickly succumbed.

Harriet Thayer, also of Hopkinton, lost her life in 1892 at the age of 16, shortly after giving birth. Inflammation of the abdominal wall, caused by bacteria entering the body, lead to intense pain and nausea before taking the teenage girl's life.

Bertha Strange died in Hopkinton in 1894 at the age of 23, following the delivery of her child. A bacterial infection caused by dirty hands or medical tools passed into her bloodstream causing sudden chills, fever, rapid heartbeat and decreased body temperature. Eventually enough toxins were present in her blood to terminate her life.

Mary Adams of Hopkinton delivered a stillborn baby boy in 1896 when she was just eighteen years old. Within hours, her blood pressure rose, her face swelled and fever set in. Bacteria had entered her body and settled in her kidneys where the inflammation quickly proved fatal.

Perhaps the saddest case of death in Hopkinton caused by childbirth is that of Elizabeth Burdick. The daughter of John and Mary Bently, she had married 21-year-old William Robinson Burdick when she was just fourteen years of age. Eight months later, she died in her bed from the trauma of her young body giving birth to twins.

MEDICAL ADVERTISEMENTS
A CURE FOR EVERYTHING

Old ad for Mug-Wump, a sure cure for disease.
Courtesy of Wikipedia.org: public domain photo.

In days of old, most people were willing to take any pharmaceutical that promised better health, long life or relief from whatever was ailing them. Sometimes the *cure* was as bad as the affliction. Following is a list of medical ads that appeared in the Hope Valley Advertiser in the year 1900. All items were available at local stores:

*U.S. Dental Association of Providence, RI: *Free! Free! Free! Painless extracting free when other work is done! $4 for full set of perfect fitting teeth. Beware of strange dentists. Investigate. We have been here nine years and enlarged our quarters four times. We can* *extract your teeth painlessly (free) and furnish new ones in six hours!*

Dr. King's Pills: Dr. King's New Life Pills cure headache and constipation. Dr. King's New Discovery is guaranteed to cure all throat, chest and lung diseases. Only fifty cents.

Cascarets: Beauty is blood deep. Cascarets Candy Cathartic cleans your blood and keeps it clean by stirring up a lazy liver and driving impurities from the body. Banish pimples, boils, blotches, blackheads and that sickly, bilious complexion by taking Cascarets. Ten cents.

No-To-Bac: It rests with you whether or not you continue the nerve-killing tobacco habit. No-To-Bac removes the desire for tobacco, purifies the blood and restores lost manhood. Leaves you strong in both health and pocketbook. One box $1.00.

Electric Bitters: Cold steel or death. There was but one small chance to save the life of I.B. Hunt of Wisconsin and that was an operation. She had consumption but her doctor had overlooked the power of Electric Bitters. She heard of Electric Bitters, took seven bottles, was wholly cured, avoided the surgeon's knife and now weighs more and feels better than ever. Positively guaranteed to cure stomach, liver and kidney troubles, including yellow jaundice so you won't need surgery. Fifty cents.

One Minute Cough Cure: You can spell it cough, coff, caugh, kauf, kaff, kough, or kaugh, but the only harmless remedy that quickly cures it is One Minute Cough Cure.

*Mother Gray's Powders: *To the mothers of this town. Children who are delicate, feverish and cross will get immediate relief from Mother Gray's Sweet Powders For Children. Making a sickly child healthy again. A certain cure for worms. Free sample.*

*Dewitt's Salve: *Poisonous toadstools resembling mushrooms have caused frequent deaths this year. Be sure to only use the genuine. Observe the same care when you ask for Dewitt's Witch Hazel Salve. There are poisonous counterfeits.*

*Hop Bitters: *Helps to restore brain and nerve waste. Cures kidney and stomach disease. If you are simply weak or low-spirited, try it. It may save your life. An absolute and irresistible cure for drunkenness, opium use, tobacco or narcotics.*

*Benson's Plasters: *Medicated corn and bunion plasters. Twenty-five cents. Beware of cheap plasters made with lead poisons.*

*Foo Choo's Balsam Of Shark Oil: *Positively restores hearing and is the only absolute cure for deafness known. Oil is extracted from a peculiar species of small white shark caught in the Yellow Sea. One dollar a bottle.*

*Kodol Dyspepsia Cure: *It artificially digests food and reconstructs the exhausted digestive organs. It digests what you eat!*

*Bucklen's Salve: *Cures old sores, fever sores, ulcers, boils and corns. Will kill the pain and heal it. Best pile cure on earth. Twenty-five cents a box.*

*Dr. Swayne's All Healing Ointment: *Cures itching piles, a very distracting scratching, as if pin worms are crawling on the body. Cures all scaly, crusty eruptions, such as scald head and barber's itch. Three boxes for $1.25.*

*Peruvian Syrup: *Has cured thousands who were suffering from debility, boils, female complaints and humors.*

*Dr. William's Pink Pills For Pale People: *Cures spinal disease and paralysis. Six boxes for $2.50.*

LEGAL DRUGS
OVER THE COUNTER OPIUM

1874 illustration of opium users.
Originally published in Illustrated London News.
Image courtesy of Nationmaster.com: public domain photo.

During the 19th century, certain things were just not tolerated; women drinking alcoholic beverages, unmarried couples having children, residents of one town moving to another. But there were other things that were perfectly acceptable, such as the marriage of blood relatives, children working in factories and opium being injected through store-bought syringes.

In 1839, the famous Opium War took place between England and China. The English, who purchased the drug from India, had long depended on the Chinese as customers. When China suddenly outlawed the use of opium, the English were not happy. Its only Chinese customers now were those who purchased the drug illegally and set up opium dens behind the facade of legal businesses.

When plans for the railroad were being established in America, word made it to China that laborers were in demand. Many men packed up their belongings and came to the States, bringing with them the opium that was completely legal here. The demand for the drug quickly began to rise and American women were urged to grow poppies along with their herbs and vegetables.

The opium was produced by slicing the seedpods of the poppy plants and allowing a white substance to ooze out. Within a matter of hours, the substance turned brown and gummy and could then be scraped from the pod and rolled into balls.

Production hit its peak during the Civil war when opium balls were handed out to soldiers in order to banish pain should they find themselves injured on the battlefield. At the war's end, 45,000 opium-addicted soldiers went home. The medical problems they had incurred from use of the drug included collapsed veins, decreased oxygen in the blood, malfunctioning of the digestive system, yellowing of the skin, and tooth loss.

Although it was known as the Soldier's Disease, opium addiction affected a wide variety of people. Politicians and mill-workers, doctors and housewives were regularly injecting the deadly substance into their veins. Sold right over the counter in drug stores, opium could be bought pure or as an ingredient in medicines. It was prescribed for those who were addicted to alcohol, pregnant women suffering from morning sickness and children who were teething.

Sold under such names as Mother's Helper, opium was a trusted substance to calm cranky children when mothers had just too many children to take care of. Children who are listed in death records as dying from *debility*, *starvation* or *weakness*, may have actually died from the effects of opium addiction.

Syringes could be purchased in stores separately, or as part of an opium kit. Opium kits were made for people of all classes. Those who had little money to support their habit could buy a simple needle. Those who could afford to splurge purchased gold-plated syringes in decorative boxes which included several glass vials. They could even have their kits monogrammed.

Edgar Allen Poe, Sigmund Freud and Elizabeth Barrett Browning were famous names known to have been opium addicts. Over time, the drug destroyed people of all races, sexes and ages. In Hopkinton, 40-year-old Cora Alma (Sisson) Crandall, widow of carriage maker Ethan Crandall, died on May 28, 1900. Her cause of death...*opium habit.*

ABUSE IN THE ASYLUMS
THE MENTALLY ILL

Old postcard of the former Dexter Asylum in Providence.
Public domain image

There was a time when medical terms such as Alzheimer's Disease and manic depression were unheard of. There was a time when there was no differentiation between the sick and the poor, the unlucky and the unwanted, the agitated and the aged. This was a time when, if you fell into any of these categories, there was a good chance you were going to be placed in your town's asylum.

The conditions at many Rhode Island asylums were not known to the masses until the state's Commissioner of the Poor & Insane, Thomas R. Hazard, conducted an investigation and presented his findings to the General Assembly in 1851. The detailed report included horrid descriptions of individuals being treated more like animals than humans.

At the Warren Town Asylum, Hazard discovered two women in their early forties, Ellen

Mason and Betsey Chase, chained to the floor beside each other. Both were unable to inform Hazard that they had been confined that way for over four years.

At the Portsmouth Town Asylum, elderly Mary Slocum had also been chained up in a small room for several years. Another inmate there, 80-year-old Thomas Durfee, displayed an injury on his head, caused by a harsh blow from the asylum keeper when Durfee accidentally got in his way.

Hannah Lawton, another Portsmouth inmate, was found to have been laying on the floor for hours after the keeper had knocked her down. Due to the fact that she was crippled, she was not able to pull herself back up.

In Foster, 40-year-old Elizabeth Hale suffered in her tiny asylum room with constant violent convulsions in her throat. Hazard Wilcox, who was chained up not far from her, had been confined there in that state for seven of his 46 years.

Conditions were just as bad at the asylum in Coventry, where 50-year-old Betsey Whitman, lay in a dirty room. At the asylum in South Kingstown, 66-year-old Sally Cory had been confined in her room for four years.

Hazard discovered a woman named Rebecca Gibbs at the Newport Town Asylum, who had been confined for thirty years. Seated on the floor with her legs drawn up to her chest, her chin rested on her knees. Her arms were wrapped around her calves and she was unable to move out of that position. Her muscles had seized up due to being confined in the room for so many years without heat.

In Jamestown, a man who had been locked up for over twenty years spent the last half of his life in a small room elevated off the ground. Beneath his feet, a slatted floor allowed waste material to drop through, thereby eliminating any need to clean the room. He ate off the floor and often rolled around in agony from lack of heat or room to move. When he died, his body was found to be imbedded with the thick splinters of those slatted boards.

While the very worst of situations were in the Providence and Newport county asylums, a total of 283 inmates throughout all the counties, were found by Hazard to be mentally ill and in need of hospitalization rather than incarceration. Hazard explained that if things were allowed to continue within the asylums as they had been, the mentally ill would continue to suffer the brutal torture he had witnessed.

Hazard attempted to convey that the mentally disabled were not to be feared. One inmate he had met at the North Kingstown asylum, 74-year-old William Whitman, had been a resident there for forty years. Hazard described watching the man bend over to pick up bugs off the ground and move them out of the way where they would not be stepped on.

What the insane needed, according to Hazard's report, was not punishment or banishment, but help. The place for them was not at an asylum, but at an established hospital specifically for the mentally ill.

Four years before, the very first Rhode Island hospital exclusively for those with afflictions of the mind had been opened in Providence. Butler Hospital for the Insane had come into existence after Hazard and his collogue Dorothea Dix discovered there was need for concern when it came to the care of the mentally ill.

Cyrus Butler, a Rhode Island resident who had inherited a large sum of money from his ship-owner father, donated $40,000 toward the construction of the hospital.

"I hope and trust that the day is near at hand when abuse (of the mentally ill) will be classed among the most flagrant crimes that are committed on earth," Hazard declared.

MALARIA
DEADLY MOSQUITOS

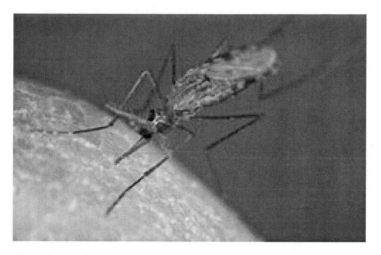

The tiny insect that brings on large epidemics.
Photo part of the collection of the Public Health Image Library.
Courtesy of Wikipedia.org: public domain photo.

William and Emeline Tefft of Hopkinton didn't know what to do. Their 7-year-old daughter Willimenia had been suffering from flu-like symptoms that wouldn't subside. A high fever, chills and aching body had taken over the little girl. January 21, 1901 was her last day to be alive. The cause of death …Malaria.

Common in areas with warm climates, Malaria hit its peak in America during the Civil War, killing thousands of men. The wet weather of the south during that time was creating more breeding grounds for Malaria-carrying mosquitoes, although no one yet knew what was causing this outbreak of sickness.

Originating in foreign countries with tropical climates, Malaria made its way to America through human immigration. When a mosquito bites a person infected with Malaria, it takes on the disease itself, passing it along to anyone else it may bite.

Just minutes after being bitten by a Malaria-carrying mosquito, parasites enter the human liver. Feeding on the liver's protein, it gains the energy it needs to move onto its ultimate goal – the body's red blood cells. It is the iron in the red blood cell which makes the parasite able to reproduce. Soon, the original number of parasites transmitted by the mosquito have doubled, then tripled. As they rob the cells of iron, the body is not able to maintain the amount of oxygen it needs. The parasites multiply in the oxygen-deprived capillaries of the spleen, the brain and the liver, turning the organs hard and black.

It can take anywhere from a week to several months for a person who has been bitten by a Malaria-carrying mosquito to notice any symptoms of the disease. Eventually, vomiting, chills, fever and body aches will begin but the infected person will usually appear to recover from the illness several times before it proves fatal in the form of anemia, kidney failure or swollen organs.

The disease affected Hopkinton in 1901 not only with the death of Willimenia Tefft, but also the death of 57-year-old tavern owner Joseph Thurston Spicer and 6-year-old David A. Greene. Five years earlier, 24-year-old Hopkinton machinist John H. Tanner Jr. also succumbed to the disease. Previous to that, in 1891, Abbie Sisson Langworthy died of Malaria at the age of 59.

It was not until 1902 that conclusive evidence showed how Malaria was transmitted. Upon the salivary glands of the Malaria-carrying mosquito lay the answer.

Malaria is still common in Africa and Asia. Over 1,000 cases are treated in America every year, most occurring after the afflicted person has returned from travels in areas where the disease is still rampant.

SEA DISASTERS

A SEA OF COTTON
THE SINKING OF THE METIS

The Metis sailed out of New York just a little after 5:00 p.m. on August 30, 1872. Carrying 163 passengers, the Providence & New York steamship headed up the coast toward Providence. Below each of the three decks, passengers amused themselves, away from the pouring rain that pounded down on the vessel.

At 3:30 the next morning, the rain was still coming down and the wind had picked up. The sleeping passengers would remain oblivious to the weather conditions for only ten more minutes. At 3:40, they would be roused from their beds to engage in a desperate struggle for life.

As the Metis sailed through the area between Montauk and Watch Hill, it collided with the schooner Nellie Cushing. Crewmembers of the Metis immediately informed their captain, Charles Burton, that the ship was taking on water. Burton did not feel the damage was severe enough to interrupt the trip. He directed his men to continue heading toward Providence.

Five miles south of the Watch Hill Lighthouse, a crewman warned Burton that water was rapidly seeping through the seams of the ship. No longer able to deny the severity of the situation, the captain ordered the crew to begin filling the lifeboats.

It was only a matter of time before the Metis would be 130 feet below the raging sea.
Passengers raced for the lifeboats as the upper deck broke away from the vessel, carrying with it fifty men and women who would not live to see another sunrise. Forty more people went down with the hull as 30-foot

waves drew those struggling in the water into a massive whirlpool.

The ship's cargo, bales of cotton bound for Rhode Island textile mills, was scattered across the water and many passengers swam against the waves to grab onto the floating debris.

Another boat captain, John D. Harvey, sighted the distressed ship from the beach and quickly launched a fishing seine outfitted with crewmen Courtland B. Gavitt, Edwin W. Nash, William H. Nash and Eugene Nash.

Lighthouse-keeper Jared Starr Crandall and lifesaving captain Daniel F. Larkin also launched a boat which included crewmen Byron D. Green, Frank Larkin and Albert D. Crandall. The men were able to pull some of the passengers out of the water alive.

The cutter Moccasin took the survivors aboard. Of those who were on the passenger list, only 32 were saved. The other 131 men and women who had boarded the Metis, were claimed by the sea.

ENCASED IN ICE
THE SINKING OF THE LARCHMONT

The Larchmont, circa 1907.
Public domain photo

On the night of February 11, 1907 at 6:30 p.m., the ship Larchmont left the dock in Providence and set sail toward New York. There were 250 passengers and crewmembers aboard the side-wheel steamer. Most of them would never be seen alive again.

The Larchmont, built in Bath, Maine in 1885 and originally called the Cumberland, was a beautiful luxury vessel with huge paddle boxes on each side of her and a large walking beam above the top deck. Purchased in 1902 by the Joyline Company, the ship made regular passages between Providence and New York.

On that fateful night in 1907, the temperature was three degrees below zero. There had been an earlier dusting of snow but now the skies were clear and starlit. Preparing to head off to bed at about quarter of eleven, Captain C.H. McVey gave charge of the wheel to Quartermaster James E. Staples and placed the ship under the supervision of Pilot John Anson.

As the ship was rounding Point Judith in Narragansett Bay, the force of 50-mile-per-hour winds began to pummel her. Suddenly something appeared in her path. Directly up ahead, another ship, the Harry P. Knowlton, had been blown off course by the gales and was heading straight for the Larchmont.

As the Knowlton was a sailing ship, she had the right of way. "For God's sake, Staples!" Anson yelled. "Port the help!" Staples swung the wheel over as far as he could, only to bring the ship closer to the Knowlton.

Down below, McVey heard four blasts of the ship's whistle and rushed back to the pilothouse. Anson pointed out the three-masted schooner in front of them. "My God, John! What have you done?" McVey shouted. Anson grabbed the wheel and turned it hard again but the Knowlton was approaching too fast. Before an accident could be averted, the bow of the Knowlton crashed into the port side of the Larchmont, slicing through half the length of the steamer.

The two ships remained locked together in the restless sea until the waves jarred them apart. Freezing water immediately began rushing into the gaping hole in the Larchmont, flooding the boiler room and sending massive amounts of steam billowing into the night sky. The impact of the collision had thrown passengers from their beds and they all rushed to the upper deck to see what had happened.

Removing the dead from the shores of Block Island.
Old postcard, circa 1907.
Public domain photo

The Larchmont was sinking fast and McVey directed his crew to begin filling the lifeboats. Hysterical passengers, who hadn't time to dress themselves against the bitter weather, huddled into the small boats as the bow of the ship sunk beneath the water. The mad dash for lifeboats and the piercing screams of men and women made for a nightmarish scene. Officers had to push people back from overcrowding the boats and many of them fell to their knees in prayer. Some jumped overboard and others were washed from the decks. Just twelve minutes after the collision, the Larchmont was gone.

McVey and six of his crewmembers attempted to row around and pick up those struggling in the water but it was of no use. The strong winds carried his small boat further from the site of the sinking and the screaming mass of people.

McVey decided to try and head for Fisher's Island, but the gales wouldn't allow that either. So they rowed in the direction of Block Island, fifteen miles away.

One of the crewmen in McVey's boat was unable to bear the torturous wind and sea spray cutting into his skin as he awaited an almost certain death. Pulling a knife from his shirt pocket, he slashed his throat.

McVey's boat reached the shores of Block Island at 6:30 the next morning. Suffering from shock and exposure, none of the men were able to speak or walk. Nearby residents ran out to the boat, gently prying loose the hands that were frozen around oar handles.

Within two hours, eight more lifeboats had reached the island, carrying both the living and the dead. Thirty-seven additional bodies washed up on the beach, all of them encased in ice nearly six inches thick.

Several boats were sent out to search for more passengers. The fishing schooner Elsie was able to collect survivors Samuel Tacunne and David Fox, who were found floating on a piece of wreckage. Mr. and Mrs. Harris Feldman of New York were also rescued. In addition to the living, the Elsie brought back a female body clad in a black skirt and short-sleeved white shirt, with two gold rings on the left hand and two gold bracelets encircling each wrist.

The schooner Clara E. retrieved seven passengers from the water, some being frozen solid. Another schooner, the Sneed, brought in the body of an unidentified man, and that of Block Island resident Harry Eckles.

Wet and frozen from head to toe, those who survived were found in a zombie-like state. As news of the event spread, it was being called the worst marine disaster in New England history. Only nine passengers and eleven crewmembers lived to tell the tale.

The Knowlton, which had been bound from South Amboy to Boston with a load of coal, sank close to shore. Captain Frank T. Haley and his crew of six were able to reach land safely.

Today, the Larchmont lies under 120 feet of water in Rosie's Ledge, just three miles southeast of Watch Hill.

FIRE & WATER
MARTHA THAYER

The Hopkinton Post Office, in Hopkinton, formerly the home of Martha Thayer.
Photographer: Kelly Sullivan Pezza

When Martha Elizabeth Babcock was just fifteen years old, her father, Simeon Babcock, drowned in the waters of Charlestown Beach. This event, a terrible shock for the young girl, was just the first in a string of tragedies that would occur in her life.

Martha was married on New Year's Day 1846 to George Kenyon Thayer. The ceremony took place just before dawn, as friends and family gathered at the Boss Meeting House in Richmond. The early hour was chosen so that the newlyweds would be able to catch the first train bound for Boston where they would be spending their honeymoon.

As a married couple, the Thayers moved to Pennsylvania where George became involved in the oil and coal industry. But in the summer of 1880, Martha felt a longing to return to Rhode Island to visit her family. George was unable to accompany her, so she decided to make the trip alone.

Martha's fare was aboard the Providence & Stonington passenger ship, the *Narragansett*. This ship was supposed to carry her safely upon the sea toward Hopkinton, but fate had other plans.

Clouds of thick fog impeded the ship's passage, making it difficult to navigate in the water. Late in the evening of June 11th, a loud crash woke the sleeping passengers who scrambled into their clothes and made their way up to the deck. There, it was discovered that their ship had collided with another steamer, the *Stonington*.

Fire was raging across the decks of the Narragansett and panicked passengers screamed and jumped from the ship into the frigid water. Clinging to floating wreckage and overwhelmed by fear, they watched the vessel be consumed by fire as they waited and prayed to be rescued.

At least forty passengers died before help arrived. Martha Thayer survived the nightmare. However her long exposure to the cold water impacted her health for the rest of her life.

After the shipwreck, George felt it was best that he and his wife move back to Hopkinton where their families were. They purchased the Jeremiah Thurston house in Hopkinton City and did their best to recover from the terrible event Mrs. Thayer had been through. But terrible events were not over for her yet.

In 1888, a massive fire, which began in the Wells Carriage Shop, swept through Hopkinton City. In its flaming path was George and Martha's house. That April day, everything the Thayers had built of their new lives, burned.

WRECKED AND DESERTED
AMOS SWEET

The California Gold Rush beckons treasure seekers.
Image courtesy of Wikipedia.org: public domain image.

Amos Reynolds Sweet died at the age of 78 in Waynesboro, Virginia. Not even two weeks before his death, he had hiked ten miles up a mountain just for the challenge of it. The experience was the summit of a life strewn with adventures.

Sweet was born in West Greenwich in February of 1829. At the age of nineteen, he married Sarah Coggshall and the family grew to include sons John and Frank, and daughter Emma. The Sweets lived in Peace Dale where Amos thrived as a farmer until a sparkling opportunity presented itself. Gold had been discovered in California. Along with thousands of others, Sweet became one of the *forty-niners* and set out to claim his fortune.

The quickest way to California was via the Panama Canal. Although the 8,000-mile journey promised hardships that the gold-hunters were willing and ready to endure, none were prepared for the extremities that were in store.

Sweet and the others left New York by steamboat and sailed easily down the Atlantic coast. Once they reached the Shagaris River, canoes met up with the boat and carried the passengers to Panama. There in the jungles, malaria and yellow fever raged. Taking such epidemics into concern, the travelers also had to be on guard against the jaguars, snakes and crocodiles that seemed to be around every corner, as horses and mules lead them through fifty miles of tropical thickets.

The Panama Canal – NASA photograph.
Courtesy of Wikipedia.org: public domain photo.

Those who made it through the jungle alive, arrived in Panama City only to be informed that there were not any boats to take them to San Francisco. Sweet and the others were forced to remain stranded in the foreign land for over two months.

Finally a boat arrived, and the travelers boarded her, expecting to finally be on their way to the gold. But the weather had plans of its own and the vessel was driven nearly 2,000 miles off course before it wrecked near the Sandwich Islands.

After being rescued, Sweet and his party at last made it to their destination where he spent the next four years searching for gold. He finally realized that he was not going to leave California a wealthy man, and he started back for home. By this time, Sweet should have been of the attitude that whatever could go wrong, would. The ship he was aboard was blown off course and wrecked off the coast of New Mexico.

When he finally returned to Peace Dale, Sweet was without riches, but with a wealth of tales to tell. He returned to farming and decided to look for adventures closer to home.

In September 1907, the widowed farmer and his daughter Emma traveled to Virginia to spend a couple months with his son Frank. They planned to return to Peace Dale the day after Thanksgiving. But on Wednesday morning, November 22nd, Amos Sweet took his last breath and died peacefully at his son's house. Word was sent to John and he immediately went out to Waynesboro to accompany his sister and their father's body home.

Sweet left his family with the legacy of a man who had been full of determination...a man rich with life.

THE TITANIC
RHODE ISLAND PASSENGERS

The Titanic.
Image courtesy of Wikipedia.org: public domain photo.

Many people know what they know about the Titanic through the technology of film-making. But beneath the magic of Hollywood, lie the true stories of those who lost their lives aboard the ill-fated ship. And the stories are close to home.

Helene Ragnhild Ostby was born in Providence in 1889. Her father, Engelhart Cornelius Ostby, was a jewelry maker who traveled the world on business trips. Because her mother had died when she was very young, Helene often accompanied her father on these trips and was with him in the spring of 1912 when he was returning home from Europe and North Africa. The two had tickets to sail aboard the new Titanic.

After spending the evening of April 14 listening to the ship's orchestra, Helene and her father retired to their cabins. Soon after, she felt the ship "bump" something and sat up in bed to listen. She could hear the noise of the engines suddenly stop and the chatter of nervous voices in the hall. Helene fetched her father and the two went up on deck where the roar of the steam pipes was almost deafening.

As Helene waited to be placed in lifeboat #5, her father went back to his cabin to put on warmer clothes. Helene never saw him again. His body was later discovered floating in the sea by a boat that had gone out on search of Titanic victims. He was identified by the paperwork in his pockets, a pair of glasses, a pocketknife, a watch chain and his gold-filled teeth.

Helene returned to Providence where she became a volunteer at Rhode Island Hospital. She died in the city in 1978 and was laid to rest beside her beloved father in Swan Point Cemetery.

Margaret Bechstein Hays was a 25-year-old from New York when she boarded the Titanic to return home from a trip she had taken with her friend Olive Earnshaw and Olive's mother Lily. Like most of the passengers, Margaret was in bed when she felt the ship hit the iceberg. After getting up and dressing herself, she wrapped her Pomeranian dog in a blanket and went up on deck. Soon, she was lowered from the sinking ship in lifeboat #7.

Titanic survivors in a lifeboat rowing toward the Carpathia.
Photo taken by a Carpathia passenger, in National Archives, Records of District Courts of the United States.
Public domain photo

By the time the rescue ship, Carpathia docked in New York, Margaret had taken on a new responsibility. Two French children, Michael and Edmond Navratil had been kidnapped by their father who planned to take them to America. Their father did not survive the sinking and Margaret volunteered to take care of the boys until their mother recognized a photo of them in a newspaper and made arrangements for them to come home.

In 1913, Margaret married Charles Easton and they lived out their lives in Providence and Newport. She died on August 21, 1956 and is buried in St. Mary's Churchyard in Portsmouth.

Twenty-four-year-old Bertha Mulvihill took passage on Titanic for her return trip to Rhode Island after attending a wedding in Ireland. Back home, her own wedding was drawing near. Engaged to Henry Noon of Providence, Bertha had collected a large assortment of linens, as well as a wedding gown while on her trip.

She escaped the wrath of Titanic on lifeboat #15, clad only in a nightgown, shoes and coat. Her linens and wedding attire went down with the ship, yet she managed to save a prayer book and a watch that her fiancé had given her as a gift. She pinned the items to her nightgown that fateful night.

Bertha was met in New York by Noon, who brought her back to Providence where they were soon married. She died on October 15, 1959 and was laid to rest in St. Francis Cemetery in Pawtucket.

Amy Zillah Stanley, a resident of England, was born in 1888. After having found work as a maid in New Haven, Connecticut, she boarded the Titanic for the journey to America. She was saved from the sinking in collapsible lifeboat "C", where she comforted other passengers and even induced a few smiles when she commented that at least they could now avoid the required vaccinations that were scheduled to be administered on the ship the next day.

Amy eventually married and settled down in Providence, where she died on April 21, 1955. She was buried in Oakland Cemetery in Cranston.

Rosa Abbott was a 35-year-old mother traveling from England to Providence with her two teenaged sons, Rossmore and Eugene, when she boarded "the unsinkable ship". Separated from boxing champion Stanton Abbott, Rosa had moved to England to be closer to her parents, but her sons were homesick and she decided to bring them back to Rhode Island.

As the ship made its final plunge, Rosa and her two boys jumped from the deck. She managed to climb onto collapsible lifeboat "A" but her sons were not so lucky. Eugene's body was never found. Rossmore's body was identified by a medal he wore bearing his name. He was buried at sea on April 24.

Ellen Bird, age 31, was making the trip from England to America with Isidor and Ida Strauss, who had hired her during their vacation to return home with them and work as their maid. When Ellen and Ida were instructed to get into lifeboat #8, Ida refused to leave her husband. She stepped back away from the lifeboat, wrapped her fur coat around Ellen, and told her to get into the boat. Both of the Strausses died that night.

Ellen married Edward Beattie and spent the rest of her life in Rhode Island. She died in Newport on September 11, 1949.

Henry Blank was born in Providence in 1872. A goldsmith, he was returning from Europe where he had gone on a business trip. Henry was playing cards in the first class smoking room when he felt the collision. Venturing into the racquet court to investigate, he noticed water seeping into the ship.

On deck, there were not enough women and children close by to fill lifeboat #7, so Henry was one of the few men afforded a chance at survival that night. He later died on March 17, 1949.

John Joseph Lamb, of Ireland, boarded the Titanic at Queenstown with his destination being Providence, Rhode Island. He didn't survive the sinking and his body was never found.

James Vivian Drew was born in Constantine, England on May 4, 1869. In 1896, he migrated to America with his brother William and settled in Suffolk, New York. There, the two men began a marble monument business.

Eventually the brothers took wives. But sadness struck when William's wife died two weeks after giving birth to their son Marshall Brines Drew. Wanting to help in this time of despair, James and his wife, the former Lulu Thorne Christian, took the child into their home. He would be with them when they boarded the Titanic. After traveling to England aboard the Olympic, to visit relatives, James and his family acquired second-class tickets on the Titanic for their return trip.

On the night of April 14, 1912, a steward knocked at the door of the Drew's cabin and told them to get up on deck because the ship was sinking. Lulu woke up 8-year-old Marshall and helped him get dressed, explaining to him where they were going. But when they arrived up on deck and stood waiting to be placed in a lifeboat, they were told that women and children were being allowed into the boats first. James stepped back as his wife and nephew climbed into lifeboat #10. As the boat was lowered from the sinking ship, James waved to them. Lulu stood staring desperately up at her husband. That was the last time she ever saw him.

James Drew, age 43, went down with the ship, buried in the waters of the icy Atlantic. His body was never found.

Memorial to Titanic passenger James Drew, at Oak Grove Cemetery in Hopkinton.
Photographer: Kelly Sullivan Pezza

As an adult, Marshall recalled how there was a malfunction with the ropes that were lowering the lifeboat he was in and that the occupants were afraid it was going to tip over and spill them all out into the sea. Once safely upon the ocean in the tiny boat, he remembered hearing a large explosion and the sound of people screaming.

One year after the sinking, Lulu married Richard Opie of Westerly. She never liked talking about the events of that terrible night in 1912. She and Richard both passed away in 1970. Their gravestone stands in Oak Grove Cemetery in Ashaway, along with a memorial to James.

THE SEA RUSHED IN
THE HURRICANE OF 1938

Billie Holiday had just been discovered. Amos 'n Andy were household names. And everyone was crooning to *Thanks For The Memory*. It was 1938 and summer had recently ended. Autumn had set in to send crisp colored leaves blowing across Rhode Island like it did every year. But the year would be like no other. Before winter came, an unthinkable catastrophe would change everything. And no one even saw it coming.

The afternoon of September 21st brought drizzling rain and chilly winds. While that type of weather was not exactly desirable, it was a lot better than what some people in other parts of the world were experiencing. Everyone knew that a hurricane had raged out of the Cape Verde Islands on September 4$^{th.}$ Moving at sixty miles per hour, it was making its way toward Canada. There, it was expected to taper off, returning the sea and the weather to normal. But at 3:30 that afternoon, several residents of Charlestown Beach looked out their windows to see a 60-foot wave racing toward the shore. No one had time to prepare for what was about to happen.

Wind gusts suddenly reached close to 186 miles per hour. The high tide rose to nearly seventeen feet. The eye of the hurricane was staring down at Rhode Island.

One by one, it began to suck up the cottages on Charlestown Beach, scattering walls, ceilings and floors in every direction. Historic homes in Weekapaug, which had stood the test of time for centuries, were smacked by the ferocious wind and reduced to rubble. Hotels, restaurants, lighthouses and bridges were crumpled as if they were made out of paper. And the Pawcatuck River backed up so far that it flooded parts of Westerly beneath four feet of water.

Twenty thousand miles of telephone and electrical lines were blown down, leaving everyone to cower in the loud and thrashing darkness. As the storm continued to lash out in fury, it took with it boats, trees, homes and bodies.

Several local organizations sprung into action, assisting the wounded and comforting the suddenly homeless. The Civil Conservation Corps from Exeter and Charlestown were called in to search the wreckage for bodies, using a building on Broad Street in Westerly as a temporary morgue where the deceased could be identified. Each body was numbered, and when someone came in to ask about the fate of a loved one, they were told to either fill out a description card, or search the pile of index cards which already bore descriptions of those who had been found.

Over 300 Rhode Island residents were killed in the hurricane. Over 200 were recovered, but the rest had been swept out to sea and remained missing forever.

Forty-year-old Havilah Moore drowned in the waters of Watch Hill. Seventy-one-year-old Jessie Mary Jackley was pulled into the sea at Watch Hill but was swept across Little Narragansett Bay into Stonington before she drowned.

Forty-year-old assistant lighthouse keeper Walter Eberle had been at Whale Rock Lighthouse in Narragansett Bay when the hurricane hit. Later, it was discovered that the lighthouse was gone, and so was Eberele.

Eighty-six-year-old Celia Elizabeth (Carr) Clark, from Shannock, was at Charlestown Beach that day with her two daughters, 58-year-old Harriet Sumner and 55-year-old Florence; and her daughter-in-law, 45-year-old Ann. They were all killed. Harriet had been the librarian at Clark's Mills Library, which was later renamed Clark Memorial Library, in her honor.

The hurricane went down in history as the worst Rhode Island disaster ever recorded.

DESTINED TO THE SEA
ALFRED VANDERBILT

Alfred Gwynne Vanderbilt.
Image courtesy of Wikipedia.org: public domain photo.

In the year 1912, the largest, most extravagant luxury liner afloat was the Titanic. While sailing from Ireland toward New York, the ship sank, taking with it the life of Newport millionaire John Astor.

In the year 1915, the largest, most extravagant luxury liner afloat was the Lusitania. While sailing from New York toward Ireland, the ship sank, taking with it the life of Newport millionaire Alfred Vanderbilt.

The similarities between the two events are like mirrored fate. And if it was fate, did Alfred Vanderbilt know that he was tempting it?

The Lusitania, a Cunard steamship liner, left New York's Pier 54 just after noon on Saturday, May 1, 1915. It was expected to dock in Liverpool, England by the next Saturday.

The 1,959 passengers aboard included poor immigrants, rich aristocrats and the ship's crew. Alfred Vanderbilt, whose late father Cornelius had willed to him the Breakers mansion in Newport, was sailing aboard the Lusitania with his valet Ronald Denyer. They were traveling to England to attend a meeting of the International Horse Breeders Association. An avid horse-lover, Alfred's estate in Newport included the largest private horse riding ring in the world.

Born in New York to Cornelius and Alice Vanderbilt, Alfred had lived a somewhat turbulent, though opulent life. When his father suffered a sudden cerebral hemorrhage at the age of 56, the bulk of his $72 million estate was left to Alfred. This enraged Cornelius's oldest son, who had been disowned by his father when he married a woman Cornelius didn't approve of. Although Alfred offered to share his inheritance with his brother, the offer apparently only added insult to injury and the brothers had little to do with each other ever again.

Alfred grew up in his family's Manhattan mansion with his widowed mother, younger siblings and staff of over fifteen servants, including maids, butlers, private physicians and cooks.

The seven-deck Lusitania was well-equipped with all the amenities a wealthy man like Vanderbilt could want. The first class dining saloon contained two interior decks topped with a grandiose domed ceiling. Menu selections included crème chatillon and bavarois au chocolat.

The first class lounge was set beneath a stained glass skylight, with thickly cushioned chairs arranged around large footstools.

The regal suites provided two bedrooms, a parlor, bathroom, pantry and private dining room. Only an option for the wealthy, accommodations in the suites carried a price-tag of $4,000 one-way.

Alfred Gwynne Vanderbilt could well afford such a luxury. He had been a child raised with wealth and was now a man who had gone on to gain even more. But his money could not save him from his fate. At the time the millionaire purchased his tickets to sail aboard the Lusitania, a lot of friction was building between countries. America remained neutral as war between Germany and England brewed.

One week before the Lusitania set out on its final sail, a notice was published in newspapers across America, warning citizens that if they embarked upon any ocean travel, they did so at their own risk. Germany had made it clear that any ship believed to be a threat to their country's security would be seen and acted on as an enemy. Adding to the danger, German officials announced that rumors were swirling concerning the allegedly neutral America supplying the British with artillery.

Among the cargo being carried by the Lusitania from the pier in New York, were crates of butter, bacon, oysters and salt. Over $735,000 worth of goods were being transported to Europe for sale there. But the Germans believed that, on this particular voyage, the ship would also be carrying six million rounds of ammunition for use by British troops.

The Lusitania itself was a British ship, built in Scotland in 1905. The 785-foot liner was, by law, equipped with fittings to carry a dozen Navy guns. As World War I simmered, a regulation was made that even ocean liners be prepared for military duty. Yet even though the Lusitania was prepared to launch attacks, it wasn't constructed to defend itself against them.

By May 7, 1915, the coast of Ireland was in sight. In just a matter of hours, Vanderbilt and his fellow passengers were to arrive in Liverpool. But the ship would not make it that far. Just 700 yards away from the Lusitania, a German submarine lurked. At 2:10 p.m., the submarine's Captain Schwieger gave the order to fire at the liner.

Aboard the Lusitania, Captain William Thomas Turner suddenly heard 18-year-old seaman Leslie Morton cry out, "A torpedo is coming!"

A brilliant trail of smoke and light blazed across the distance between the two vessels and exploded as it hit the right side of the Lusitania. The force violently threw the ship into a leaning position.

As passengers rushed to the decks to see what was happening, seamen Morton and Joseph Perry immediately began to ready the lifeboats. Although there were enough boats to carry every passenger, launching them proved almost impossible. Those on the port side were hanging on to the deck, while those on the starboard side were hanging too far out over the water to be reached.

As the seamen struggled to lift the first lifeboat off the deck, it slipped from their hands and swung away from them, crushing the hysterical passengers standing behind it. The second boat was loaded but then was unable to be lowered from the ship and instead flipped over and spilled its human contents into the ocean sixty feet below. While the passengers struggled in the water, the ropes of the lifeboat hanging over them snapped, and the boat smashed down upon them.

A third boat was filled and lowered but before it had a chance to touch down, another full boat was lowered directly above it. Suddenly the upper boat broke free of its ropes and landed on those underneath.

The scraping and scratching of lifeboats, the snapping of ropes and the steam shooting out of the dying ship accompanied the chorus of screams piercing the spring air.

It is said that Vanderbilt kept his cool throughout it all. He instructed his valet to assist him in gathering up all the children they could find. Rushing into the nursery, the two men began tying life jackets to the bassinets of each infant. When Third Officer Alfred Bestic ran into the room urging the two men to get off the sinking ship, Vanderbilt paid no attention. He continued to outfit each baby with a chance of survival. Once finished with that task, he and Denyer went up onto the deck to help finish loading the children there into lifeboats.

Only when he was sure he had helped everyone he could, did Vanderbilt make an attempt to save his own life. He couldn't swim and was attaching a life jacket to himself as he hurried down a corridor when a hysterical young woman ran up to him crying that there were no more life jackets left. Vanderbilt immediately untied his own and put it on the girl.

Less than 18 minutes after the torpedo blast, the bow of the Lusitania was submerged. As the front of the ship struck the sea floor, the stern rose high in the air, standing almost straight up. By 2:28, the entire ship had disappeared from sight. Today she lies in complete darkness at the bottom of the ocean.

Of the 1,195 dead, 123 Americans were included. This blatant attack on innocent American civilians almost insured that the United States would become involved in the war, fueled now by a bitter resentment toward Germany. Recruitment posters began bearing the words, "Remember the Lusitania!"

Those who were rescued from the wreck were treated at a Queenstown hospital. The known dead were returned to their families while the unknown dead were buried at Old Church Cemetery in Ireland.

Apparently the mirror of fate reflected on Alfred Vanderbilt. He had allegedly received a telegram in his hotel room the night before the Lusitania set sail. The message held a warning that he should not sail aboard the ship because she was destined to sink. Vanderbilt chose to ignore the warning. The body of the 37-year-old man was never found.

A LIGHT UPON THE WATER
THE GHOST OF THE PALATINE

The Princess Augusta sailed out of Rotterdam in the fall of 1738. Bound for New York, her passengers included a large number of immigrants from the Palatine area of Germany.

From the very beginning, the journey was anything but smooth sailing. Frigid winds, high seas and blinding snow slowed the ship's pace, dragging out the trek for longer than planned. The food supply was diminished and the crew asked Captain Andrew Brooks if they could break open the cargo of rations being delivered to New York. Brooks refused to allow what edible cargo they had to be consumed.

Sick, starving and frost-bitten, the crew and passengers could do little more than try to endure the frozen hell they were sailing through. Drinking water had long been depleted and many passengers began to die. For those who survived the dehydration, the lack of nourishment and the harsh climate, there was still more of hell to be seen.

On December 27, a snow storm began to rage. The ship was blown off course and the captain was left to decide which port he should attempt to head for. But the ocean swelled and the waves smacked up against the ship, making it impossible to maneuver in any specific direction. At 2:00 p.m. that afternoon, the Princess Augusta wrecked against the rocky shores of Block Island.

Water began to pour into the cracked vessel and island residents who witnessed the wreck ran out to help the passengers to safety. Those who were still alive weakly made their way onto the beach.

One woman, who refused to leave her possessions on the ship, opted to stay aboard. The crew and residents urged her to quickly come ashore but she was relentless. Suddenly, a fire erupted. As the flames raced across the deck, the woman began to scream for help. But it was too late for anyone to save her.

The Princess Augusta has gone down in history as the Palatine, due to the nationality of those who had last sailed upon her. And the strange phenomenon that has been occurring for centuries in the waters around Block Island has come to be known as the Palatine Light.

Over the years, dozens of people have witnessed a glowing light in the shape of a ship, drifting aimlessly across the sea. The light then sinks beneath the surface of the water. The phenomenon has never been explained, and many believe that the ghost of the last passenger aboard is reliving her ordeal again and again...for all to witness.

RELIGION

THE SHAKERS OF HOPKINTON
FOLLOWERS OF ANN LEE

Nineteenth century engraving of a Shaker meeting.
Image courtesy of Wikipedia.org; public domain image.

In days gone by, religion played a huge role in the lives of basically everyone. Locally, we had Baptists, Quakers and a variety of other religions. In fact, the town of Hopkinton seemed to be a magnet for those wanting to branch out into new or little-known religious sects.

In 1774, a religious group from England called the Shakers arrived in the colonies. The most outspoken of the sect was Joshua Birch, who settled in the house later owned by Peleg Clarke, on Kuehn Road in Hopkinton. This large house provided more than enough room for Shaker meetings, which were anything but quiet affairs. The Shakers believed they could reach the height of religious enlightenment by shaking and dancing themselves into a frenzy.

Legend has it that during one of the meetings at Birch's house, his wife threw her gold necklace on the floor and the hysterical dancers smashed the necklace to powder with their fancy footwork.

The rules of the sect included separation of the sexes, even between members who were married, and celibacy was strictly enforced. Their meetings, in addition to wild dancing, included public confessions of sins as well as speaking in strange tongues.

The Shakers believed a woman named Ann Lee to be the female embodiment of Christ. Lee had been brought up in a poor English family, spending her childhood working in a textile mill to help the family make ends meet. Perhaps it was being forced into marriage with a man she didn't love or the subsequent deaths of all four of her children, that drove her to find spiritual comfort.

After becoming friends with a Quaker couple, James and Jane Wardley, Lee decided to begin following their faith. However the Wardleys were a bit obsessed with the art of prophecy. Lee submerged herself in their beliefs, and eventually she and other Quakers who were less typical members of the religion, broke away and formed their own sect. They called themselves the United Society of Believers in Christ's Second Coming.

Lee and other members of this sect were often arrested and imprisoned for their demonstrations and bold attempts to convert others. After one such arrest, Lee reported that, while confined in her jail cell, she had a vision. During this experience, she was informed that she was the reincarnation of Christ. In light of this information, Lee became the sect's leader.

While her followers saw her as their savior, members of other religious groups saw her as a false prophet and were determined to rid themselves of her evil presence. They continuously found reasons to whip and ridicule her and her followers. Finally, she had another vision. This time she was told to take her sect elsewhere.

On May 10, 1774, Ann Lee and eight of her followers boarded a sailing ship, the Mariah, at Liverpool. Their journey across the Atlantic would take three months.

On August 6, the Mariah docked in New York. Lee and her brother William, along with James Whittaker, John Townley, John Hocknell and four others immediately began searching for a place to live. They discovered a swampy tract of land in Niskeyung, New York. Just as Lee's followers had financed the entire journey, they paid for the tract of land.

The members built cabins upon the property and planted crops. They also spread the word to neighbors that the Messiah had arrived. It wasn't long before hundreds of people were flocking to the settlement to follow the teachings of Lee.

She demanded communal living within the sect, and complete disconnection with the outside world Separation of men and women was strictly enforced, as anything leading to procreation was viewed as one of the worst sins a person could commit.

There were rules to be followed by every single person, at every single moment of every single day. Members were to rise at 4:30 in the morning during the summer months, and 5:30 in the winter. They were then to kneel and pray before getting dressed, stripping their beds and opening all the windows in their dormitory-like sleeping quarters.

Breakfast was to be eaten exactly one hour after waking. Following that, every member was expected to work without stopping except for meals and prayer. All members had assigned jobs. Some were housekeepers, others were cooks, animal caretakers, wood-choppers or farm workers. Men and women had to use separate stairways and doors, and were not allowed to speak to each other for any reason without a chaperone present.

The workday ended at 6:00 at night and bedtime was set at 9:30. On Sundays, the entire day was spent worshipping.

Worship was cause for this completely serene group of people to become transformed into part of a wild spectacle. Loud singing and dancing was interrupted by members suddenly being seized by hallucinations, twisting and contorting their bodies. Strange languages were spoken before members fell to the floor, spun around and finally collapsed into a deep trance.

When Lee died in 1784, her sect, which by this time had become known as the Shakers, did not die with her. By 1860, the group had over 6,000 followers with settlements in New York, Massachusetts, Connecticut, Maine, New Hampshire, Ohio, Indiana and Kentucky. The religion lasted another hundred years before the last Shaker settlement, in Massachusetts, closed down. The strict membership rules had long been severing families, not to mention prohibiting any chance of producing offspring. So the wild dances and deep trances ceased, and the teachings of Ann Lee were left to history.

FROLICKING & FIDDLING
QUAKERS AND CONTROVERSY

A Quaker Cemetery in Hopkinton.
Photographer: Gregory Pezza

Centuries ago, in England, certain people took it upon themselves to break away from widely accepted religions of the time. They formed a society which they called the Friends and began to follow their own religious path, which later became known as Quakerism.

With their strict rules of moral conduct, the Quakers separated themselves from the majority. Persecution followed and most members of the society fled to the colonies, hoping for greater religious freedom.

In 1750, local Quakers requested that a meetinghouse be erected for them in Richmond *"on the highway which leads from John Knowles' house to Mumford's Mills"*. The 32 by 24 foot structure was cold and unembellished, in keeping with the Quaker's rules of simplicity and absence of adornment.

Quaker meetinghouses also sprung up in neighboring towns and the Friends held meetings at each of them on an alternating basis.

Certain members of the society were elected Overseers and their duty was to regularly visit the homes of other members to make sure they were abiding by all of the society's rules. Members who were suspected of any wrongdoing were put before an elected disciplinary committee where they were expected to account for their actions in writing, as well as verbally apologize for their behavior. Sometimes forgiveness was granted. Sometimes it was not.

Records show that some local Quakers did not seem to be quite as God-fearing as the Society expected them to be. Some members went before the disciplinary board for breaking the rule that prohibited one Friend from taking another into court. John Barber, of Hopkinton, was one such person called before the board to explain why he sued a fellow member. The parents of Charles Bowen were asked to repent for the same misdeed when they encouraged their son to bring legal action against John Collins.

Others were called in to apologize for missing meetings, even when the absence was due to the hardship of traveling on horseback through cold, winter nights.

Sometimes it was felt that one member had somehow cheated another, as when John Congdon of Charlestown was placed before the board to answer for treating Simeon Tucker *"hardly in bargaining"*.

Friends who did not make good on their debts were also faced with discipline. Thomas Hazard, John Collins and Thomas Wilbore were at one time elected to look into the affairs of member Robert Knowles who was in a financial dilemma. He was instructed by the committee to sell off his worldly goods, and then his house in order to pay off his debts. Knowles was allowed to stay at his brother John's house where he was provided the use of one cow and 1 ½ acres of farmland.

It was against Quaker rules for any member to marry out of the Society. This was usually a reason for immediate dismissal. Friends who had intentions of marrying were expected to inform their fellow members of their wish at the beginning of a meeting. Consent was not given for one month. This allowed plenty of time for a group of elected members to closely inspect the lives of both parties and decide whether or not the union was appropriate.

Weddings were held at one of the meetinghouses with all members in attendance. Attending weddings of any other faith was looked down upon. In 1757, Jonathan and Samuel Perry who resided in South Kingstown, found themselves before the disciplinary board for *"being at an entertainment subsequent to a marriage at which there was vain recreation"*. Jonathan wrote a letter asking for the Society's forgiveness, stating that although he was at the wedding, he would have rather been at a Society meeting. But Samuel stated in his own letter that he did not feel he had done anything wrong.

The next year, Jonathan was once again discovered to be acting in an unacceptable manner. This time, not only for attending a non-Quaker wedding, but for actually taking part in the festivities that followed, dancing *"in a light and airy manner"*.

But the Perry boys were not the only local Quakers caught in the act of failing to restrain themselves from *"undue liberties."* The three daughters of Hezekiah Collins were also at the above-mentioned wedding and were called before the disciplinary board to explain why they were at an event where there was *"frolicking and music, fiddling and dancing"*. Hezekiah received a letter from Jonathan Perry's father Jacob.

Fearing for his son's ultimate destiny, Jacob hoped this letter might help remove all temptation from his son's mind. It seemed that the young Jonathan had a mad attraction to Hezekiah's daughter Alicia.

"On the first of the year, the Gardners of Boston Neck had a gathering, indulging in practices forbidden by our Society," wrote Jacob. *"My misguided son, instructed by thy daughter, joined in the dancing and, I am informed, excelled all the young men present. When asked to condemn his conduct, he boldly justified it. I entreat thee to warn thy daughter as to the danger of beguiling a youngster from the light of truth."*

Although the Society of Friends is still in existence, its number has dwindled over the years. Most of the old meetinghouses have been torn down and the descendents of former Quakers have taken the paths of Baptists, Catholics and other religions. But those who "saw the light of truth", or at least tried, still remain here, resting beneath stones in Quaker burial grounds. And records of their lives, their meetings and their concerns remain also, a comforting reminder that no one is perfect.

PUBLIC PROPHET
JEMIMA WILKINSON

In 1776, a Quaker by the name of Jemima Wilkinson, whose father was cousin to Governor Stephen Hopkins, came down with a serious fever. As she lay in bed at her home in Cumberland, she began to have hallucinations and hear voices.

To those around her, it appeared that Wilkinson's mind was becoming affected by the fever. But once she recovered from her illness, she began to claim that her former soul had departed and that she was now a prophet inhabiting Wilkinson's body. Her new name, she proclaimed, was the Publick Universal Friend.

Wilkinson began preaching sermons throughout Cumberland before moving on to Kingston and Hopkinton. Many of her followers had been lifelong Quakers until trading their former beliefs for Wilkinson's. But most Quakers in Hopkinton frowned upon her beliefs and forbid any of their members from attending her sermons. Jeremiah Browning secretly attended two of her sermons and was only forgiven by the Quakers when he asked them in writing for forgiveness for what he had done.

Wilkinson was in her late twenties when she began spreading her warnings of the judgment day to come. She was described as a beautiful woman with long, curly black hair who often dressed in men's clothing. While her followers believed her to be the second coming of Christ, others believed her new self-designated position to be that of massive fraud.

In 1779, a Providence book publisher published a book Wilkinson claimed to have written. Later, upon examination of the book, it was found to be a copy of another religious publication. Wilkinson was charged with plagiarism.

While holding her sermons on Tower Hill in Kingston, she was given full reign of the home owned by Judge William Potter, whose entire family had left their Quaker beliefs to follow her teachings. At that time, Potter's daughter Alice was telling anyone who would listen that Wilkinson truly was the son of God, and that anyone who did not believe it was eternally damned. Wanting to prove to the naysayers that she was in fact, the chosen one, Wilkinson shared with them the date on which doomsday would occur. According to the Publick Friend it would take place in April of 1780.

She also tried to offer proof of her status by appearing at local funerals and trying to raise the dead. Never once was she successful in this endeavor, and she blamed her inability to complete the miracle of resurrection on the lack of faith in those around her.

During a large local gathering where several speakers of different religions had come to spread their beliefs and garner new followers, one pastor spoke to the crowd in a foreign language. Wilkinson stepped up and asked the pastor if he might translate what he had just said. "If you are Christ, then you know what I just said," he replied.

Wilkinson held meetings in Hopkinton at a structure near the Connecticut state line. She would ride on horseback to and from the meeting, with her twelve disciples, wearing colored robes which would float upon the wind. Her sermons included subjects such as the importance of celibacy and she made it clear that she was not fond of the idea of marriage.

By the late 1780's, she had more than 200 followers and decided it was time to move her entire establishment to the wilds of Pennsylvania, far from the evils of the world. They remained in Pennsylvania for four years before Wilkinson announced that it was time to relocate to New York and build a new Jerusalem.

There, she explained, they would live together as a family, segregated from civilization.

Because Wilkinson did not believe in owning earthly possessions, the compound's land in New York was put in the name of one of her followers, Sally Friend. A few years later, when Friend died, her will directed that ownership of the land be passed into the hands of her daughter. This daughter, just sixteen years old, and disliking the strict rules of Wilkinson's sect, climbed out her bedroom window one night and eloped with a man. The law at that time determined that a woman who owns land then takes a husband does not own the land any longer...he does. Her husband began to sell off parcels, eventually forcing the sect from their homestead. Twelve years worth of court litigations were about to begin. ..ending only after all those involved were dead.

Joseph Phillips of Richmond left his wife in 1803 to join Wilkinson in New York. He never returned and is buried there. His wife Susannah, who did not share his belief in Wilkinson, is buried in a cemetery off Punchbowl Trail in Richmond.

Jemima Wilkinson died in 1819. By that time, she had lost most of her followers and many even tried to have her arrested. She was buried in New York in an unmarked grave.

MOTHER OF THE MONSTER
MARY DYER

Illustration of Mary Dyer being led to her execution.
Courtesy of Wikipedia.org: public domain image.

The Hazard family of Charlestown may trace their roots back to a frightening piece of history. Joseph Hazard, who resided in that town in the 1700's, was a descendent of Mary Brownell. Mary's sister married Charles Dyer, the sibling of a historically documented "monster".

William and Mary Dyer settled in Boston, Massachusetts after sailing from England to escape religious persecution. Once Puritans, they eventually found themselves drawn to the Quaker faith and under the spell of religious leader Anne Hutchinson. Against all commonly accepted religious beliefs, Hutchinson preached that it was not necessary to find God through a clergyman, but that an individual could find God themselves and be assured of salvation.

On March 22, 1638, the Puritan Church of Boston excommunicated Hutchinson for those beliefs, and began calling her a witch. As she walked out of the crowded church that day, Mary Dyer rose and followed her. "Who is that woman accompanying Anne Hutchinson?" one church member asked aloud. "She is the mother of the monster!" another member answered.

In the summer of 1637, Mary Dyer had learned that she was pregnant. The baby was not due until December but Mary went into pre-mature labor on October 17.

Hutchinson and two other women stood at the bedside as Mary endured several hours of painful labor. When it was discovered that the child was in a breach position, Hutchinson reached inside and turned the fetus around. But it was of no use. The baby girl was born dead.

The child was buried and the three women made a mysterious pact of secrecy concerning the birth. But one of them was not able to keep what she knew to herself and soon rumors were circling the town.

The woman confessed to authorities that Dyer's baby had been born with a face but no head. That its ears, similar to those of an ape, grew from its shoulders. And that there had been four horns above its protruding eyes. The child was also described as having sharp, prickly scales all over its body and that *"it's naval and belly were where the back should have been"*.

She went on to describe two mouths between the child's shoulders, *"in each of them, a piece of red flesh sticking out."* Its arms and legs, she continued, were of normal shape and size, yet there were no toes. Instead, three sharp talons grew from each foot. The authorities ordered that the body of the child be exhumed for examination.

Governor John Winthrop penned in his diary that rumors of a monster being in the grave needed to be proven or disproved. There was widespread belief that Anne Hutchinson had bewitched Mary Dyer and caused her to breed the horribly deformed child. *"Before the birth, the bed whereon the mother lay did shake,"* Winthrop wrote. *"And withal here was such a noisome savor as most of the women were taken with extreme vomiting and purging."*

When the body of the Dyer baby was exhumed, it was found to be just as the female witness had described.

Hutchinson was banished from Boston and Mary Dyer followed her to Newport. Religious freedom was greater in Rhode Island, but Mary refused to stay put. Upon learning that two fellow Quakers had been imprisoned in Boston, she went there to visit them. She was immediately placed in prison with them and sentenced to be hanged.

On October 27 of that year, the prisoners held tightly to each other's hands as they walked towards the gallows. Mary was forced to watch the others hanged first and then instructed to climb the ladder. Her hands and feet were then bound, a blindfold placed over her eyes and the noose tightened around her neck. At that moment, someone in the crowd cried out that Mary had been granted a reprieve. Her life spared, she was ordered to leave Boston and never return. But she decided that being a martyr was more important and on June 1, 1660 at 9:00 in the morning, she was once again lead to the gallows in the Boston Common. There, she was given a chance to repent, but refused. The hangman's noose was once again slipped around her neck and this time the execution was not stopped. She was later buried there in the Common in an unmarked grave.

Mary Dyer left behind seven children, hundreds of future descendents, and a mysterious legend.

MARRIED TO THE MARTYR
HUMILITY GREENE

1901 illustration of Anne Hutchinson on trial
Artist: Edwina Abbay.
Courtesy of Wikipedia.org: public domain image.

When Humility Greene of North Kingstown married Joshua Coggeshall, she became forever linked to one of the most infamous religious events in history.

Joshua was a Quaker who had been imprisoned in Boston and robbed of his horse because of his beliefs. The son of John Coggeshall, his father had begun a relationship with someone which would forever affect the family.

Anne Marbury was born in Lincolnshire, England in 1591. The daughter of a church deacon who had been thrown in jail for claiming that most ministers were not fit to guide the souls of others, Anne grew up strongly attached to her father's convictions. Her life was so deeply rooted in religion, when her favorite Puritan minister, John Cotton, removed to the colonies, she packed up her belongings and followed.

With her husband William Hutchinson, Anne boarded the Griffin and sailed toward the shores of Massachusetts in 1634. What she found there was disappointing. It seemed to her that the ministers of Boston were speaking as if they themselves were the Lord. Anne was so bothered by this Puritan attitude that she began to hold small religious gatherings at her own home. There, five or six locals would gather to hear Anne's interpretations of the Bible.

Anne did not believe that the positive or negative actions of one's life would determine whether or not God would save one's soul. According to her teachings, good deeds did not bring salvation anymore than evil doings brought damnation. True Christians, she believed, had the light of God inside them and were therefore guaranteed salvation, despite anything they were to do here on earth. Under such a belief, one did not have to read the Bible or go to church on Sundays to please the Lord. She also believed that child baptisms were un-necessary because the child had no understanding of what was happening. The teachings of the Bible, she said, were meant to be interpreted differently by everyone.

It wasn't long before Anne's small weekly group of listeners turned into a following of over fifty people who met at her house twice a week. As she was still a member of the Boston Church, which held strong to the Puritan beliefs that she was undermining, an outrage erupted in Massachusetts and Anne was put on trial in Boston.

She was called a witch and her teachings were deemed to be above the scripture. Many witnesses at the trial spoke out against her, claiming that she had trained her followers to draw others to her. One man testified, "Having gotten them into her web, they could easily be poisoned by degree."

Some also claimed that Anne and her followers went out of their way to acquaint themselves with as many people as possible by showering them with affection, offering them free room and board and attempting to comfort those in despair by convincing them they had been following the wrong road toward joy.

In her defense, Anne's husband referred to her as "a dear saint". But a Massachusetts pastor called her "a most dangerous sprit."

The Puritans viewed Anne as pure evil in human form. Since her arrival in Boston, strange events did indeed occur. Experienced as a mid-wife, Anne was present at the laboring of Mary Dyer, the mother of the proclaimed monster child. The frightening birth was brought up at the trial and Anne explained that the descriptions of the event were all true and that she had wanted to inform authorities immediately but that the Pastor Cotton had urged to keep quiet about the matter and simply bury the child. Cotton admitted she was telling the truth.

During the trial, Anne was pregnant with her 15th child. While giving her testimony, she became wracked with pain and eventually expelled a premature fetus. She continued to proclaim her innocence and told the court that she could see into the future and though she was not evil herself, a real and true evil was about to befall the colonies. She announced that God had assured her he would deliver her out of their hands and that a curse would befall Massachusetts. Branded a heretic, she was banned from the state. "I deliver you up to Satan," the judge told her before she left the courthouse.

Anne and her family removed to Rhode Island and helped found the area of Portsmouth. By 1643, her husband had passed away and she had relocated to New York. Six of her children went with her. That summer, several Indians broke into her home and murdered Anne and all but one of her children.

Though many stood up to persecute Anne Hutchinson, there were many others who stood up to defend her. One of those people was John Coggeshall. A Boston deacon, he so solidly stood behind Anne throughout the trial that the courts decided he had been brain-washed and ordered him and 58 other men to turn over all their guns and ammunition to authorities. Nineteen of those men removed to Rhode Island, including John.

His son Joshua was raised to believe in the principles of Anne Hutchinson. Believing her teachings to be stronger than the banishment imposed on his fellow believers, he ventured back into Boston and was imprisoned. But his return to Rhode Island and marriage to Humility created a bloodline that carries on through our local counties to this day.

MORMONS
THE TANNER FAMILY

Old postcard of the Mormon Temple in Salt Lake City, Utah.
Public domain image

On August 15, 1778, Joshua Tanner and his wife, Thankful, of Hopkinton, welcomed a baby boy they named John. Their son would not grow to follow the traditional religions of the colonies however. He would take a path of his own choosing.

In 1830, a man named Joseph Smith founded an organization in Ohio called the Church of Jesus Christ. Smith felt that true Christianity had been lost over time, as religion had branched out, creating several different churches and a wide variety of different beliefs. He felt that one true religion needed to be established and he took the task upon himself. He decided to call the group the Seekers. Later, they would become known as the Mormons.

Within one year, over 1,000 people counted themselves as members of this church. Yet devotees of other churches did not want Smith diminishing the numbers in their congregations, and conflicts began. Smith opted to move his church from Ohio to Missouri. But no sooner had he arrived there when tensions and violent eruptions started anew, forcing him to relocate again. Not long after settling in Illinois, Smith was assassinated.

John Tanner had moved to New York while in his early twenties, There, in 1800, he married Tabitha Bentley. When she passed away the next year during childbirth, John married 28-year-old Lydia Stewart and the couple worked their farm, not much differently than his parents had done in Hopkinton.

When Lydia died in 1825, John took Elizabeth Besswick as his third wife, and seven years later, a decision was made between them that would change life as they knew it. John and Elizabeth joined the Mormon Church under the leadership of Joseph Smith. They followed him from Ohio to Missouri to Illinois and were there with him when he was killed.

A man named Brigham Young took over leadership of the church and led the group to Utah. By this time, John Tanner had over twenty children. His son Myron took a wife of his own in Salt Lake City in 1856, a fellow Mormon named Mary Jane Mount. Ten years later, Myron, who was employed as a gristmill operator, decided to marry again. That May, he exchanged vows with English-born Ann Crosby. However, he was still married to Mount.

Statue of Mormon leader, Brigham Young.
Public domain photo

The Mormons believed in a spiritual union called polygamy. Men were urged to marry as many women as they liked, as this insured that everyone would have the opportunity to be part of a religious merging.

When Myron married Crosby, he had already fathered five children by Mount. In 1867, both women gave birth to more children, one on March 16 and the other two weeks later. For the next several years, the two women seemed to take turns giving birth to Myron's babies, and two more times both women were pregnant at once, in 1872 and 1875.

By 1890, the federal government took a stand against this marriage practice. The right to vote was denied to anyone who took more than one wife at a time. The Mormons agreed to abandon the act of polygamy, but the decision did not affect Myron Tanner. Mary Jane Mount had died that year, leaving him with just one wife.

BLESS THE CHILD
SARAH CORNELL

Nineteenth century illustration of Ephraim Avery and Sarah Cornell. Public domain image

Doctor Wilbur of Tiverton was a respected member of the Quaker religion's Society of Friends. It was perhaps for this reason that Sarah Maria Cornell turned to him when those of her own religion turned away.

In October of 1832, Sarah went to Doctor Wilbur to confide in him about a problem she had. She feared she was pregnant and, if she was, the father of the baby was a married man who already had several children. Worse than that, he was a Methodist minister.

Doctor Wilbur examined Sarah and, sure enough, found her to be with child. The single, 30-year-old woman was so distraught that she broke down in tears over her hopeless situation. Doctor Wilbur advised her to send a note to the alleged father-to-be, Ephraim Kingsbury Avery, inform him of her condition and ask him for financial assistance so that she could give up her strenuous factory job. But Sarah knew it would not be as simple as that.

Sarah explained to the doctor that she had recently been expelled from the Methodist Church for "lewdness and lying". After such an expulsion, no other Methodist church was willing to accept her into their congregation. She had gone to Avery for his help.

After learning that the minister was going to be a speaker at a church camp meeting, she had taken a trip out there to meet him, filled with the hope that he would be the kind of person who would assist her in getting the expulsion reversed. She said that she begged Avery to help her clean up her reputation by burning the letters of sinful confession her former church had asked her to submit. Avery allegedly agreed to help her on one condition: that she have a romantic interlude with him. She agreed and was now carrying the result of the deal in her womb.

Taking Doctor Wilbur's advice, Sarah went to Avery and told him of her predicament. Avery allegedly forbid her to have the child and directed her to take thirty drops of fluid from an herb called tansy. The yellow-flowered, bitter-tasting plant was well-known for inducing uterine contractions that would eventually bring on abortion. A few days after this meeting, she received a note from Avery asking if he could see her in private.

Sarah showed Avery's note to Doctor Wilbur and he urged her to refuse a private meeting with the minister. The next day, December 21, 1832, Wilbur awoke to find a crowd of people rushing past his house. He ran out into the yard and inquired as to what was taking place. "A young girl has hanged herself!" someone yelled to him.

Local farmer, John Durfee, had gone out into his farmyard that morning and found a young woman hung from a rope which had been secured to one of his haystack poles. Among those who later gathered around the tragic scene was Avery. He identified the body as that of Sarah Cornell.

Sarah's death was recorded as a suicide and she was prepared for burial. However, her banishment from the congregation coupled with the stigma of self-murder made it against the law of religion for her to be buried in the sacred grounds of a church cemetery. Taking pity on the poor girl, Durfee afforded a grave for her in his own family cemetery.

Despite his good deed, Durfee didn't feel that he had done enough to insure that Sarah Cornell would rest in peace. Thoughts of her filled his head and he was overcome with a nagging suspicion that there was more to her death than a simple suicide. He decided to file an official complaint stating that he wanted the death investigated.

Officials went to Sarah's house where they found an old trunk filled with letters. One, written the day before her death, was in her own handwriting. *"If I should be missing, enquire of the Reverend Mr. Avery of Bristol. He will know where I am. S.M. Cornell."*

After the discovery of the letter, Sarah's body was exhumed for an examination. The town was shocked to hear that the body contained the fetus of a five-month-old baby, and that there were indications of violent attempts to bring about an abortion.

Avery immediately fled the state of Rhode Island and bunked down at a cottage in Rindge, New Hampshire. When police found him, he was placed under arrest and brought back to Rhode Island to stand trial.

The trial lasted for 27 days and testimony against Avery was strong. Sarah had been wearing white gloves at the time of her death and, even though the rope secured around her was dirty, her gloves remained perfectly clean. The rope itself contained a double knot, something that would have been quite difficult for a person trying to hang themselves to accomplish.

When the judge noticed that Avery had been wearing a single glove throughout the trial, he asked him to remove it. The minister did so and there on his hand was a partially healed human bite mark.

Yet, even with so much evidence against him, Avery continued to maintain his innocence, proclaiming that he was alone in Portsmouth at the time of Sarah's death. The jury deliberated for 16 hours. They returned with a verdict of *not guilty*.

The Methodist Church welcomed Avery back to the pulpit and he continued to preach the word of God. In 1834, he retired from the ministry and removed with his wife and children to Ohio. He died in 1869, and if he had a murderous secret, he took it to the grave.

A CHOSEN ONE
MARIE FERRON

Stigmatists bleed from the areas of Christ's crucifixion wounds.
"The Crucifixion" painting by artist Matthias Grunewald.
Courtesy of Wikipedia.org: public domain photo.

Since the year 1222, records have been kept about the mysterious phenomenon known as stigmata. When stigmata affects an individual, he or she suddenly notices wounds appearing upon their body in the exact places Christ was wounded while being put upon the cross.

Over 345 documented cases of stigmatists include saints and devout Catholics in many countries including France and England. However one case is very close to home.

Marie Rose Ferron was born on May 2, 1902 in St. Germain de Gratham. Along with her parents, Jean-Baptiste and Rose Delima Ferron, she immigrated to America from Quebec in 1925. After settling for a while in Fall River, Massachusetts, the family moved to a home on Providence Street in Woonsocket.

Jean-Baptiste was a blacksmith and his wife was a homemaker. Deeply religious, they raised their children under the strict words of God. After each birth, Rose asked the Lord to place her new child under the protection of the Mystery of the Rosary. As Marie was the tenth child, she was under the protection of the tenth symbol of the Mystery, "the crucifixion".

Crippled with arthritis since shortly after birth, Marie was also overcome with Polio as a child and was unable to walk without the aid of a crutch. Believing strongly in miracles, her parents finally took her to visit Brother Andre, in Montreal, who was known for his gift of healing. After that visit, Marie no longer needed the crutch.

Then at the age of six, something began to happen to the young girl that would place her in the pages of religious history forever. That year, she claimed to have had a vision of Christ. In the vision, he was hanging on the cross and looking at her with sadness in his eyes.

The next year, Marie claimed she had seen the Lord again. This time he taught her a prayer which she would recite every day for the rest of her life. The prayer included the line, *"Many are called but few are chosen."*

Most likely few people outside of her family knew about the things Marie was experiencing. But in 1916, her name and all that was happening to her would be known throughout the world. On March 17 of that year, wounds began to appear on her body for no apparent reason. By 1927, the wounds were appearing upon her flesh every single Friday. Deep gashes swelled upon her arms as if she had been whipped. Holes appeared in the centers of her palms as well as on her feet, gushing blood as she writhed in pain. Those who witnessed this were rendered speechless by what was taking place right before their eyes.

On December 8, 1929, Marie made her vows as Foundress of the Sisters of Reparation of the Sacred Wounds of Jesus. But the following year, Marie began to question her condition. Within the throes of yet another bout of stigmata, she cried out, "How long do I have to suffer?!" She then became quiet and listened as if the Holy Spirit was answering her question. She finally asked out loud, "Seven years?" Marie died in her bed at her family's Woonsocket home on May 11...seven years later.

No other documented case of stigmata has been as severe as that of Marie Rose Ferron. While most stigmatists exhibit one or two wounds which mirror the crucifixion wounds of Christ, Marie suffered them all. In photos of her on her deathbed, there is clearly an indented line which runs across her forehead and resembles a crown of thorns. Five small holes, the circumference of nails, dot the indentation.

Thousands flocked to Marie's bedside when she took ill and it was trusted that she would be canonized after her death. However Bishop Russell McVinney was vehemently against the idea. Under his direction, the Diocese of Providence conducted an investigation into the validity of Marie's stigmata. The result of their investigation was that there was no real proof.

Her casket was carried into Holy Family Church by six women dressed in white. Thousands attended the funeral. She was then laid to rest in Precious Blood Cemetery in Woonsocket. Her gravestone reads, in French, *"Victim of her Jesus."*

HALLOWED GROUND
RHODE ISLAND BURIALS

Plain, simple fieldstone graves at a burial ground in Hopkinton.
Photographer: Kelly Sullivan Pezza

Beneath fieldstones sprawled across Rhode Island lie the remains of our forefathers. The stones bare no names or dates. Who lies where is unknown. Turned to dust, most traces of their existence is unembellished, just as it was intended.

The Quakers and Puritans of early New England did not allow images to be placed on their burial stones. Death, though a solemn event, was simply the end of a life and the deceased was not to be idolized or memorialized in any way, as their fate in the afterlife was unknown. The stone markers of early centuries were simply to serve the purpose of pinpointing where human remains had been placed in order to prevent exhumation by farm animals.

It wasn't until the beginning of the 18th century that New Englanders began to change their views toward the burial of loved ones. For the first time, Rhode Island had its very own professional stone carver in John Stevens of Newport. Working with slate,

Stevens became well known for his carved image of a skull. His sons John, William and Phillip eventually joined their father in the business, adding images such as cherubs to the choice of designs.

Grave of a twelve-year-old boy in Chestnut Hill Cemetery in Exeter, depicts engraving of an angel with a lamb and the message, "You will always be here..."
Photographer: Kelly Sullivan Pezza

Seth Luther of Providence gave families an even greater range of images to choose from in the mid-1700's. His work included portrait-like carvings with protruding eyes and scroll lettering.

Black slate remained the stone of choice for carvers until the mid-1800's. Comprised of very small crystals of sand, it was highly durable and allowed great ease in carving out minute details and deep engravings.

By this time, gravestones had taken on the English custom of being sold in pairs, consisting of a headstone and a footstone. Laid out, the stones would be in proportion to the height of the deceased. The headstones were usually placed facing east so that the dead could rise to face the Lord on judgment day.

Stones also began to include quite a bit of information about who lay beneath them. Names, birth dates, death dates, names of parents, names of spouses and sometimes even the cause of death, were carved alongside epitaphs and effigies.

Teenage girl's grave in Chestnut Hill Cemetery in Exeter, with a color photograph of the girl upon the stone. Her graduation robe and dozens of momentos adorn the grave.
Photographer: Kelly Sullivan Pezza

Grave in Old Fernwood Cemetery in Kingston, engraved with the couple's wedding date, the image of a bird, and musical notes.
Photographer: Kelly Sullivan Pezza

Purchasers of gravestones could view pre-carved stones with verses and images already on them, browse through a carver's catalog of designs, or suggest an original design of their own. Effigies, meant to honor the departing soul of the dead, were symbols of grief. Skulls, urns and weeping willows were the most common symbols used by carvers in this representation.

Eventually other types of stone, less durable than slate, but more affordable, were available to customers. Gray granite, comprised of very large sand crystals, did not allow for the fancy scroll of the past. Sandstone, with its soft elements, sugared and crumbled over time. But at least now, even those with meager incomes could afford to memorialize their loved ones.

Franklin Cooley of Providence, John and Henry Bull of Newport, and R.A. Crandall of Wakefield were just a few of the many Rhode Island carvers who made their fortune in gravestone design. Their artistic ability made it possible for our ancestors to replace the fieldstone with beautiful markers inscribed to preserve the memory of those who had gone before them.

However, the sprawling of stones across the state is not an accurate representation of how many have lived and died here. Many stones have sunk beneath the ground, been removed or stolen, or weathered and destroyed. All around us, within the depths of Rhode Island soil, lie bodies of those who were here before us, with nothing at all to mark their burial places.

Old records indicate that William Boss, who died in 1889, his son William Wayland Boss, who died in 1916, and other members of their family are interred *"on the family farm in Rockville"*.

Buried *"somewhere near Rockville"* are the bodies of two children of Hazard and Marcelia Burdick. Ferdinand H. Burdick, who died at the age of six, and

Lydia W. Burdick, who died at the age of seven, were buried in a now unknown place in the village in 1861.

Over thirty members of the Tanner family are buried *"on the family farm"* in Hopkinton. Abel Tanner, who died in 1802, his wife Phebe, their children and over a dozen others lie together in some unmarked place.

Elizabeth Perry, who died in 1778 and Martha Perry, who died in 1789 are recorded as having been laid to rest *"near the house"* in Hopkinton. Which house, is no longer known.

And just as the absence of a gravestone does not mean the absence of a body lying beneath the ground, the presence of a gravestone does not mean that the person it memorializes is really there. Often, the burial of a human being did not constitute a *final* resting place. Before large community-type cemeteries existed, families buried their deceased loved ones right in their yards. When property changed hands, that often brought about the need for exhumation and removal of bodies, as families did not want to leave their relatives behind.

Even after public or church burial grounds were established, the desire to remove bodies occurred for a variety of reasons. Perhaps the upkeep of the cemetery was not thought to be suitable. Or later generations of the family of the deceased felt that the interred had not been placed where he or she rightfully should have been. In any case, the removal of the contents of a grave from one place to another, were usually subject to town ordinances and state laws.

In order to move a body, a petition was supposed to be filed by those desiring the relocation, and all living relatives of the deceased were to be notified of the potential move and given the opportunity to voice their opinions on the matter. Petitions for removals were not always approved. Those which were, were granted a removal permit.

In 1939, Alice Norris petitioned the town of Hopkinton for permission to remove the body of her mother Hannah (Spicer) Barnes from the Spicer family cemetery on North Road. Apparently permission was granted but records do not indicate where the body was removed to.

When Hazard Gates, a Hopkinton farmer, died of Pneumonia on April 3, 1896, the 68-year-old man was laid to rest in the Hoxie family cemetery on Canonchet Road. Four years later, his body was exhumed and moved to Oak Grove Cemetery to be placed beside that of his wife, Sarah (Edwards) Gates.

In 1910, John Barber petitioned the Hopkinton Town Council for permission to have the bodies of his grandparents Noah and Roxa (Lewis) Palmer exhumed from the Palmer-Burdick-Appley Cemetery on Kenney Hill Road. He also asked that the bodies of his uncles Silas and Anthony Palmer, as well as that of his cousin Allen Caswell be removed. Barber felt that the family cemetery was neglected and wanted his relatives interred in a place where better upkeep was afforded. However John's aunt Lavina, who was Noah and Roxa's daughter, fought his petition. She stated that she did not want the graves of her parents and siblings disturbed. Lavina lost her battle and Barber was granted permission to move the five bodies to Pine Grove Cemetery.

In 1883, the bodies of Thomas Potter and his two wives, Mary (Babcock) Potter and Judith (Rogers) Potter were exhumed from the 50-grave family cemetery in Hopkinton where they had lain for over a hundred years. Their descendents desired that all the generations of the family be interred together in one place and the three bodies were removed to the 4,000-

grave First Hopkinton Cemetery where five other generations of Potters were interred.

The Joseph Burdick Cemetery on Burdickville Road has had at least two graves removed from it over the years. Thirty-five-year-old Benjamin Franklin Burdick was laid to rest there in 1875 after succumbing to heart disease. But his wife Martha later had his body moved to the sprawling River Bend Cemetery in Westerly. And Lizzie (Bentley) Burdick, a fifteen-year-old wife who died while giving birth to twins in 1892, was also buried in the Joseph Burdick cemetery and later moved.

The Deake-Utter house in Hopkinton City once marked the burial place of Abram, Esther and Edwin Utter, who all passed away between 1810 and 1815. The Utter family petitioned the town in 1955 to have the bodies removed to River Bend Cemetery and their wishes were granted.

In 1905, eleven bodies were moved from the Cole Farm in Hopkinton and reburied in Ashaway's Oak Grove Cemetery.

Although Rhode Island law states that the burial marker of a deceased person is to be moved along with the body after an exhumation and reburial, the law wasn't always followed. Many times a new stone was placed at the site of the new interment and the old stone left behind at the former grave.

The ornate gravestones of Rhode Island tell us where many of our descendents lie. But then again, so do simple, ordinary fieldstones, although their message is silent. Old grave markers that should have been removed falsely tell us the ground beneath them contains remains. And bare grounds, with no markers of any kind, lead us to believe that the dead are not secretly all around us.

Child's grave in Chestnut Hill Cemetery in Exeter, with the figure of a lamb atop it and a verse below attesting to the young age of the deceased.
Photographer: Kelly Sullivan Pezza

LOVE

CAUGHT BETWEEN SISTERS
BERIAH LEWIS

Thomas Wells of Hopkinton was the father of two beautiful girls named Lois and Sally. Sally had long been courted by a young man named Beriah Lewis who seemed every bit as smitten with her as she was with him. His intentions toward Sally appeared devotional, as he had asked for her hand in marriage. Therefore it came as quite a shock to Sally and her entire family when Beriah suddenly disappeared.

Deeply depressed over losing the man she so loved, Sally was reluctant to even consider new romantic prospects, as her family encouraged her to do. However, a Connecticut schoolteacher named Linden Fuller eased Sally's heartache. Fuller eventually fell in love with her and asked her to be his wife. Thomas Wells could not have been happier.

Sally's wedding dress was prepared and all plans for the wedding set. Yet before the vows were exchanged, Beriah Lewis reappeared, more than a year after he'd left. He showed up on Sally's doorstep with the intention of reaffirming his love for her and continuing their engagement. Not knowing how to handle the situation, Sally went to her father for advice. Her marriage to Fuller was close at hand. Fuller had loved her and stood beside her through her emotional pain. Beriah Lewis had abandoned her and broken her heart. But it was Beriah her heart still beat for.

Sally met with Fuller and gently explained to him that she could not marry him because she was still in love with another man. Fuller was understanding. His wedding plans with Sally were cancelled and he left town.

No sooner had Fuller departed when young Beriah had a change of heart. He suddenly realized that maybe it wasn't a good idea for him and Sally to be together after all. They had been apart for quite some time and things between them had changed, he explained.

In a panic, Thomas tracked down Fuller, hoping he was still interested in marrying Sally. The confused and heartbroken schoolteacher explained that he simply could not go through with the marriage after all that had just transpired.

On April 28, 1770, Sally did indeed become a bride...to Beriah's older brother Israel. Beriah himself was married the next year...to Sally's sister Lois. Beriah finally admitted that it had always been Lois he was in love with. The couple went on to have eleven children.

LOVE KNOWS NO BOUNDARIES
TALES OF ROMANCE

In 19th century Charlestown, George C. Perry was a man who had a lot of experience walking down the matrimonial aisle. His first wife, Thankful Carpenter, was four years younger than he was. His second wife, Sally Browning, a year older. But his third marriage was to 32-year-old Eliza Tucker, deaf and dumb, and young enough to be the daughter of either of his first wives. When Eliza gave birth to the couple's daughter Clara, she was 35 years old. George Perry was 67.

In the mid-1700's, Benjamin Barber of Richmond was faced with the task of caring for his ailing wife Mary (Tefft) Barber. The woman had fallen ill and 76-year-old Benjamin realized he could not take adequate care of her by himself. A 35-year-old nursemaid, Mary Perry, was thereby hired to come into their home and take care of Mrs. Barber. Apparently she made Mr. Barber feel better also. After the death of Mrs. Barber, the nursemaid married her employer. Two years later, she became a mother at the age of thirty-seven. The proud papa was one year shy of his eightieth birthday.

During the late 1600's, in the town of Hopkinton, lived an unfortunate woman by the name of Joan Greene. After marrying Henry Gardiner, she discovered that she was unable to have children. Unknown to her, her husband was having children with another woman, a widow named Abigail Remington.

In 1694, the affair was brought to light when Ms. Remington sued Henry for the support of her one-year-old son Ephraim and her three-year-old son Henry. The town of South Kingstown, where Remington lived, was sympathetic to her plight and ordered Henry to pay up. However the embarrassing and uncomfortable legal proceedings did nothing to smother the flames of their affair, as three years later Remington gave birth to another child whom she claimed was Henry's. Offspring from the secret union continued as in 1703 Remington had yet *another* child, a daughter Hannah, whom she also claimed was Henry's

Twelve years later, Joan died, childless of course, and most likely unaware that she had been sharing her husband with another woman for over twenty years.

DIVORCE
UNTIL THE LAW DO US PART

Divorce was more common in the olden days than people think. In 1811, Susan Perry Lewis of Charlestown married Jeffrey Hazard Browning. Their life was not one of wedded bliss and eventually Jeffrey filed for divorce. He claimed that he had *"expected to participate in the happiness of a matrimonial state, but Susan is in no way regarding the marriage contract and has frequently violated it by abandoning the house and refusing to return."*

Jeffrey also claimed that his wife had attached her affections to other men while excluding him and that he had done everything in his power to clean up his wife's reputation. In addition to the accusations of abandonment and adultery, Jeffrey also told the court that his wife *"frequently assaulted and beat"* him without provocation. The divorce was granted.

Many locals can trace their lineage back to a woman named Herodias Long. Herodias married John Hicks in the early 1600's when she was just thirteen years old and the couple settled in Massachusetts. There, Herodias became acquainted with a man named George Gardiner. It wasn't long before John Hicks obtained a divorce from his wife, and Herodias married George.

After twenty years of living together in a matrimonial state, Herodias left her second husband. She petitioned the courts to make George provide her with money and property but the courts convinced the couple to instead give the marriage another try. George agreed to take his wife back into his home but she absolutely refused.

When George asked to be granted a divorce, Herodias claimed that wasn't necessary and swore that their marriage hadn't even been legal. Deemed a terrible scandal by the courts, a divorce was in fact granted and both parties fined twenty pounds each.

And shortly before the death of Christopher Potter of North Kingstown in 1747, his wife Mary was granted a divorce after telling the court that she would rather slit her throat than remain married to him.

A FAIRYTALE GONE WRONG
HANNAH FOSTER

The Deake house in Hopkinton City.
Photographer: Gregory Pezza

Once upon a time, as the story goes, George Deake and his brother Richard jumped ship and avoided the law by heading to the wooded havens of the colonies.

While the tale of the Deake brothers arrival in what is now Hopkinton carries with it no hard facts, town records present us with plenty of facts concerning their children. Facts that tell a story without a happy ending.

At the time of George's death in 1746, he and his wife Susannah had four sons and sixty-three acres of land in Hopkinton. The Deake house still stands near the junction of North Road. The land was divided between the boys, but son Charles bought his brother's shares.

Son John had become a physician and made his calls around town on horseback. Revered for his skill in medicine, it seemed unlikely that anything could mar his reputation. However a wealthy businessman named John Foster lived in nearby Richmond. He and his wife Margery possessed a beautiful plantation, as well as a beautiful daughter.

Hannah Foster was just seventeen. She was enamored with the good doctor...and pregnant with his child. Once John Foster learned of this news, he shunned his daughter. Hannah married Deake and the couple went on to have nine children, including a set of twins in 1753. But two years after their last child was born, Deake passed away at the age of thirty-seven. The inventory of his Hopkinton estate proved that the doctor had not been as financially prosperous as was believed.

Owning little more than some farm equipment, 14 spoons, 1 old tin kettle and 1 pickle pot, there was not enough money to pay off all his debts after everything was sold.

The beautiful and once-wealthy Hannah Deake was now a 32-year-old widow with several children to support, and not a dime to her name. The hardships of her situation continued until the town council voted that John Foster be contacted and ordered to support his daughter and grandchildren.

Foster's wife had since died, but he agreed to take in Hannah and her six oldest children. Five-year-old Foster Deake was sent to live with his uncle Charles. Two-year-old Martha and three-year-old Mary were taken in by John and Abigail Langworthy. The rest of the children moved into John Foster's house, but Hannah refused to live with her father again.

Hannah took a room at the home of Peter Main in Hopkinton, but it wasn't long before Main felt the financial burden of her residence and appealed to the town for help. Town officials, as well as her father, refused to support Hannah unless she moved back into her father's house as ordered. Finally, she consented.

Soon after, John Foster died. With him went Hannah's financial support. After long arguments with the town council, Hannah was successful in having some of her children returned to her. But her life never returned to the fairytale it had been growing up. The daughter of the wealthy plantation owner, and wife of the dashing doctor, did not see her story end with the words *"and they lived happily ever after."*

THE CRUEL HAND OF FATE
HANNAH ROBINSON

The Rowland Robinson House in North Kingstown, where Hannah grew up.
Originally published in the 1902 book State of Rhode Island and Providence Plantations: A History.

The home of Rowland Robinson was one of the most beautiful around. With fireplaces ornamented in Chinese tile and exquisite artwork hung upon the walls, it caused its share of envy. Likewise, the daughter of Rowland Robinson was one of the most beautiful women in town. With her delicate skin and graceful manner, she also caused a good deal of envy. However, being a Robinson daughter and living on the Robinson estate was not a fate to be envied. In fact, it brought about one of the biggest local scandals to occur during the colonial era.

As a Quaker and respected young lady of society, great things had always been expected of Hannah Robinson. She had been given the best of everything and her father trusted she would remain in the wonderful style of life he had provided for her. But it was not riches that Hannah wanted. It was love.

Dr. William Bowen was a friend of Rowland's, who would often pay friendly visits to the family. But it eventually became obvious that his intentions there were focused on his friend's beautiful daughter. Finally, the wealthy physician proposed to the girl he had become so enamored with. Hannah felt she needed to be completely honest with the good doctor. She told him she was flattered by the proposal but that she was already engaged.

This news came as a total shock to her father. And when he found out who is future son-in-law was, that shock turned to explosive anger.

Peter Simon had been his daughter's tutor. He had no money, no social esteem, no chance at giving Hannah the kind of life her father wanted her to continue having. But the couple had been secretly in love for eight years and Hannah was determined that nothing was going to come between them. She begged her father to reconsider his feelings toward Peter but Rowland would not be swayed. He forbid his daughter to ever see Peter Simon again.

John Gardiner, Hannah's uncle, was sympathetic to the plight of the young lovers. Going behind his brother-in-law's back, he set up secret meetings between Hannah and Peter. Late at night, the young girl would sit in her bedroom and profess her undying love while Peter listened from his hiding place in a nearby tree.

Finally, neither could take the forced physical separation any longer. The few stolen moments they were allowed once her father had gone to sleep were no longer enough. Hannah made plans to visit her aunt in Wickford. As her father did not trust her to abide by his rule concerning Peter, he sent a servant along with her on the trip.

When Hannah arrived at the Wickford estate, Peter's carriage stood there waiting outside the gate just as they had planned. The servant became very upset at this blunt act of deceit and warned Hannah that if she went through with the caper, her father's wrath would fall upon her. Ignoring the warnings, Hannah climbed into Peter's carriage and the couple sped away.

Peter and Hannah were married in Providence the next day. Rowland offered a reward to anyone who would bring his daughter back home but there were no takers. The newlyweds moved into a house on Bridge Street in Newport and Rowland disinherited his daughter.

Love did not conquer all. Peter soon deserted the woman who had given up everything for him. Hannah's health began to decline immediately after her husband's departure. Only in her thirties, she had been abandon by the two men who were supposed to love her the most.

Destitute and seriously ill, she was brought back home to her family. On the way through town, she asked the driver to stop at McSparran Hill. There, she stepped out onto the rock which would later go down in history as Hannah Robinson's Rock. Sadly, she gazed out across the vast ocean. Whatever thoughts she had there in her silence were among her last. She died soon after. The physician who attended to her listed her cause of death as a broken heart.

HANGED HUSBANDS
SARAH GREENE

In 1668, Sarah Greene exchanged marriage vows with a man named Thomas Flounders of Narragansett. Two years later, not long after their first child was born, Flounders made a decision what would leave his offspring fatherless.

A land dispute between Flounders and one of his neighbors, Walter House, had been boiling for quite some time. Determined to put an end to it, Flounders walked to House's shop near Devil's Foot to confront him. The two men exchanged words before Flounders got a stick and proceeded to beat House with it. When House raised his arms to protect himself, he lost his balance, fell backwards and slammed his head against a rafter. Instantly, he was killed.

Flounders admitted to his fatal deed and was arrested. After standing trial for manslaughter, he was found guilty and sentenced to be hanged. On October 26, Sarah Flounders became a widow. Her late husband's land and household were confiscated, leaving both her and her baby homeless and penniless. Two male friends petitioned the courts to have sympathy on the young mother and finally they relented and allowed her to keep one cow, one hog, some bedding and some corn.

Hope for a happy life was instilled once more when Sarah met and married a North Kingstown man by the name of Joshua Tefft. The couple had a child on March 14, 1672 which they named Peter. But two days after his birth, Sarah died. Perhaps it was for the best that she did not live long enough to see history repeat itself.

During the Great Swamp Fight of 1675, Joshua Tefft was believed to be fighting on the side of the Indians. He was captured by the English and ordered to stand trial for treason. Found guilty, he would go down in history as the only Rhode Island man ever drawn and quartered.

And Sarah would go down in history for being the only Rhode Island woman to have two husbands sentenced to death.

LOVE IS DEATHLESS
SULLIVAN BALLOU

Sullivan Ballou
Public domain image

Sullivan Ballou was born on March 28, 1827 in Smithfield. The son of Emeline and Hiram Ballou, he grew up without a man to look up to, as his father passed away when he was just six years old. But with his mother's rearing, he became an adult filled with love and respect for women, God and his country.

Ballou married Sarah Hart Shumway in New York on October 15, 1855. Shumway was just 19 years old and Ballou 28, but they both knew that they had found the love of a lifetime in each other.

Ten months after their marriage, the couple welcomed a son, Edgar Folwer Ballou. Less than three years later, another son, William Bowen Ballou, was born to them. Life undoubtedly seemed perfect for the family. But something beyond their control loomed on the horizon.

When Abraham Lincoln called for soldiers to take part in the Civil war, Ballou heard the call loud and clear.

> *My very dear Sarah, the indications are strong that we shall move in a few days, perhaps tomorrow. Lest I should not be able to write again, I feel impelled to write a few lines that may fall under your eye when I shall be no more...*

The 2nd Rhode Island Infantry, under the command of Colonel John Slocum, trained in Providence for less than a month before donning their issued uniforms and marching toward battle.
Ballou and the rest of the infantry reached Washington D.C. on June 22, 1861. The next day, they set up camp quarters in an oak grove known as Gales Woods.

> *If it is necessary that I should fall on the battlefield for my country, I am ready. I have no misgivings or lack of confidence in the cause in which I am engaged, and the courage does not falter...*

On July 15, the 1st RI, along with the 2nd RI, the 2nd NH and the 71st NY, were given orders to pack up camp and begin marching toward Manassas, Virginia. Under the command of Ambrose Burnside, the men set out the next day at 3:00 p.m. with rations of salt pork, hardtack and coffee.

> *I know how great a debt we owe to those who went before us through the blood and sufferings of the revolution. And I am willing, perfectly willing, to lay down all my joys in this life to help maintain the government and pay that debt...*

The day before the orders were given for the troops to begin heading toward Virginia, Ballou sat down and penned a letter to his wife. For reasons only known to him, he never sent it, but placed it in a trunk with the rest of his personal belongings.

The memories of the blissful moments I have spent with you come creeping over me and I feel most gratified to God and to you that I have enjoyed them so long. It is hard for me to give them up when we might still have lived and loved together and seen our sons grow...

On July 21 at 9:15 a.m., as the troops headed toward the railroad junction at Manassas, they were met by enemy fire. After Slocum ordered the men to advance, he and Ballou immediately snapped the reins of their horses and galloped straight for the Southern troops. Less than three minutes later, Slocum was hit by enemy fire and killed. Ballou was hit just seconds later as a cannonball exploded into his horse, killing the animal and tearing open the soldier's leg.

If I do not return, my dear Sarah, never forget how much I love you. When my last breath escapes me on the battlefield, it will whisper your name...

Ballou was carried to the field hospital at Sudley Church, his leg so mangled that surgeons decided the chance of gangrene and infection were too high to take any risks. After anesthetizing Ballou with chloroform, they employed a saw to remove the leg.

If the dead can come back to this earth and flit unseen around those they loved, I shall always be near you. If there is a soft breeze upon your cheek, it shall be my breath. As the cool air fans your temple, it shall be my spirit passing by...

Sullivan Ballou died from his injuries on July 29 at the field hospital. He was buried in a grave nearby.

Several months later, Governor Sprague visited Virginia to collect the remains of the fallen men. When he inquired as to the resting place of Ballou, he was told a grisly story about the Rebels digging up one of the graves and burning the body. When the grave of Ballou was opened, Sprague found nothing but ashes.

The ashes were placed in a coffin and transported to Providence. On March 31, 1862, a funeral with military honors was held for Ballou at Grace Church. The remains of the 35-year-old man were then interred in Swan Point Cemetery.
Eventually Ballou's personal belongings were sent home to Sarah. It was then that she read his last letter to her.

Sarah never remarried. She died in East Orange, New Jersey in 1907, at the age of 81. Today, she lies beside her husband, sealing the love that was deathless.

Sarah, do not mourn me dead. Think I am gone and wait for thee. For we shall meet again...

A DEVELISH ROMANCE
THE TALL STRANGER

Hannah Maxon and Comfort Cottrell were two young girls swept up in the romance of the future. Both in their early 20's the friends were staying with the elderly Mr. and Mrs. Clarke in Westerly when their curiosity about fate changed their young lives.

One late afternoon during the latter part of the 18th century, Hannah and Comfort talked excitedly to each other about the young men their hearts beat for. They suddenly got an idea. Instead of waiting on destiny, they would try to create their own. One of the girls had heard about a mystical way to attract the one you loved. They searched the house for a ball of yarn which they carried out to the well. They dropped the ball into the deep, dark hole while holding tightly to the end piece. As they slowly wound the yarn back up out of the water, they thought about the two men they were enamored with and quietly chanted a verse from the Bible backwards.

Convinced the spell had worked, they anxiously ran out to the front yard to await the arrival of what they had just summoned. But what they had summoned was not a couple of love struck young men. It was a being straight from the depths of hell. Coming slowly up the road was a figure about nine feet in height. With a heavy stride, it walked toward them, its eyes large and glowing. Hannah and Comfort screamed wildly as they turned and ran into the house.

Mr. Clarke barely had time to ask what was happening before he looked out the door the girls had just darted through and saw the creature coming up onto the porch. The old man stood rigid, watching it as it pressed its face against the window of the door and peered into the house. A deeply religious man, Mr.

Clarke closed his eyes and prayed fervently. When he opened them, the monster was gone.

In just a matter of hours, news of the event was making the rounds of Westerly and Hopkinton. Residents were convinced that Hannah and Comfort had unwillingly contacted the devil and brought him to the streets of their towns. The two girls prayed for forgiveness and vowed to commit themselves to the teachings of the church.

Both women eventually married and moved on with their lives. But the warnings about what they had done that one afternoon were passed down through generations.

It wasn't until over half a century later that a new chapter was added to the story. Mrs. Rogers, a widow from Newport, ventured into Westerly one day to seek out members of the Clarke family. As her husband had recently died, she was making good on her promise to him to confess his most disturbing secret.

Her husband, Daniel, had been a young man staying with the Hiscox family of Westerly that fateful day all those years ago. With a sense of amusing mischief, he had decided to play a trick on the two young girls down the street. Garbed in a hideous monster costume, his plan was for nothing more than a little fun.

Once Daniel discovered his prank had caused massive alarm throughout Westerly and its neighboring towns, he immediately departed for Newport where he spent the rest of his life, never being able to forgive himself for the panic he had caused. Mrs. Roger's admission to her husband's secret changed local history. The devil had not, in fact, been walking the streets of Westerly.

THE UNEXPLAINED

GHOSTS AT THE INN
THE STAGECOACH HOUSE

Old postcard from the former Dawley's Hotel & Tavern in Wyoming, now the Stagecoach Bed & Breakfast.
From the collection of the author: public domain Image.

An innkeeper sees a ghostly figure during an electrical outage. A guest of the establishment flees after hearing unexplained voices. Who, or what, is inhabiting the Stagecoach Inn located near the Wyoming Dam, is yet to be determined.

The inn has gone through several renovations and owners since its original construction in the late 18th century. At different times it has served as a stagecoach stop, a hotel, tavern, antique shop and jewelry store.

The area where the inn stands was once known as Brand's Iron Works. Samuel Brand, who owned the large manufacturing plant beside the dam, lived in a house where Woodmansee Insurance now stands. Brand deeded a part of his land to his son-in-law, Francis Brown, and there Brown constructed a tavern where stagecoach drivers could pause in their journeys to partake of a meal or drink, spend the night or get a fresh change of horses from the livery stable across the way. The tavern contained a kitchen, bar and rooms for sleeping, as well as Brown's jewelry and buckle shop.

In 1820, the Providence –New London Turnpike was built, snaking through Wyoming to provide easy access from Providence to New London and Boston to New York. Business at Brown's thrived. Near the tavern, Albert and Clarke Niles had set up the Niles Wagon Shop. A sawmill and grist mill were also built close by. Suddenly, Wyoming was a bustling center of activity.

By 1845, Brown's Tavern had become known as the Halfway House, as it was the midway point between the major cities. That year, the building caught fire and had to be rebuilt. The new structure contained 26 rooms including a large great room with a fireplace and vaulted ceilings.

The inn was eventually sold to Joseph Irish, who in turn sold it to a Mrs. Fields. The next owner, Matthew Wilbur, ran the inn as a temperance house and imposed strict rules against alcohol consumption on the property for the next fifteen years.

Silas Kenyon then took over the property but became so deeply in debt, he sold it to Amos J. Dawley. Re-establishing the business as Dawley's Inn, the stop once again became popular for travelers.

Over the years, the building suffered several fires and became a dilapidated eyesore. When Kenneth and Diane Boucher bought the property, they took great pains to restore the structure to its original beauty and reopened it as a bed & breakfast. During the massive restorations, many items were discovered hidden within the walls of the old inn. Whiskey flasks, old medicinal containers, belt buckles and shoe molds were pulled from concealed spaces. But the renovations also seemed to pull something else out from the dark silence.

One night during a snowstorm, the electrical power in Wyoming was knocked out. As the desk clerk at the inn prepared to close up the office for the night, a woman suddenly appeared at the desk. He later described her as African-American and dressed in a long nightgown and sleeping cap. She asked him what was happening. As he began to explain that the storm had made the electricity go out, she disappeared as quickly as she had arrived.

The Stagecoach House Bed & Breakfast in Wyoming.
Photographer: Alecia Keegan

A few weeks prior, a man and his wife who had just checked into the honeymoon suite were preparing to go out to dinner when they heard a noise outside their door. They later described the disturbance as sounding like two or three small children laughing and running up and down the hall. When they opened the door to see what was going on, there was no one to be seen. As they left the inn for dinner, they stopped at the desk to ask the clerk how many guests were registered at the hotel. There to relax, the couple was a bit miffed that anyone would let their children be so disruptive. There were no other guests, the clerk explained.

An antiques dealer who once ran his business out of the old inn was not surprised by the reports of ghostly sights and sounds there. He had experienced them himself. He explained that often, while opening up his shop for the day, he would find all the light bulbs unscrewed. And every once in a while, a strange cold presence would make the hair on the back of his neck stand up.

Death records show that Mr. Dawley's three children died at the inn during a cholera epidemic. The inn was also home to a young woman who was raped and impregnated by a friend of her father's. This we know. But whose spirits remain and why, are questions yet to answer.

ALLEGED VAMPIRE
MERCY BROWN

*Mercy Brown's gravestone in Chestnut Hill Cemetery in Exeter.
Photographer: Alecia Keegan*

Following the death of Dracula author, Bram Stoker, an interesting discovery was made by family members sorting through his research notes. Several newspaper articles dated in the 1800's and hailing from Rhode Island were found stashed away in his collection of vampire information. Rhode Island holds a history of being home to more accused vampires than any other state in the country.

A vampire is described as being an undead creature which rises from the grave at night to suck the blood from unwilling victims. The word is believed to be a translation of the Slavic word *Nosufur-atu*, which means *plague carrier*.

In the 1800's, having little understanding or means of preventing disease, residents of this area could only incorporate what they knew to explain the unexplained. And what they knew best was religion.

When people began dying off in quick succession after suffering terrible pain and bleeding, it was a mystery that could only be regarded as the work of the devil. Herbs, precious elements and Christian symbols were placed throughout local houses in an effort to protect the living from those who supposedly refused to stay in their graves. But to no avail, it was believed that vampires were still prowling the streets and that extreme measures had to be taken to get rid of them.

New England can claim 15 alleged vampires, perhaps the most well-known being Mercy Lena Brown of Exeter, who died at the age of 19 in 1892. Her mother Mary had passed away nine years earlier, and her sister Mary Olive, eight years earlier.

When Mercy's brother Edwin fell sick shortly after her death, townspeople began to believe that vampirism was the cause. One cold night in March, several men took shovels in hand and headed into Chestnut Hill Cemetery to dig up the graves of the Brown family. Mary and Mary Olive were much decomposed, but blood still filled the heart of Mercy. Immediately, the men decided that Mercy was a vampire. They cut out her heart and burned it on a nearby rock.

The ashes were collected, mixed with a liquid and given to the ailing Edwin to drink. But the cure didn't take, and two months later Edwin died at the age of 24.

The graves of Mercy Brown, her mother, father and sister, in Chestnut Hill Cemetery in Exeter.
Photographer: Kelly Sullivan Pezza

Mercy was the last alleged vampire to be exhumed in Rhode Island. Medical discoveries have allowed us to base our explanations on scientific evidence rather than the supernatural. A highly contagious disease known as Tuberculosis or Consumption entered America in 1793. With symptoms such as pressure on the chest, coughing up blood, sweating and painful breathing, the disease is fatal without antibiotics.

A chronic bacterial infection, Tuberculosis causes tumor masses to grow in the lungs. Wheezing, coughing and sneezing passes the microscopic bacterial particles into the air where they are transmitted via inhalation to new victims. The disease may attack the body immediately or lie dormant and without symptoms for years.

Before the practice of embalming, all dead bodies were buried with blood still in the heart. After several years, the blood as well as the rest of the body decomposes. Temperature plays a part in the length of the decomposition process. Mary had been buried for nine years. Mary Olive, for eight. Their bodies had decomposed over time. But Mercy had been placed in the frozen grounds of January a mere two months before she was exhumed.

Stukely Tillinghast, another Exeter farmer, had engaged in the burning of his own daughter's heart some years earlier. After having a dream that half his orchard died, six of his fourteen children succumbed to a strange illness.

Townspeople convinced Stukely that a vampire was killing his family off and that it would be necessary to unearth his six deceased children to find out which of them was the culprit. After examining the exhumed bodies, it was decided that 19-year-old Sarah was the vampire, her body intact, her heart filled with blood.

In 1874, William G. Rose of Peace Dale dug up the body of his 15-year-old daughter, Ruth Ellen, after members of his family began falling ill. Yet another fire was built, another young girl's heart set aflame.

Often our lack of knowledge leaves us with sad pieces of history. Not only did these poor young girls suffer terribly at the end of their short lives, their memories will carry on through time based on the wrongful assumptions of their ancestors.

GRAVE DISTURBANCES
NELLIE VAUGHN

The boarded up church beside the cemetery on Plains Meetinghouse Road in West Greenwich.
Photographer: Kelly Sullivan Pezza

Along Plains Meetinghouse Road in West Greenwich, businesses used to thrive. The homes of residents used to line the street and the sound of horse's hooves and rattling carriages used to be common among the bustle. Today, the center of that bygone activity stands hauntingly silent. Nothing but the boarded up West Greenwich Baptist Church remains. But for those buried in the small cemetery beside the church, even the silence has not brought peace. Throughout the years, a disturbing legend about one of the women interred beside the church has been woven, making this part of town nationally famous as a place of haunting.

The West Greenwich Baptist Church was built in 1825 and Allen Tillinghast was elected its deacon, a position he held until his death in 1879 at the age of 83. Tillinghast's farm adjoined the church property and he had given a small portion of his land to be used as a

251

burial ground. At his own expense, a stone wall was built around the growing number of graves, presently at 320.

The cemetery contains the bodies of Tillinghast family members as well as that of a young woman named Ellen Vaughn. Better known locally and nationally as Nellie, the vampire, this girl has become the focus of a tale which has caused horrible acts of vandalism within both the cemetery and the church.

Several years ago, a local teacher was telling students about a supposed vampire being buried in West Greenwich. Most likely she was talking about 19-year-old Mercy Brown, who is buried in Chestnut Hill Cemetery in Exeter. But when students began searching for the alleged vampire's grave, they came upon the grave of 19-year-old Nellie Vaughn and believed they had found the subject of their teacher's story.

Since that time, destruction of the graves and the church has become a sickening activity for the evil-minded, the curious and the bored. A crypt within the cemetery has undergone years of abuse as people continually chip off pieces they believe to be souvenirs of a vampire's grave. The crypt, however, contains the bodies of two males. Nellie's grave is unmarked, her stone removed by caretakers to protect her body from being disturbed.

Nellie was born Ellen Louise Vaughn on June 6, 1870 in West Greenwich. She was the daughter of farmer George Burton Vaughn and his second wife, Ellen Louise Knight. Nellie had a half-sister Georgianna, who was thirteen years older, and a half-brother John, who was four years older. Her siblings were the children of George and his first wife, Mary Ann Harrington.

Nellie died on March 31, 1889 of pneumonia, not tuberculosis, as the legend goes. She was originally buried on her family's farm on Robin Hollow Road.

At a time when many people were laid to rest upon their own property, as opposed to a public burying ground, families were forced to leave their loved ones behind when the property was sold. Nellie was indeed exhumed, but not for the reason legend tells us. She was taken from her grave, not in order to have her heart burned or to arrest any blood-sucking activity. She was exhumed so that her parents could place her body in the public cemetery of West Greenwich where they felt it would be forever protected. The town gave their permission for transfer of the body seven months after Nellie's death.

Over the years, church windows have been smashed and satanic propaganda spray-painted on the walls, pews stolen, blood smeared around and even an axe driven through the door. Trespassers have been arrested on the grounds, carrying with them such objects as knives, crucifixes and chalices. A grave has even been dug up, the coffin lifted out and the lid opened to expose the body inside.

The cemetery on Plains Meetinghouse Road in West Greenwich where Nellie Vaughn was laid to rest.
Photographer: Kelly Sullivan Pezza

For those who lie interred beside the church, they have become the unwilling victims of lies, distortions and misunderstandings. They are simply former church members, farmers and store-keepers, deacons and blacksmiths. They are mothers, fathers, children. They are people who deserve to sleep peacefully.

ACCUSED WITCH
ELIZABETH SEGAR

The Segar family members of Richmond were known for being honest and prosperous business-owners, maintaining one of the most popular stores along the stagecoach route from Westerly to Kingston. But though their reputations were gleaming, their family history held a dark page.

In 1662, news spread through Connecticut and Massachusetts that the devil had descended upon New England. Signs of the alleged evil first became apparent at Hartford where several female residents were believed to be possessed. These women were accused of having the mark of Satan on their bodies, in the forms of moles or scars, of being able to communicate with animals, and having the ability to perform such inhuman feats as flying. Ousted from society and seeing fingers pointed at them wherever they went, these women who were once merely mothers, wives or daughters were now branded with a new title...witch.

History tells us about the witch trials in Salem and surrounding areas. And about how a servant girl named Tituba was believed to have introduced her knowledge of voodoo to the women of Connecticut and Massachusetts. Many women were tried and hanged for the crime of witchcraft in those states.

The first of several witch trials was held in 1662 in Hartford. Among the accused was Elizabeth Moody Segar. The charge against her was based on her close association with the other women on trial. The first two times she faced the court, she was found not guilty of the charges against her. But the third, time, she was not so lucky and was sentenced to death by hanging.

Accused witches on trial.
Artist: William A. Crafts, 1876.
Image provided by Wikipedia.org: public domain image.

The governor of New York stepped in just in time to save Elizabeth's life and although she had already spent three years in prison, she was finally set free. The stigma never left the poor woman and in 1678, she and her husband moved to Westerly. There, she had children and grand-children, her fourth great-grandson eventually becoming the proprietor of Segar's Store in Wyoming.

The Wood River Inn in Wyoming, formerly Segar's Store.
Photographer: Kelly Sullivan Pezza

DRUID'S DREAM
JOSEPH HAZARD

Image of Joseph Peace Hazard.
Originally published in The History of Kent & Washington Counties,
1889, by J.R. Cole.

Thomas Hazard came to America from Wales in 1630. Nine years later, he settled in the colonies where his surname would one day fill the pages of history books.

The name Hazard, of Welsh origin, means one of a high nature. Thomas's descendents certainly lived up to that meaning, as they donated buildings, bridges and artwork to their hometown of Kingston. But aside from being generous, the Hazard family was once known for something else...the eccentricities of Thomas's great-grandsons Joseph and Thomas.

Joseph Peace Hazard was raised in a strict, religious household. His father, a member of the Society of Friends, founded the first mill in Peace Dale, a village named for his wife, Mary Peace Hazard.

Joseph worked in the mill as a teenager and later erected a woolen mill of his own. But the urge to travel lead him to give up the business and go off to other parts of the world.

In 1884, Joseph supposedly had a dream in which a Druid appeared to him and instructed him to build a stone house on a piece of land near Narragansett Pier. He quickly hired Narragansett Indian John Noka to construct the massive granite home modeled after an English abbey. The building contained two towers, one being a hexagonal tower dedicated to his mother, and the other being a square tower dedicated to his ancestors. Joseph named his ornate house Druid's Dream.

Joseph most certainly had learned about Druidism during his travels. Those of an ancient Celtic religion, Druids believed that life was to be lived in pure truth and in accordance with nature. They followed a strict code of morals which they trusted would establish a positive karmic pattern. They also believed in transmigration of the soul, otherwise known as reincarnation, which made their way of living essential to the well-being of every human on the earth.

Joseph may have visited Stonehenge on his journeys, the sacred English meeting place of the Druids. Believed to have been built as early as 3500 BC, Stonehenge is comprised of stones and pillars all set in specific alignment to each other. The circle in which they are set, is a shape used widely in Druidism, representing the ongoing cycle of life, death and rebirth.

Not far from Druid's Dream is Kendal Green, a construction strangely reminiscent of Stonehenge. The name Kendal Green comes from the coarse green fabric made in the borough of Kendal for the clothing of bow-hunters. Its Baron once owned Barton Manor, which stands near a large circle of stones believed to have once been a Druid's temple.

Kendall Green, with two of the columns visible in the foreground and the ceremonial chair in the distance.
Photographer: Gregory Pezza

Joseph built Kendal Greene himself, setting out the four-foot tall, rounded stone pillars in a circular pattern. A large stone slab, raised about a foot off the ground, is surrounded by the eight pillars. The number eight was held in high esteem by the Druids. Their secret alphabet, the Ogham, was written to go in eight directions. Time was told by dividing each day into eight tides and measuring the horizon by one-eighths. The Druids also believed that every human being was made up of eight essential parts.

Before entering Kendal Green, one must first pass through an opening in a stone wall. Druids trusted stone walls to separate sacred grounds from the external world. To the left side of Joseph's creation stands four square stone pillars. In Celtic terminology, these are called *dressed stones* and represent east, west, north and south. The inscription on the first pillar takes up all four sides and reads: *This pillar, erected by Joseph P. Hazard upon Kendal Green (that is named for Kendal Green), in the year 1886. It is dedicated to the memory of John Wakefield, Banker of Kendale who died in 1811, aged 73 years, and to Isabella Wakefield, for whom my sister Isabella Wakefield Hazard was named, and is buried at Vaucluse on the island of Rhode Island.*

Behind these four pillars is a massive slab of stone shaped like a chair. Ancient Druids used such chairs to accommodate authority figures. It was believed the chair would transfer the strength of the rock to whoever sat upon it, giving them the ability to see great visions.

Just prior to the construction of Druid's Dream, Joseph and his brother Thomas began holding séances at Thomas's house. Thomas lived on an estate called Vaucluse, which was interwoven with mazes and pathways. The loss of his wife in 1881 threw Thomas into such a state of despair that he began to look to the unknown for answers. When he invited a psychic medium to come and stay with him for two weeks, he also invited Joseph to be present as the spirits of his wife and deceased children were summoned.

In all, thirteen séances were held and Thomas later described the materialization of his beloved wife and his two daughters, Fanny and Gertrude. Five years later, Thomas joined them in the other world.

Joseph died in 1892, leaving behind a family history of charity, goodwill and mystery.

THE TESTIMONY OF A GHOST
REBECCA CORNELL

The winds outside were chilly that February night in Portsmouth, but the home fires were burning. A few hours before dinner time, Thomas Cornell decided to go into his 72-year-old mother's room to visit with her. Rebecca Cornell was keeping herself warm in front of the stove in her bedroom, while she conversed with her son for about an hour and a half. Thomas then joined his wife and children in another part of the house.

When it was the usual time for the family to eat their evening meal and Rebecca had not emerged from her room to cook it, Thomas's wife Sarah became impatient. She ordered her son Edward to go ask his grandmother if she planned on boiling any milk for dinner. Edward went to Rebecca's bedroom and opened the door. There, on the floor, lay a burning body.

Edward quickly fetched his father and they returned to the room together. Surely some drunk must have come into the house and fallen on the floor in front of the stove, Thomas rationed. But upon closer inspection, the identity of the person became clearer. "Oh, Lord! It is my mother!" Thomas cried.

Officials deemed Rebecca Cornell's badly burned body and subsequent death the result of an accident. Common theories were that she had been smoking her pipe and haphazardly caught her clothing on fire, or that she'd suffered an attack of some kind and fallen into the stove.

A funeral was held, Rebecca was buried and everyone prepared to go on with their lives. But then Rebecca's brother, John Briggs, had a dream.
In the dream, the ghost of Rebecca appeared to him as a fiery apparition standing beside his bed. "I am your

sister," the apparition told him. "See how I was burnt with fire."

The next day John went to the authorities claiming that he had very pertinent information concerning his sister's death. According to his statement, the ghost had informed him that she had been murdered. And that the killer was her son Thomas.

Rebecca's body was exhumed and an examination conducted. It was discovered that the upper portion of the woman's stomach contained a stab wound. Thomas Cornell was immediately placed under arrest for the murder of his mother.

During the trial, several witnesses testified against Thomas. One of those witnesses, John Russell, told the court that just before her death Rebecca had commented that she wanted to move out of Thomas's house in the spring and into the house of her son Samuel. But she added that she was afraid she may not live long enough in Thomas's house to ever leave.

John's wife Mary told the court that about four years earlier she had gone to Thomas's house to find Rebecca weak and dirty from taking care of the farm animals all day. Rebecca was apparently very distraught due to all the work that was expected of her and she cried to Mary that she never received any help and was considering stabbing herself in the heart to bring an end to her misery.

Another witness, Mary Almy, testified that Thomas was well known for neglecting his mother's needs and that Rebecca often complained of having to sleep in a cold bed on dirty linens and was often forced to go to sleep hungry.

The testimonial evidence against Thomas was astounding. But there was not a single piece of physical evidence linking him to the crime. The jury was left to go on character assessments made by witnesses after the ghost of the dead woman allegedly made an appearance in John Brigg's bedroom.

That was apparently all the jury needed. At 1:00 p.m. on May 23, 1673, Thomas Cornell was hanged from the gallows in Newport, on the charge of murder. He was 46 years old.

Shortly after his death, his wife gave birth to a baby girl. She named the child "Innocent".

CREATURE IN THE WOODS
BIGFOOT IN SOUTH COUNTY

In the 1500's, English adventurer Andrew Battel visited Africa for the purpose of documenting the types of animals he saw there. According to his records, those animals included one known to the natives as the pongo. Battel described the beast as looking like a human covered with hair.

The Indians of California had documented the same type of creature which they called the omahah. Apparently the same such animal was native to British Columbia, as the Indians there also talked of a furry manlike being they called the tsookwa. Canadians who saw this kind of animal in their homeland called it the weekatow. And those who claim to have seen such a sight in America, call it bigfoot.

Despite the different names used, sightings of this creature have been documented all over the world, with descriptions being nearly identical no matter where the witnesses lived.

Standing nearly eight feet tall with red, gray or white fur, the bigfoot is consistently described as having a receding forehead, a wide nose with large nostrils and very thin lips.

Most alleged sightings are reported to have taken place at night, as the animal roamed through the forest, hunched over with its long arms hanging down past its bent knees.

Casts of what are said to be bigfoot prints show all the toes to be of the same short length with the big toe containing a double pad. Flat arches, a very large heel and long claws are also evident in the prints, which span about 18 inches long and 8 inches wide.

Purported handprints show the bigfoot's thumb to be much thinner than a human's and just as long as its four fingers, which contain flat, yellow fingernails.

The palms are described as being thickly padded, which may mean that the animal occasionally walks on all fours.

Witness sightings tell of the bigfoot's eyes, glowing with a reddish tint, square white teeth and hair on the creature's head being much longer than that on the rest of the body.

Most alleged sightings have come from loggers, fisherman, campers and hikers. And most of these witnesses claim that the bigfoot did not appear to be afraid of human presence, but instead seemed very curious and interested in observing human behavior. It was also noted that when a bigfoot departs after having made human contact, it does not run, but walks away slowly while regularly looking back over its shoulder.

Massive hands, legs and shoulders are said to be extremely out of proportion with the bigfoot's small head and very short neck. A large barrel chest is often described, and could mean that the animal has an incredible breathing capacity which would allow it to move over rocks and cliffs easily, lift heavy objects, swim great distances and jump several feet.

Blood and hair samples taken from sighting areas, show that the materials are not human nor from any animal on record. Its DNA characteristics show it to be a combination of both homo sapien and primate.

The bigfoot appears to have no violent tendencies toward man and there are rarely any accounts of bigfoot attacks.

Dozens of sightings have been reported as near to us as Connecticut, New Hampshire, Maine, New Jersey and Massachusetts. Yet records show only one reported sighting in Rhode Island. The event allegedly took place in South County in 1973.

If bigfoots are roaming the world, including the east coast, why would they seemingly refrain from crossing the border into the ocean state? Maybe they don't. Maybe those Rhode Islanders who have crossed paths with a hairy beast in the woods prefer to keep mum.

CREATURES IN THE SEA
AQUATIC MONSTERS

Beneath the sea, we have found ancient cities never known to have existed. We have discovered sunken treasures, statues and ships which human eyes have not set upon for centuries.

Why then is it so hard for some to believe that the sea may hold secrets of the living kind...prehistoric creatures that dwell within watery depths and make their existence known every now and then?

The first recorded sighting of an unknown animal appearing in a body of water took place in Scotland in the year 565 A.D. Over the years, there would be dozens more sightings there and eventually the mysterious creature would come to be known as the Loch Ness Monster.

The same type of reports describing an unidentified monster from the deep have come out of Brazil, Africa, and right here in the United States.

In June of 1996, two fishermen out for monkfish just off Block Island pulled up a 14-foot skeleton in their nets. The bony spine resembled a massive snake with a very large head.

Experts all had their own idea of what the creature may be. A decayed shark, a manatee, squid, seal, porpoise, otter, eel or slug. But many agreed that if the creature was indeed any of these things, it appeared to differ from any form of the species we had ever seen before.

In August of 2002, a couple swimming in Portsmouth came face to face with something in the water which they described as being fifteen feet long with four-inch teeth and dark green skin.

One of the most interesting things about reports of sea monsters is that virtually everyone, no matter where in the world the sighting takes place, gives the same physical details. The snakelike monsters have dark skin on the tops of their bodies with lighter skin on the underbelly, a large head and whiskers growing from each side of the snout.

If it is possible to believe that these animals are an undocumented species of shark, squid or slug, then why is it so far-fetched to believe they are an undocumented species of an animal we have never discovered?

Perhaps all the dinosaurs are not really extinct. Perhaps something is silently slithering along the ocean floor, keeping man guessing as it dwells within underwater worlds we have yet to explore.

FAMOUS NAMES

A RICHMOND LEGEND
JESSE JAMES

Jesse James photo from the Library of Congress.
Image courtesy of Wikipedia.org: public domain photo.

All towns have their legends, stories in which the boundary between fact and fiction is often straddled by those who are determined to believe.

Shelved in the memories of our elders, and the tales they left behind is the legend of one Mr. James, a gun-slinging bandit who carved a name for himself in the annals of crime. Yes, according to local legend, the famous Jesse James was born and bred right here in Richmond, Rhode Island.

In the James family cemetery, off Gardiner Road in Richmond stands a stone marker upon which is carved the names *James B. James* and *Anthony James* with the notation that they *left home for California in 1849 and are supposed to be dead.* It's been passed down through the generations that this stone is actually a memorial to the famous James brothers, known to the rest of the world as Jesse and Frank. The legend says that kinship to the duo has passed down through the local Sherman and Woodmansee families. But historical facts tell a different story.

Jesse Woodson James was the son of Reverend Robert Sallee James and Zerelda Elizabeth Cole. His birth record, in Clay County, Missouri, states that he was born September 5, 1847. Originally from Kentucky, Robert and Zerelda relocated to Missouri shortly after their marriage. In 1843, their first son, Alexander "Frank" was born. Their second child, Robert, died as an infant. Following Jesse's birth, a daughter Susan Lavenia was born in 1849. This was the year of the massive rush for gold in California and Jesse's father decided to leave his family in order to go seek his share of the wealth. But within a matter of months, Robert contracted food poisoning and died in Placerville Gold Camp. He was buried there in an unmarked grave.

Zerelda then married Benjamin Simms, who was soon killed in a horse mishap. Dr. Reuben Samuels became her third husband and she gave birth to four more children; Fannie, Sarah, Archie and John.

At the beginning of the Civil War, Jesse and Frank were quick to join the Confederate cause. Jesse was so enthralled by this new power to shoot 'em up, that his interest continued long after the battles were over.

Designating Frank as his right-hand man, he organized a gang of vigilantes and his life became one that must have had his Baptist minister father rolling over in his grave. In 1874, Jesse married Zee Mimms. In 1875, he saw the birth of a son, Jesse Edwards James. And in 1876, he robbed the First National Bank of Northfield, Minnesota.

For the next five years, Jesse divided his time between bank hold-ups, train robberies and stagecoach rip-offs. At the end of his rampage, he had succeeded in 24 acts of theft and killed at least a dozen men.

His last robbery, on the Chicago and Alton Train, was carried out with the help of five other men, including his cousin Bob Ford. But seven months later, Ford would prove that in the world of banditry, blood was not thicker than water. By the spring of 1882, there was a heavy bounty out on the head of Jesse James. A $10,000 reward was being offered to anyone who could bring in the great hold-up man, dead or alive. Ford saw this as the perfect opportunity to score some more easy cash.

On the morning of April 3, Ford walked into Jesse's home on the outskirts of St. Joseph, Missouri. He aimed his revolver at the back of his cousin, who was straightening out a picture on the wall. Suddenly a shot rang out, a bullet collided with Jesse's head and one of the most famous villains in history fell dead.

From Jesse's death, a number of legends sprung to life. Men from around the country came forward to proclaim that they were the real Jesse James, while others claimed to possess knowledge that the shooting on April 3rd was staged and that a different man was put to rest beneath Jesse James's headstone. And then there is Richmond's legend. But, like all the others, the pieces of the puzzle do not fit.

According to Missouri birth records, Jesse Woodson James was born there in 1847. According to

Rhode Island birth records, James B. James was born in 1811, the son of Jonathan and Ruth James, not Robert and Zerelda. If the Richmond legend bares any stitch of truth, it is apparently masked like an elusive bandit.

FENCING & SWORD SWALLOWING
LOCAL PERFORMERS

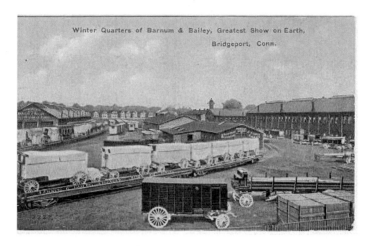

Old postcard depicting the Bridgeport, Connecticut winter quarters of the Barnum & Bailey Circus.
Public domain photo

If you've heard the phrase 'go run and join the circus', it may not be so far-fetched to assume that one of your ancestors may have done just that. If so, they didn't have to run far, since Hope Valley was once the home of several real-life show-stoppers.

Many years ago, the area now known as Canob Park was nothing more than a spacious field. It was the perfect place for a circus. At least the Ringling Brothers and Barnum and Bailey thought so. It was here they would pitch their striped tents and exhibit a menagerie of exotic animals and astounding humans. Many of their attractions lived right down the road.

Nationally renowned sword swallower Marie DeVere of Hopkinton, joined up with the circus in 1897. As a child she dreamed of performing under the big top and finally paid an actress friend a substantial amount of money to teach her the secret of sword swallowing.

Helen Englehart, who was born in Switzerland and ran a Hope Valley boarding house, developed a fondness for sharp-shooting at a very young age. In addition to becoming an expert shooter, she also became an internationally known fencer.

By 1946, both DeVere and Englehart had retired from the circus life and taken up residence together on a large farm on Tefft Hill Trail. Living there with them was the famous circus strongwoman Betty Rose. Working the farm for a living, the women would tend the animals and the garden, chop trees and stack wood. That year, the members of the Gordon-Greene American Legion Post of Hope Valley paid Englehart a visit and asked her to grant them a favor. They were planning a benefit concert and hoped she would help them out by performing her fencing act one more time.

Englehart explained to the men that she was sixty-nine years old and retired from the sport. But they were persistent. She had, after all, been a legend. She had been known all over the world as "Englehart the Great" and "Fencing Champion of the World." Of the 48 contests she had entered during the span of her career, she had lost just one. Englehart finally relented and agreed to perform at the benefit. She had one question for the men however, that being how they were ever going to find a suitable opponent. But there was an answer to her question. Englehart would face off against another Hope Valley resident, the 1888 Yale Fencing Champion, Edward M. Tillinghast.

Nearly 1,000 people packed into the large brick building at the old Bank Block to watch Englehart lunge and jab for the first time in decades. It took just three bouts before Tillinghast quit and handed the victory to his opponent.

The old circus performers are now gone, and the ground where the big top stood is built up with houses. The days are over when the train would stop at the

Hope Valley depot to drop off clowns and acrobats. And the sounds of local children shouting, "The circus is coming!" have dissolved into the silence of history.

ENGRAVED IN STONE
JOHN PALMER BROWNING

John Palmer Browning's masterpiece at First Hopkinton Cemetery in Hopkinton.
Photographer: Kelly Sullivan Pezza

Hopkinton possesses its share of interesting monuments, however there is none so unusual as that which stands in the First Hopkinton cemetery in the village of Ashaway.

An assemblage of nearly fifty granite markers, which look as if they are planted in a sea of glistening rock, make up what can be described as a massive piece of artwork.

The man responsible for the monument was John Palmer Browning, a resident of Hopkinton who acquired a love of granite-working from his many years of toiling in the quarries.

When he wasn't working, Browning, who was born in 1886, ventured from his house on Laurel Street down to the Bonner Monument Company in Ashaway, carrying with him different religious verses he wanted engraved in stone. He would stay and watch the carvers work their magic and then carry each stone to his family's burial lot in the cemetery. Some of the stones were set out to memorialize loved ones, while others were simply placed there to convey a message to those passing by.

In his younger years, Browning had fallen in love with a girl from New Orleans. Because he did not have enough money to travel out and see her, the long-distance relationship continued through letters. By the age of 24, he had saved enough to make the trip to Louisiana, but before he got there, the girl died. Browning purchased an enormous piece of granite, had it inscribed with her name and shipped to New Orleans. Placed atop her grave there, his love for her was forever carved in stone.

Described by those who remember him as an eccentric loner, Browning was well-known for doing things his own way. From placing three dampers in his chimney instead of relying on just one, to walking the roads with his wheelbarrow in tow instead of driving his truck, he left a permanent image on everyone who knew him.

Browning committed most of his life to working on the monument in the Hopkinton cemetery. Finally, he committed his body. He rests alongside his mother Annie and father John, as a life-size statue of the German Maid of the Seas watches over them all.

A devoted son, an eccentric loner, an imaginative individual, John Browning is now immortalized by the granite he loved.

THE MYSTERIOUS ENGLISHMAN
THEOPHILUS WHALEY

King Charles I
1635 oil painting by Anthony Van Dyck.
Image provided by Wikipedia.org: public domain image.

When King Charles I stood trial in England, he was accused of using tyrannical power to overthrow the people. After having levied war against parliament, he was branded a traitor who cared more about himself than the rights of the people. His trial resulted in a death sentence and 59 people signed the order of execution, including three judges named Whalley, Goffe and Dixwell. At the Palace of Whitehall, on January 30, 1649, the 49-year-old king placed his head on the chopping block, stretched his arms out and was decapitated with an axe.

After the Restoration of Charles II in 1660, many of those who had participated in handing down the death sentence were threatened with their own death if they were found. Fifty-two of them were pardoned. But the other seven were not. Those seven included Whalley, Goffe and Dixwell. Fearing for their lives, they fled to the colonies. According to an account published by the governor in 1764, a ship had arrived in Boston on July 27, 1660 with Goffe and Whalley aboard.

An interesting story in itself, it becomes even more interesting when one considers the secretive man who lived hidden in a small area on a Narragansett farm. His name was Theophilus Whaley.

Coming into town after King Phillip's War, Whaley obtained a small portion of land from the Willet family, just north of Pettaquamscot Pond. There, he built himself an underground shelter along a hillside. The large, six-foot tall man was very well educated and fluent in Greek, Latin and Hebrew. The few who knew of his presence and talked to him would often ask him why he lived the way he did.

But Whaley chose to dodge such questions, only reporting that he had previously lived in Virginia but relocated because he felt he was in danger there.

Francis Willett, who was just a boy when his father let the land to Whaley, later recounted that he remembered men from Boston coming to the Willett farm annually to check on the well-being of Whaley. According to Willett, the men always acted very affectionate and caring toward the recluse and that Whaley was always in possession of a great deal of money after they left. He also remembered a man coming to the house claiming to be a relative of Whaley's who was looking for him. The man was a captain on a ship of war and invited Whaley to come onto the boat. Whaley refused.

Born in Screveton, England in 1616, Theophilus Whaley was the son of Richard and Francis Whaley. He married Elizabeth Mills in Virginia in 1670 and the couple had two children there; Joane and Mary Elizabeth. Five other children were born in Narragansett.

In 1709, Whaley obtained a 20-acre tract of land in West Greenwich and relocated there with his family. His wife died in 1715 at the Hopkins Hill Road home. Five years later, Whaley followed her to the grave, at the age of 104. He was buried in the Judge Hopkins lot in West Greenwich.

Several people had come right out and asked Whaley if he had been one of the judges who took part in the trial and execution of the king. He would never answer the question.

RUM-RUNNER
DANNY WALSH

U.S. Coast Guard patrol boats were used to catch rum-runners.
Photo taken by U.S. Coast Guard.
Image courtesy of Wikipedia.org: public domain photo.

No person shall, on or after the date when the 18th Amendment to the Constitution of the United States goes into effect, manufacture, sell, barter, transport, import, export, deliver, furnish or possess any intoxicating liquor except as authorized in this act...National Prohibition Act, January 16, 1920.

An abrupt change in American life was brought about when the Prohibition Act went into effect. For brewers and saloon owners, it meant a sudden end to business. But by alcohol being designated an illegal substance, a massive window of opportunity opened for others. Speakeasies, which allowed customers in as long as they knocked the secret knock, became a risky business that made their owners rich. And bootlegging became one of the most prosperous businesses of all time.

Danny L. Walsh was born in Cumberland in 1893. The son of poor mill workers, he spent his early years employed as a clerk in a Pawtucket hardware store. His job, though respectable, was hardly one that would net him a fortune. The inevitable wealth that rum-running would bring was something that he could not ignore.

Walsh started out on the lower rung of the business, working as a driver for established bootleggers. But it wasn't long before he had earned enough money to start conducting his very own illegal enterprise. He had an entire fleet of rum-running boats constructed and bought a sprawling horse-breeding farm on Charlestown Beach Road in Charlestown. Employing a private housekeeper Etta M. Gorton, chauffer Herbert W. Johnson, estate hostlers George A. Gorton, William Welch and John J. Grogan, and even a private estate cook George Freeman, who all lived with him, Danny Walsh had become one of the most prosperous rum-runners in America, before the age of forty.

The coast of Rhode Island was famous as a drop off point for booze which had been smuggled in from other countries. Large ships transported crates of alcohol to areas not far from shore, where smaller boats would venture out to make the transaction.

The U.S. Coast Guard was well aware of what was going on and was authorized to shoot at the occupants of any vessel taking part in rum-running. Walsh managed to outsmart the authorities long enough to become a very rich man. His convoy of secret transportation grew to include planes and cars, and his circle of friends widened.

But Walsh's luck ran out in 1933. On February 2nd of that year, he joined six acquaintances for dinner at the Bank Café in Pawtuxet Village. When the meal was over, he bid the others good-bye and left the premises. No one ever saw him again.

To this day, the fate of the famous Charlestown rum-runner remains a mystery. Rumors have circulated that have him being placed in a barrel of cement and dumped off the coast of Block Island by business rivals. Others rumors have him being killed and secretly buried on his own Charlestown farm.

Ten months after Walsh's disappearance, Prohibition was repealed and the sale and manufacture of alcohol was once again legal. But the history concerning the end of Prohibition in Rhode Island can not be completely written until certain questions of that era are answered. Where is the body of Danny Walsh?

LESSONS TAUGHT
PRUDENCE CRANDALL

The Hezekiah Carpenter house in Hope Valley where Prudence Crandall was born.
Reprinted from the History of the Town of Hopkinton, published by the Town of Hopkinton in 1976.

Six days before Christmas, in the year 1799, 21-year-old Pardon Crandall and 15-year-old Esther Carpenter exchanged wedding vows before Baptist minister Ellet Locks. The couple moved into the house which Esther's father Hezekiah had built in Hope Valley in 1778. Their first child, a boy named after Esther's father, was born on September 22, 1800. On September 3, 1803, the Crandalls welcomed a baby girl into the family. They named the child Prudence, and little did they know that one day their little bundle of joy would claim a major place in history.

By the time Prudence was nine years old, she had another sibling, Reuben, born on January 6, 1806, and their mother was pregnant again. Pardon enjoyed his growing family but he was becoming bored by what he perceived to be a lack of opportunity in Hope Valley. Just days after Hannah Almyra was born, on June 27, 1812, the family packed their belongings and relocated to a new home in Canterbury, Connecticut.

Having exchanged their Baptist beliefs for Quakerism, the Crandalls sent Prudence to the Friend's Boarding School in Providence. Upon graduation, she decided to become a teacher and, in the fall of 1831, several well-to-do residents of Canterbury began asking Prudence if she would be interested in starting a private school there in town.

Prudence Crandall
Public domain image

After taking the idea into consideration, Prudence took out a loan and purchased the Paine Mansion in which to run the school. The Canterbury Female Boarding School was thereby established with Prudence as its director.

A number of young women from the most prosperous families in town enrolled, including Eliza and Phebe Howe, Frances Ensworth, Sarah Adams, Frances and Sarah Coit, and Hannah Pearl. Tuition, including room and board, was $25 per quarter. Basic subjects were taught, with specialty subjects being available for an extra fee.

Prudence's teaching ability and wide range of knowledge garnered her much praise from the community. But being revered was not something she was going to enjoy for long.

Prudence employed an African-American woman by the name of Marcia Davis to keep house for her. Marcia was close friends with 17-year-old Sarah Harris, the sister of her fiancé Charles. Originally from Norwich, the Harris family had relocated to Canterbury where Sarah worked as a servant in the home of Jedediah Shephard.

The South County Art Association Workshop in Kingston, formerly the home of Sarah Harris and her husband.
Photographer: Kelly Sullivan Pezza

Sarah often came to the school to visit Marcia and one day she began talking to Prudence about her education. She said she had attended the Norwich public school but that she would like to further her education so that she could one day become a teacher. Prudence asked Sarah if she would like to enroll in Canterbury School. Sarah said yes and was enrolled as a student.

When the parents of the other students learned that an African-American would be attending the same school as their daughters, they caused a furor and threatened to withdraw their children from the school if the dark-skinned girl was not dismissed.

Rather than cater to their wishes, or risk having an attendance of just one student, Prudence simply changed the type of school she was running. Advertisements now publicized the educational center as being for *"young ladies and little misses of color."*

The parents who had issued the threats were shocked and angered when their children were suddenly refused admittance. Prudence penned a letter to the town authorities explaining why she would no longer teach her former students. *"I had a nice colored girl as help in my family,"* she wrote. *"and her intended husband regularly received the Liberator newspaper. The girl took the paper from the office and loaned it to me. The condition of the colored people, both slave and free, were most truthfully portrayed. Having been taught from early childhood the sin of slavery, my sympathies were greatly aroused."*

Prudence went on to explain that her housekeeper was often called upon by the young Sarah Harris. *"During these calls, I ascertained that she wished to attend my school,"* she wrote. *"So I allowed her to enter as one of my pupils. By this act, I gave great offense. I very soon found that some of my school would leave and not return if the colored girl was retained. Under these circumstances, I made up my mind that I would teach colored girls exclusively."*

Over twenty African-American girls from Massachusetts, Pennsylvania and New York arrived for admittance at the school. The first to arrive was Ann Eliza Hammond, who came in from Providence on April 12, 1833. Soon, Prudence had a total of 24 new students, including Harriet Lamson, Theodosia DeGrass, Mary Harris, Eliza Glasko, G.C. Marshal, Amelia Elizabeth Wiles, Mariah Robinson and Ann Peterson. But it was not a situation that residents of the town were going to accept.

Ann Hammond was warned by authorities, less than 24 hours after her arrival, that unless she left town, she would be publicly whipped. Then, on May 24, 1833, the state of Connecticut passed a law that stated it was illegal to establish a school specifically for the education of blacks. Prudence ignored the law and continued holding classes. She was arrested and placed in jail on June 27th.

On August 23rd, her trial resulted in a hung jury. Two months later, she was tried again and found guilty, a decision which she appealed. Three months later, before the case had returned to court, residents made an unsuccessful attempt at burning the school down.

Over the course of the next six months, Prudence and her pupils were harassed and threatened unmercifully. Local stores and businesses refused to sell them food or supplies. Rocks and eggs were tossed at them. Animal feces was thrown into the school's drinking water, and the students were threatened by authorities that they would be arrested for vagrancy and subjected to public whipping if they did not leave the school and go back home. Prudence and the girls endured the torture, and finally the prevailing court case was dismissed due to a technicality.

On August 12th of that year, Prudence married a 46-year-old Baptist minister named Calvin Philleo. Hailing from Brooklyn, New York, he had taken an interest in the case and sat in the court room during the trial. Reverend George Tillotson performed the ceremony between the controversial teacher and the recent widower with three children.

Less than a month later, on September 9, residents ambushed the school with iron bars and wooden clubs. Over ninety window panes were smashed out of the building while Prudence and her students sat inside trembling with fear. The next morning, Prudence gave up what seemed to be a hopeless battle. With her students' lives in jeopardy, she dismissed them all and closed down the school.

Prudence and her husband relocated to a small farm in Boonville, New York. In 1838, she received word that Reuben had died in Jamaica on January 6, at the age of thirty-two. Six months later, her father passed away.

The couple then moved to the Troy Grove, Illinois farm her father had owned and Prudence obtained a job teaching in the local school. She remained in Illinois until three years after Calvin died on January 5, 1874. She then purchased a small farm in Elk Falls, Kansas with her widowed brother Hezekiah. He died there in the spring of 1881. She followed on January 28, 1890 and was buried in the Elk Falls Cemetery.

Toward the end of her life, the State of Connecticut offered Prudence an annual pension of $400. She took the offer, but explained, "I accept this not as a deed of charity, but as restitution for the property that was destroyed."

In the midst of the tortures of 1833, Marcia had married Charles Harris. Sarah was also married that year, to 30-year-old George Fayerweather. Grandson of an Indian princess and great-grandson of one of the slaves belonging to the Reverend Samuel Fayerweather, George worked as a blacksmith. He and Sarah spent the majority of their lives in South Kingstown. The couple had several children before Sarah's death in 1878. She was buried in Old Fernwood Cemetery in South Kingstown.

Grave of Sarah (Harris) Fayerweather in Old Fernwood Cemetery in Kingston.
Photographer: Alecia Keegan

LOVE VS. FAME
JOHN L. SULLIVAN

John L. Sullivan
Courtesy of Wikipedia.org: public domain photo.

Annie Bates was born in South Kingstown in 1845. She spent her early adult years working as an operative in one of the local cotton mills and, like most women of that time, she probably expected she would marry a farmer and live a simple life. But one day a young man appeared across the street from her sister's house in Centreville. From a window, she watched him roping off a small vacant area where he was planning on holding a little sparring match. Something about him impressed her. Something about him would soon impress the whole world.

John Lawrence Sullivan was born in Boston, Massachusetts on October 15, 1858 to Irish immigrants Michael and Katherine Sullivan. Because his parents were strict Catholics, a problem arose when his love for Annie Bates reached the point of a marriage proposal. Annie would have to give up her own religion and become a Roman Catholic if she wanted to marry him, John told her. Annie had no idea that this was just the first of many sacrifices she would make to be the wife of the future boxing champ, John L. Sullivan.

Watching her fiancé prepare for his bout with Paddy Ryan in February of 1882, she could not bear to remain a witness to his training as he knocked out man after man with the utmost of brutality. Sullivan not only won the bout with Ryan, but took home the Heavyweight Champion of America title.

On May 1, 1883, John and Annie were married at St. Patrick's Church in Roxbury, Massachusetts. The ceremony was anything but romantic. Fans of the "Great John L.", as he had come to be known, packed into the church and lined the road that ran past it just to get a glimpse of their hero. The new Mrs. Sullivan was appalled by the intrusion.

Four months later, Annie accompanied John when he left their home in Rhode Island to begin a tour. For Annie, married life had been over-shadowed right from the beginning by her husband's larger than life persona and the tour proved almost unbearable for her.

John had a habit of challenging anyone, anywhere, to fight him. Calling himself "The Boston Strongboy", John swore he could beat anyone alive. His wife couldn't stand to watch the duels that were constantly provoked by him. The way he physically battered his opponents made her feel ill. But what bothered her the most was the knowledge that one day John would undoubtedly meet his match and end up lying pulverized at her feet.

During the tour, Annie discovered that she was pregnant. She announced to her husband that she was returning home to await the birth of their child. He agreed that was probably for the best. On April 10, 1884, "Little Johnnie" Sullivan was born.

The boxing champ immediately returned home upon hearing of the birth. Yet, he brought with him a crowd of reporters, photographers and fans.

Annie lay in bed with her newborn child as dozens of strangers crowded into the house, popping flashbulbs in her face. Shocked and irate, she ordered all of them off the property. The order did not sit well with her husband. He sternly explained to her that she must be polite and accommodating to his public at all times. Annie had finally had enough. She told John to make a decision: it was boxing or her. John packed his belongings, exited the house, slammed the door and never returned. He resumed his tour and won a bout with Pete McCoy in Louisiana two days later.

On October 28, 1886, Little Johnnie died of Diphtheria. Annie tried again and again to make contact with John and let him know of his son's death but he never responded to her messages. All she ever knew of her husband's whereabouts or his life was what she read it the papers. And what she read was that the Great John L. had won a bout with Steve Taylor three days after his son's death and that he was busily training for another spar with Paddy Ryan in San Francisco. The stories were accompanied by a nice photo of John in California with burlesque dancer Ann Livingston, who was identified in the caption as his wife.

Annie became deeply depressed. She convinced herself that she had over-reacted to the pitfalls of being Mrs. John L. Sullivan. She convinced herself that he still loved her and would return to her someday.

On September 7, 1892, she was still clinging to that belief when she traveled to New York City to watch her husband defend his Championship of the World title against Jim Corbett. She left after the 21st round when Corbett knocked Sullivan to the ground and he was unable to get back up. The Boston Strongboy had finally met his match.

John had long been having divorce petitions sent to Annie but she refused them all. For over twenty years, she contested his every action for legal separation. Alone in her small West Warwick cottage, Annie Sullivan had spent her life hoping for a happy ending to all the madness she had endured. On December 13, 1908, another divorce petition arrived at her door. The 63-year-old woman finally picked up a pen and signed it.

John was quick to marry again. His new wife was Kate Harkins and the couple settled on a farm in West Abington, Massachusetts. John retired from boxing, began raising poultry and settled into a life of quiet solitude. On February 2, 1918, he died at the farm of a heart attack.

John was inducted into the International Boxing Hall of Fame in 1990, titled as one of the most successful heavyweight champions in the world. Annie passed away one year before John. She was interred beside her son in Woodland Cemetery in Coventry, *her* only title being that of the ex-Mrs. John Sullivan.

THE REALITY OF SURREALISM
H.P. LOVECRAFT

On August 20, 1890 at 9 a.m., Howard Philips Lovecraft was born in his parent's house on Angell Street in Providence. His mother, Sarah (Phillips) came from a prominent New England family. His father, Winfield Lovecraft, knew a life less extravagant. As an employee of Gorham and Company Silversmith's, he supported his family by working as a traveling salesman.

When Howard was just three years old, his father suffered a minor heart attack in a Chicago hotel room while there on business. He returned to Rhode Island and was admitted to Butler Hospital for the Insane. It was believed Winfield was suffering from some form of nervous agitation, as he had begun to have hallucinations.

Howard's father remained in Butler Hospital for five years, unable to speak or move, passing away on July 19, 1898 at the age of 45.

The raising of young Howard fell to his mother, and her father Whipple Van Buren Phillips. At the Phillips home, Howard struggled to come to terms with the recent deaths in his family. There was no better place to do that than at Whipple's fairytale estate. The wealthy 65-year-old was a retired real estate industrialist and former president of the Owyhee Land and Irrigation Company. Well-traveled and highly educated, Whipple had a staff of servants at his command.

There, Howard traveled in private carriages and walked the winding pathways of the yard which snaked around fountains and through orchards. Most importantly, he had the use of his grandfather's extensive library.

Whipple had married his first cousin, Robie Alzada Place in 1856. When she passed away in 1896, Howard was forever marked by the stigma of loss. *"The death of my grandmother plunged the household into a gloom from which it never full recovered,"* he wrote in a letter to a friend years later. *"The black attire of my mother and aunts terrified and repelled me to such an extent that I would surreptitiously pin bits of bright cloth or paper to their skirts for sheer relief."*

His grandmother had died just two years before his father, and he eventually began to feel that gloom was never-ending. Subconsciously the child began to take permanent notes in his head which were later reiterated on paper for the masses.

Howard began to have terrible nightmares after Robie's death and forced himself to stay awake rather than enter the terrifying world of sleep. During the day, he would struggle through classes at Slater Avenue School. Although he was somewhat of a child prodigy, having learned to read and write by the age of four, and received good marks in school, his lack of attendance affected his grades. Nervousness, fatigue and other psychological afflictions often kept Howard out of class and in the solitude of his over-protective mother.

Yet even without the benefit of the classroom, Howard went on to learn all he could. In his grandfather's library, he would peruse gothic thrillers and the works of Edgar Allen Poe. He would then retreat to his bedroom to write essays about science and the art of composition. But his secure world fell apart on March 27, 1904 when his grandfather suffered a stroke. A few hours later, the 71-year-old man died.

Whipple had intended for his family to inherit his wealth but mismanagement of the funds brought about a total loss. The servants were let go, the carriages sold and the grounds of the three-story, fifteen-room Victorian closed up.

Howard and his mother were forced to move into much more modest quarters, at the other end of Angell Street. The trauma of constantly losing loved ones caused Howard to contemplate ending his own life. *"My grandfather was the center of my entire universe,"* he later wrote to a friend, claiming that he longed for a *"long peaceful night of non-existence"*.

In the small apartment he now shared with his mother, the boy struggled to go on living, in a world seemingly overshadowed with loss. He entered Hope Street High School, where his interest lay heavily in chemistry. But once again, physical and psychological ailments would prevent him from receiving a normal education. Two years into high school, he dropped out after suffering a nervous collapse.

It was at this time that Howard P. Lovecraft took what may have been his first major step in the world of composition. After reading an article about astronomy in a local paper, he wrote a letter to the editor, expressing his dismay at the opinions of its author. The letter was published and gained the attention of literary bigwigs. Soon he was writing columns for several newspapers.

In 1913, he was invited to join the United Amateur Press Association. This allowed him to expand on his talents. While he continued to put together educational pieces for the papers, his stories of fantastic imagination were now being published in magazines such as Weird Tales and Amazing Stories.

Most of Howard's fiction was told against the backdrop of the Providence he loved. It was dark and thrilling, a mixture of the styles of writers he admired and the shades of death that had colored his own life since he was a child. His nightmares of funerals and mental hospitals and the inevitable dark corners of the future had long ago laid the foundation of his life's work.

Little did he know that the gloomy experiences forced upon him were not yet over. His mother suffered a nervous breakdown in 1919 and was admitted to Butler Hospital, the very place where his father had died. Two years later, she remained there, suffering from gall bladder problems. On May 24, 1921, she died from complications during surgery.

At just 31 years old, Howard had already lost the four people he loved most in the world. All he had to keep him from voluntarily following them to the grave was his love of writing. On July 4, 1921, he attended a journalism convention in Boston, Massachusetts.

There, he met Sonia Haft Greene, a widow from Brooklyn, New York. Howard left the Rhode Island he so loved to move in with Sonia, who owned a hat shop on Fifth Avenue. On March 3, 1924 they were married. But the cruel hand of fate was not done with Howard. Soon after the couple married, Sonia's business went bankrupt. The loss caused her to suffer an emotional breakdown and she was admitted to a New Jersey sanitarium.

Although Sonia's health improved and she was released from the hospital, the marriage took a downward spiral. Howard had refused a position as editor of Weird Tales because it would have necessitated a move to Chicago. Yet Sonia had no qualms about relocating when she was offered a job in Cleveland. They had been married less than a year when she accepted the job and left her husband behind.

Howard continued to try to find good-paying work in New York, but for someone whose only experience was writing, any other job was out of his grasp. In the spring of 1926, he returned to Providence and he wrote some of his best work.

But however deep his dreams were, or however long his plans, they were not to be. In 1936, he began suffering from pain in his abdomen. When he finally saw a doctor in the spring of 1937, he was diagnosed with intestinal cancer. Having progressed for so long, there was little the doctors could do except try to make him comfortable. Five days later, on March 13, 1937, Howard Phillips Lovecraft died at the age of 47.

He was buried in the Phillips plot at Swan Point Cemetery in Providence, and his name added to the family stone. In 1977, literary scholar Dirk Mosig raised funds to purchase a separate marker for Howard, one that would let all who passed know they were in the midst of the man who left the world with volumes of his creative ingenuity. His gravestone is carved with the appropriate statement, *"I AM PROVIDENCE"*.

During his short life, Howard had composed over a hundred literary articles, several hundred poems, more than fifty short stories, four short novels and 24 collaborative writing efforts, most published in obscure magazines. Two years after his death, his former writing colleagues August Derleth and Donald Wandrei founded a publishing company called Arkham House. Their main objective was to publish the collected works of Howard. That year, "The Outsider and Others" hit bookstore shelves, compiling the great works of the late author.

Today, his following reaches a number of astounding proportions. His works are translated into several languages. Fan clubs are devoted to him, film festivals held in his name. Just the name H.P. Lovecraft evokes an image. *"Men of broader intellect know there is no sharp distinction betwixt the real and unreal,"* he once wrote. His own reality was one the average person sees only in his darkest dreams.

KEEPER OF THE LIGHT
IDA LEWIS

Ida Lewis standing beside the lighthouse.
Old postcard, circa 1910.
Public domain photo

She was born in 1842 in Newport, the oldest of Hosea and Zoradia Lewis' four children. Her father was a seaman, long-drawn to the translucent waves of the Atlantic.

In 1853, Hosea was given the appointment of the first lighthouse keeper of Lime Rock, a tiny island situated one-third of a mile from the shores of Newport. Packing his family and belongings into a boat, they sailed to the isolated bit of land to begin a unique and solitary way of life.

However things did not go as Hosea planned. Four months into his duties, he suffered a stroke and became unable to continue the work his position required. Ida cared for him, adding to the responsibilities she had already grown accustomed to. Her little sister, who was seriously ill, needed Ida's constant attention. The two other children, who attended school on the mainland, were rowed daily by their older sister across the stretch of water and back.

Ida's own education had been aborted, as her devotion to her family required nearly all of her time. Now, with her father unable to maintain the lighthouse, she took on yet another job. She filled the beacon light with oil every night at sundown, refilled it at midnight, trimmed the wicks at regular intervals, kept the reflectors free of carbon, and rose at dawn to extinguish the light before taking her siblings to school. Her duties also included saving lives.

One day, four prominent young men had taken their boat out on the water for a leisurely sail. But, being boys, they were not content to merely float along. One of them jumped up onto the mast of the boat, flipping it over and throwing himself and his friends into the water. From the island, seventeen-year-old Ida saw the boys splashing about in distress. Quickly, she pushed her little row boat off the shore, climbed in and brought them all back safely.

Yet another amazing recovery took place one snowy day in 1869. Two soldiers sailing through Newport Harbor toward Fort Adams, were caught in a storm. Suddenly their boat capsized, sending them into the icy ocean. Zoradia saw the commotion and screamed to Ida, who was sick in bed. Without stopping to put on her shoes or coat, Ida raced out to her snow-covered boat and commenced to save the soldiers. One of them gave her a gold watch in appreciation. And so thankful were the other soldiers at Fort Adams that they raised $218 among them and presented it to their heroine.

Another soldier was saved after Ida had rushed out to help the drunken man, who had gone for a sail and fallen from his boat. As the man was too heavy for her to lift him into the safety of her own boat, she tied a rope around his waist and carefully pulled him to the shore.

Ida was also keeping a careful lookout the day three men were attempting to transport a prize sheep across the harbor. When their boat flipped over, both the men and their cargo were submerged. Within minutes, Ida had pulled them into her boat and deposited them back on land. She even went back for the sheep.

Because of her heroic efforts, Ida was given the honor of being the first woman in history to receive a Congressional Medal for bravery. The Life Saving Benevolent Society of New York also presented her with a gold medal and a check for $100. During that year's town-wide Fourth of July celebration, Ida was publicly honored and given the gift of a new mahogany rowboat.

As news of this amazing woman reached the far corners of the world, crowds began to flock to Lime Rock. One year, more than 9,000 strangers pulled their boats up along the shores of Ida's secluded family home. Mrs. John Jacob Astor and President Ulysses Grant were among those who came to meet her. But there were also throngs of newspaper reporters, magazine journalists and men desperate to marry this amazing woman.

Ida shirked from the attention, the proposals and the praise. However, she did agree to marry Captain William Wilson of Black Rock, Connecticut, leaving Lime Rock and the lighthouse to live with him at his far off home.

The marriage did not last. Perhaps she missed the sea that she had once gazed out across from the bed she had positioned beside the window. Perhaps she missed maintaining that beacon of light. Perhaps she missed being the beacon of hope.

Ida returned alone to Lime Rock in 1879 and was finally granted not only the title of lighthouse keeper, but the pay as well, which had been going to her mother since her father's stroke. She was now to receive $500 a year for her work. And, again, she was lighting the flame daily and pulling drowning souls to safety.

In 1881, she was awarded the highest medal of bravery ever awarded by the U.S. Lifesaving Service. "When in danger, look for the dark-haired girl in a rowboat," one sea captain commented after she had guided his distressed vessel to shore.

At the age of 63, Ida made her last rescue as a friend who was coming to visit, stood up in her boat and fell overboard. Just as spryly as ever, Ida rowed out and pulled the woman into her own boat. When reporters wanted to know where a lady of her age got the strength to accomplish such a feat, Ida replied, "I don't know. I ain't particularly strong. The Lord Almighty gives it to me when I need it."

The next year, she became a lifetime beneficiary of the Carnegie Hero Fund, which sent her a monthly pension of $30. In all, she had saved almost twenty lives during her many years on Lime Rock.

In the early hours of October 25, 1911, Ida awoke feeling ill. Still, she got out of bed, got dressed and put out the beacon light, not knowing it would be the last time. That afternoon, she died.

The bells of every vessel in Newport Harbor tolled their sad bells that night. Flags were flown at half-mast and another lighthouse keeper, Edward Jansen, was appointed. A few months later, when Jansen's wife gave birth to a baby girl, she was christened Ida Lewis Jansen.

In 1924, the Rhode Island legislature officially changed the name of Lime Rock to Ida Lewis Rock.

And the Lime Rock Lighthouse became the Ida Lewis Lighthouse.

"Sometimes the spray dashes against these windows so strong that I can't see out," she had once written. *"But I am happy. There is peace on this rock that you don't get on the shore. And it's part of my happiness to know they are depending on me to guide them safely…"*

A WOMAN'S VOICE
MARGARET FULLER

Margaret Fuller
Engraving from the Library of Congress.
Image courtesy of Wikipedia.org: public domain image.

At a time when many women were unable to read or write, she spoke fluent French, Italian, German, Greek and Latin. And by the time she died, she had not only become just a wife and mother during her short existence. She would forever be known as a writer, editor, teacher, activist, and a woman who spoke out when the world seemed to be against women having a voice.

Margaret Fuller was born on May 23, 1810 in a large house on Cherry Street in Cambridge, Massachusetts. The daughter of Timothy and Margaret (Crane) Fuller, she was the first-born child of the couple.

Timothy Fuller was a renowned lawyer and congressman and wanted to bestow the very best education upon his offspring. However, education was reserved for male offspring while daughters were expected to stay at home and help with cooking and cleaning. Mr. Fuller decided to bend those rules when he enrolled his daughter in Cambridge Private Grammar School. At the age of 11, she moved on to Dr. John Park's School in Boston. Two years later, she was a student at Miss Prescott's Seminary in Groton, Massachusetts.

By 1833 the Fullers had welcomed seven more children and moved to a new home in Groton. But their happiness would be short-lived. On October 1, 1835, Timothy Fuller succumbed to cholera. It was now up to 25-year-old Margaret to take care of her mother and siblings.

Margaret took a job teaching languages at The Temple School in Boston. From there she went on to teach at the Greene Street School in Providence. At the same time, she started giving lectures and seminars for women.

By that time, Margaret had been writing for several years and had an article published in the Boston Daily Advertiser in 1834. She had become friends with such future legendary figures as Bronson Alcott, Ralph Waldo Emerson and Henry David Thoreau. In 1840 she decided to put her writing talent to work for herself when she and Emerson started up a transcendentalist magazine called The Dial. For two years, she acted as the magazine's editor then took a job as literary critic for the New York Tribune and moved her whole family to the city with her.

In 1844, Margaret published her first book "Summer on the Lakes." In 1845, "Women in the Nineteenth Century" hit the store shelves. The following year, her "Papers on Literature and Art" was published.

Following the third book, she traveled to Europe as a foreign correspondent for the Tribune. Her treks through France, England and Italy filled her with romantic creativity and a pull so strong that she decided to move to Rome in 1847.

There, she fell in love with the Marchese Giovanni Ossoli. His involvement with the dangerous politics taking place in the foreign land intrigued Margaret and she began work on a book manuscript concerning the situation there.

Only months into the new subject and her relationship with Ossoli, Margaret found herself pregnant. The two were quickly married and Angelo Eugenio Ossoli was born on September 7, 1848. On May 17, 1850, the couple and their baby son boarded the Elizabeth and set sail for a visit to America.

The two-month long trip took its toll on everyone aboard, as Small Pox had been brought onto the ship by an infected passenger. Angelo became ill but Margaret was able to nurse him back to health. The captain however, was not so lucky and succumbed to the illness, leaving an inexperienced first mate to take over control of the ship.

On July 19, as the vessel made its way through stormy weather toward Fire Island, it struck a sandbar. Waves crashed up against the Elizabeth, spilling over the deck until she began to sink. Margaret, her husband and their baby jumped overboard with the rest of the passengers and were never seen again.

A monument erected in Mount Auburn Cemetery in Cambridge pays tribute to the family, and immortalizes the brilliance of the 40-year-old woman who had spent a lifetime making her voice heard.

TREASURES OF THE EARTH
ORLANDO SMITH

Orlando Smith of Ledyard, Connecticut earned his living by laying the foundations for local mills and houses. It helped make ends meet until the quantity of available granite began to run out and he was left to search the neighboring state of Rhode Island for additional building material.

Venturing into Westerly, he happened upon the Babcock farm. The two and a half story Georgian dwelling that stood upon the farm was built in 1734 for Dr. Joshua Babcock. Little did the doctor know that there was buried treasure on his property and that in 1846 a man named Orlando Smith would become famous by discovering it.

A small rocky outcropping on the farm immediately caught Smith's eye. When he investigated further, he found that he was standing upon a massive amount of what would prove to be some of the most sought after granite in the world. He offered the owner $8,000 for the property. Upon agreement of the sale, he handed over a $2,000 down-payment. The 32-year-old stonemason, along with his wife Emeline (Gallup) and their children, relocated to Westerly and he began to withdraw the crystalline material from the earth.

Glistening in shades of red, white, blue, gray, black and pink, the highly polished ledges produced some of the heaviest and densest granite ever discovered. With a crushing resistance that was unmatched by any other building material, the granite was nearly indestructible and orders began to pour in for the construction of banks, town halls and churches. Too beautiful to be hidden beneath houses, more and more customers began requesting that Smith embellish their house interiors and exteriors with his incredible stone.

Because the granite was so tolerant to harsh New England weather, hundreds of people began ordering grave markers made of Smith's material. And then orders began to come in from around the world. Customers wanted memorials, monuments, statues and grand buildings. Smith's stonemasonry career had exploded and Westerly granite was being coveted from the four corners of the earth.

The 23-foot-high Antietam Soldier was carved from a single 60-ton block of Westerly granite and transported to Antietam National Cemetery in Maryland. More orders were filled and more monuments transported. Gettysburg Battlefield was eventually able to claim over seventy percent of its granite memorials as hailing from Westerly, Rhode Island.

Hundreds of men were hired to help fill the orders that continuously rolled in. Immigrants were arriving for the sole purpose of obtaining work in the Westerly quarry. Artists and laborers from Ireland, Scotland, England and Italy hauled the granite, cut it, designed and sculpted it, then packed it onto railroad cars for delivery. By the late 1880's, the Smith Granite Company employed over 1,200 men who were earning up to $2.50 a day.

Orlando Smith did not live long enough to see the real height of his discovery. He passed away in 1859 and the granite company passed into the hands of his son Orlando Jr.

By 1955, the amount of granite left in Smith's quarry had considerably diminished. What was left was very deep and difficult to get to. Because of this, the price of it rose and consumers began to look elsewhere for the material they needed.

The quarries in Vermont had much more granite in them, closer to the surface and easier to remove. The financially savvy began taking their business to

Vermont as opposed to Rhode Island. The Smith Company employees were let go and the quarry closed that year. Yet all around the world stand pieces of the Orlando Smith story. Indestructible, unforgettable treasure, glistening in the sun.

WHEN THE MOON FELL
EDGAR ALLEN POE

I saw thee once, only once
Years ago
I must not say how many, but not many
It was a July midnight...

     Edgar Allen Poe was born in Boston, Massachusetts on January 19, 1809. He was not yet two years old when his mother died and he was sent to live with a foster family.

     Poe grew to have an interest in writing and eventually enrolled in the University of Virginia.

Upon graduation, Poe had plans to marry his childhood sweetheart, Elmira Royster. But when he returned from school, he discovered that Royster had gotten engaged to another man.

Poe eventually fell in love again and was married in May of 1836. The bride was his 13-year-old cousin Virginia. The couple moved to Fordham, New York and there Virginia died of tuberculosis at the age of 24.

The distraught Poe began to concentrate on a writing career and spent his time traveling in the circles of other writers. During a visit to Providence, he decided one evening to go for a quiet walk. As he passed the two-story gable-roofed house at #88 Benefit Street, he suddenly stopped. There, in the rose garden, illuminated by the moonlight, stood the poet Sarah Helen Power Whitman. Poe was captivated.

Little did the writer know that Sarah had read his work and was intrigued by him as well. Not long after he watched her dreamy figure walking about the rose garden, he received a Valentine's Day poem from her. He responded by penning a poem of his own called "To Helen."

For the next several months, Poe urged Sarah to marry him. She refused his proposals again and again until one evening when they were standing together in St. John's Cemetery behind her house. There, the highly educated Quakeress finally agreed to become his wife on one condition; that he give up his drinking habit.

Poe agreed to Sarah's demand and, the following autumn, he took a break in his travels to visit his fiancé and her family at their home in Rhode Island. For three days Sarah waited, but he never arrived. When he finally did show up, he was drunk. Sarah made him leave and the desperate man attempted suicide by ingesting opium.

With another engagement aborted, Poe once again invested all his energy in his writing career. Traveling to Richmond, Virginia, he attempted to raise money for a magazine he hoped to publish. In a strange twist of fate, he ran into his old sweetheart Elmira, now the widow of a Mr. Shelton.

The two rekindled their romance and Elmira again agreed to marry him. Determined to finally secure a happy future, Poe joined the Sons of Temperance and swore off intoxicants.

Less than two months later, Edgar Allen Poe was found lying on a Boston street. He was transported to a hospital where he drifted in and out of consciousness for four days. On October 7, 1849, he passed away at the age of 40. The probable cause of his death was alcoholism.

Following Poe's burial, an ornate stone was carved to mark his grave. *"Here at last, he is happy"*, it read. But before the marker could be transported to the cemetery, a train de-railed, hit the completed stone and smashed it to pieces.

Clad all in white
Upon a violent bank,
I saw thee half reclining
When the moon fell
On the upturned faces of the roses...

FALLEN STAR
EVELYN NESBIT

Evelyn Nesbit
Image courtesy of Wikipedia.org: public domain photo.

The first word that entered your mind when you looked at her was 'beautiful'. With flawless skin and wavy red hair that reached to her waist, teenage Evelyn Nesbit was the very definition of physical perfection.

The daughter of Winfield Scott Nesbit, Evelyn was born on Christmas day 1884 in Tarentum, Pennsylvania. While in her early teens, her father passed away, leaving Evelyn and her mother nearly destitute. The only thing they had to cash in on was the young girl's beauty.

At just fifteen years old, she became the "Gibson Girl" model, a symbol that epitomized what every young girl of that era wanted to be. Modeling lead to theater and by the next year, Evelyn was working as a showgirl upon the stages of New York.

The city was full of interesting characters, both on the stage and off. There were young women looking for rich men, and aged men seeking beautiful young girls.

Stanford White, the son of Richard Grant White, was 31 years old when Evelyn was born. By the year 1900, he and his wife Bessie were living in luxury, thanks in part to his massive success as an architect. Well-known for designing many Newport, Rhode Island mansions for the elite, Stanford also designed Madison Square Garden in New York City. There, he kept the tower apartment for himself, regularly hosting scandalous parties that made fodder for the gossip magazines. His wife seemed oblivious to rumors of Stanford carousing with young girls and jumping from one short affair to another.

One night, while watching a spirited song and dance number on Broadway, his eyes fell upon a redheaded performer. He asked a friend who she was. Evelyn Nesbit, he was told.

Stanford invited Evelyn to visit him for lunch at his tower apartment. Mrs. Nesbit saw nothing wrong with her 16-year-old daughter dining with the 47-year-old man. He was rich, talented, and successful. Apparently it did not matter that he was someone's husband.

Stanford White
Photo courtesy of Nationmaster.com: public domain photo.

After lunch, Stanford showed Evelyn around his luxurious hideaway. From the ceiling in one room hung a red velvet swing. Enticing his guest to change into a Japanese Kimono, Stanford then suggested she climb onto the swing. With her long hair flowing out behind her, Evelyn giggled like a school girl while she swung back and forth for her host's amusement. The two then shared a bottle of champagne.

Evelyn awoke the next morning in Stanford's apartment, no longer the innocent child who had arrived there the day before.

For several years, Stanford continued to be in awe of Evelyn. He paid for private schooling, and even rented an upscale apartment for her and her mother. But eventually the carousing side of Stanford over-powered his obsession with the chorus girl. He grew bored with the relationship and the two parted ways amicably.

While attending a New York party, Evelyn met Henry Kendall Thaw. The millionaire was heir to his father's Pennsylvania railroad fortune and was seeking a beautiful young woman to have on his arm. The showgirls, however, wanted nothing to do with Henry. He had a long-standing reputation of being viciously cruel and demonstrating an explosive temper. While a student at Harvard, he had been expelled for holding a taxi driver at gunpoint.

When Henry began exhibiting an interest in Evelyn, the other girls warned her to stay away from him. She did as they suggested but Henry would not take no for an answer. He had grown up in a 10-room mansion with cooks, housekeepers, servants, waiters and coachmen. He was used to getting what he wanted. He baited Evelyn with gifts which won the praise of her mother, and eventually Evelyn gave in. Soon after, she became his wife.

On the evening of their honeymoon, Henry was disgusted to learn that his bride was not as pure as he'd thought. He demanded to know every detail of her relationship with Stanford, the man who had ruined her.

On June 25, 1906, Henry and Evelyn walked into a musical review on the rooftop club of Madison Square Garden. At the front of the club sat Stanford White. Henry approached him, reached into his long black overcoat and pulled out a pistol. Holding it just inches from Stanford's head, he fired three shots.

Screams rang out over the music as the architect slumped onto the floor.

Henry then turned to leave the club, meeting up with his wife by the elevators. "My God, what have you done?!" Evelyn cried.

Henry was tried for murder and found not guilty by reason of temporary insanity. However, Evelyn quickly obtained a divorce.

In later years, she married her vaudeville partner Jack Clifford, but that union also ended in divorce. The innocent and beautiful young woman who once held the future in her hands died alone in a nursing home at the age of 82.

ALL THAT GLITTERS
THE ASTORS & THE VANDERBILTS

Old postcard of the Breakers in Newport.
Public domain photo

Take a step back in time. You are about to visit one of the most elegant houses in Newport. Known as "The Breakers", the mansion began to go up in 1893. Constructed for millionaire Cornelius Vanderbilt, it reached it's completion in 1897.

Cornelius Vanderbilt II
Image courtesy of Wikipedia.org: public domain photo.

Built on one full acre of land, the five-story structure contains 72 rooms, 33 of which are the servant's quarters. Like most of the summer homes in Newport, "The Breakers" was designed by Richard Morris Hunt.

As carriages approach the wrought iron front gate, which weighs seventy tons, resembles intricate black lace, and carried a price tag of $75,000, four footmen stand ready to allow entry.

All the rooms of the house are built around a two-story internal courtyard called the Great Hall. This 45-foot high open space is visible from the second and third floor interior balconies. The high ceiling is painted to look like a bright blue sky with billowy clouds floating across it.

Your hostess is the highly esteemed Alice Vanderbilt. The tiny five-foot tall Sunday school teacher has a reputation for wanting things to be perfect. The maids here could tell you stories about her slipping on a white glove every morning to run her delicate fingers across every nook and crevice of the house to be sure the dusting has been done. However, she is also known for being very cordial to guests and you are welcome to stroll through the two-story dining room where twelve red alabaster columns topped with bronze are set about the 2,400 feet of space. The ceiling depicts a painting of the goddess Aurora and deep red draperies flow over the windows.

Hunt modeled the mansion after the 16th century Italian palace of a Genoese merchant prince. Workmen from Italy were hired to complete the project. At a cost of seven million dollars, without furnishings, the structure includes stone from France and marble from Africa.

You can make your way into the library, which is paneled in walnut and wraps around a massive fireplace. The white marble mantel was purchased from a 16th century chateau in France.

The billiard room, paneled in Cippolino marble, is crowned with a ceiling mosaic of a Roman mother and child in a bath.

As you move past the grand staircase, the enormous fireplaces, mirrored walls and grandiose chandeliers, you make your way toward the ballroom, where the events regularly held there cost the Vanderbilts an average of $100,000 per party.

Party-goers are always the high society members and proper etiquette is essential.

At parties in Newport, the rule of thumb is to maintain a quiet demeanor. Loud talking or laughing will insure that you do not receive an invitation to the next event. It is also expected that you refrain from talking to members of the opposite sex whom your host has not formally introduced you to. And crossing the room without an escort will bring stares and disdain.

Guests at these lavish parties always receive gifts from the hostess. Women may be presented with ruby brooches while the men are likely to be handed quality cigars wrapped in one hundred dollar bills.

Cornelius Vanderbilt is a New York railroad magnate. The spectacled, gray-haired legend and his wife bred seven children, two of whom passed away prior to the turn of the century. All the children but one have a close relationship with their parents. Cornelius III has married Grace Wilson, eight years his senior, and the family does not approve of the match. Grace had been engaged to Alice and Cornelius's son William when he died of Typhoid Fever in 1892. She then latched onto their other son. Alice and Cornelius refuse to even see their new grandchild as he is a product of that "money-chasing" woman.

When Alice's husband dies suddenly in 1899, Cornelius III will not even be allowed to pay his last respects. Nor will he receive a fair share of the family fortune.

Once she becomes a widow, Alice will wear black for the rest of her life. And although the other society women will politely offer their sympathies, they will still try to outdo her parties, her dresses and her circle of friends. That is the way of life here in Newport. Yet there is one woman who seems to consistently hold the title of "Most Popular" and that is Mrs. Astor.

Caroline Astor and her husband William own the Newport mansion "Beechwood." Built in 1851 for New York merchant Daniel Parrish, and designed by architects Andrew Downing and Calvert Vaux, the mansion was sold to the Astors in 1881. They employed the talents of famed architect Richard Morris and invested two million dollars in renovations.

Caroline Astor
Image courtesy of Wikipedia.org: public domain photo.

The Astors spend only eight weeks out of the year at "Beechwood." Like most everyone else who has summer "cottages" in Newport, they spend the remaining months on Fifth Avenue in New York City.

William Backhouse Astor is the son of a German immigrant who made his riches by investing in real estate. Mrs. Astor has strong feelings concerning one's finances. "New money" is not quiet as respectable as "wealthy blood" and if she had her way, people would not be able to buy their place in society. Recently she helped writer Ward McAllister compile a list known as "The Newport 400". The names on the list are of those in Newport whose families have been rich for generations. If you're not on the list, don't expect to be invited anywhere by the high-brows.

As you walk along the two-mile footpath which runs past the house and is known as the Cliffwalk, you may ponder what Mr. Astor does for fun while his wife is hosting the most lavish get-togethers in all of Rhode Island. Many of the Newport men enjoy spending time at the Casino where tennis matches are regularly held.

Membership at the Casino costs several thousands of dollars, but that is spare change for the Astors when you consider that they regularly budget nearly $300,000 every year for entertainment purposes. And no one else had better even consider holding their own lavish events on a Monday. That is Caroline's day for parties and all of society knows it. No one would dare to upset the woman who insists on being called THE Mrs. Astor. But that does not stop the other women from trying to rise to her status, especially when it comes to Mrs. Astor's sister-in-law Alva.

Alva Erskine Vanderbilt and her husband William Kissam Vanderbilt, have just had their own Newport mansion constructed. Alva had gone to her husband literally crying about the necessity of the eleven million dollar Newport cottage because the Astors had one. She even demanded that it be built right next to door to the Astor's.

Richard Hunt was employed to design the structure and Alva stood right beside him throughout the four years of construction, approving or disapproving of every little detail. Finally "Marble House" was a reality.

Five hundred thousand tons of white marble had been shipped in from a quarry on the Hudson, to make up the mansion's façade. Four towering Corinthian columns, modeled after those at the Temple of the Sun at Heliopolis, stand guard at the front of the house.

As you pass through the Entrance Hall, you are immersed in a buttery yellow aura, due to the fact that several tons of Sienna marble imported from a quarry in Italy line the walls and the floors.

Marble House, Newport, RI circa 1911.
Public domain photo postcard.

Near the large bronze fountain filled with fresh flowers stands your hostess. She is short and stocky and although young in years, her waist-length brown hair is already tinged with gray. She leads you to the ballroom, the most impressive room of the house, where marble walls with gilded trim are literally crowded with detailed carvings of cherubs and mythological figures.

Lined with hundreds of sheets of gold leaf, the construction of this room alone cost two million dollars.

Modeled after a Louis XIV structure at Versailles, the mirrored surfaces and delicately molded wood provide a luxurious backdrop for the exquisite statues atop marble pedestals.

William Kissam Vanderbilt
Image courtesy of Wikipedia.org: public domain photo.

Alva got her ideas for the construction of her mansion during a visit to Greece. When she returned, she announced that what she wanted was a temple of white marble that outshone the Acropolis in brilliancy.

But what is a woman like Alva Vanderbilt to do when she just needs to *get away*? Well, sail out on her yacht, of course. The "Alva", which was built at a cost of $500,000 in 1886, contained mahogany-paneled staterooms, each with its own private bath.

The library, constructed of walnut, included a large fireplace and a variety of expensive oil paintings. The dining room, 32 feet wide, 18 feet long and 9 feet high was constructed of white enamel and its woodwork trimmed in gold. All the decks were covered with Oriental rugs and, in addition to the many people who kept the boat clean, the on-board staff included a surgeon and an ice machine engineer.

But the "Alva" ended up at the bottom of the sea. After colliding with another yacht, she sank and there was little that could be done except to go out and simply obtain another custom-built yacht. The sleek black Valiant weighs 2,400 tons and, at 312 feet long, is the largest private yacht ever built.

Alva's parties stretch the limits of excess. Meals consist of eighteen courses, with the last being served at 7 a.m. Oysters, cream of celery soup, poached salmon, French peas, lamb with mint sauce and cucumber salad may be topped off with raspberry éclairs or some other rich delicacy.

Alva's husband is second vice president of the Central New York Railroad. But let's take a step forward in time now because she is about to leave him for his best friend.

It is 1895 and Alva is now Mrs. Oliver Belmont. Just a few years ago, Oliver employed Richard Hunt to design "Belcourt Castle" for him. Built in the style of a Louis XIII hunting lodge, the mansion contains 52 rooms. The interior, which is completely medieval, includes a Gothic ballroom. With tall 13th century stained glass windows along its walls, and circular stained glass windows along the ceiling, the ballroom has the aura of a church. Two stuffed horses, mounted with dummies clad in suits of armor, stand in a corner of the room which can comfortably accommodate 500 guests.

Carriages actually drive right into the house, as the ground floor is merely a multitude of indoor stables. Each stable is individually tiled and upholstered, paneled and equipped with sterling silver harness fittings. Three times a day, English groomers change the horses' pure white linen towels.

A Grand Staircase leads to the living quarters, where the doors to each room contain solid gold hinges and knobs. As a wedding gift, Oliver gave Alva the deed to the mansion. It is here that she now holds her tea parties, soirees, balls and dinners. Her wealthy guests enjoy the best food money can buy. They coif and smile. They gossip about each other while following the strict rules of etiquette. They marry, they divorce, they marry again. And a wonderful musical ensemble is always there to provide the background music for the drama of the elite.

ASSASINATION MYSTERY
JOHN WILKES BOOTH

John Wilkes Booth
Image provided byPDimages.com: public domain photo.

As President Abraham Lincoln sat watching a performance of "Our American Cousin" at Ford Theatre in Washington, a horrendous piece of history was only moments away from being made.

It was April 14, 1865 and a Shakespearian actor named John Wilkes Booth was in the theatre that night. But he wasn't there to act out a tragedy. He was there to commit one.

Angry about Lincoln's stand on slavery, Booth jumped into the president's theatre box and shot him in the back of the head with a .50 caliber gun. As the leader of our country lay dying, Booth rushed to center stage and announced to the stunned crowd, "Thus always with tyrants." He then ran out of the theatre, climbed atop the horse waiting for him in a back alley and fled into the night.

The President's box in Ford's Theater where Lincoln was assassinated.
Image provided by PDImages. public domain photo.

For the next twelve days, Union troops searched for Booth. At 2:00 a.m. on April 26, the New York 16th Cavalry finally tracked him down at the Richard Garratt farm in Bowling Green, Virginia. Booth and one of his conspirators in the assassination plot, David Herold, were ordered to come out of the barn they were hiding in. Herold complied but Booth refused.

The soldiers warned that if he did not surrender, the barn would be burned down.
Moments later, after Sergeant Boston Corbett had set fire to the straw around the barn, Booth attempted to flee the blaze and was shot in the back of the head by Corbett.

Booth was carried to the porch of the farmhouse where he drifted in and out of consciousness until death came at 7:00 that morning.

Abraham Lincoln
Image provided by PDimages.com: public domain photo.

The Secretary of War ordered that he be buried beneath the floor of a cell at the Old Penitentiary in Washington. Two years later, the body was exhumed and buried in a storeroom at the prison. In 1869, the US government relinquished ownership of the body, exhuming Booth once again and turning his remains over to his family.

The body was interred in the Booth family plot in Green Mount Cemetery in Baltimore, Maryland, on June 22 of that year. But all was not laid to rest with the burial. There are many who believe that the man captured and killed that day was not John Wilkes Booth.

In May of 1995, twenty descendants of Booth, including one Hopkinton resident, appeared before a judge in Maryland, asking that the buried body be exhumed and examined by scientists. The group presented what they presumed to be compelling evidence supporting their belief in the misidentification of their ancestor.

One piece of evidence concerned a man named Fennis Bates who had purchased a mummy in 1903 to use in his traveling carnival show. The preserved body was that of a man called David E. George who committed suicide on January 13 of that year in Enid, Oklahoma. A book written by Bates claimed that before the man took his life, he confessed that he was, in actuality, the real John Wilkes Booth.

Faced with disbelieving scrutiny by the public, Bates had the mummy examined by medical experts in 1931. Results of the examination showed the body to have a fracture of the left leg. It was a noted fact that the president's assassin had fallen to the floor while making his escape and had visited a doctor later that evening to have a bone in his left leg set.

The mummy also showed a scar on its neck. John Wilkes Booth had once had a large fibroid tumor removed from the very same spot.

However, those who were against exhuming the body had compelling evidence of their own. Many who had witnessed the autopsy of the man shot while escaping from the barn, had left statements concerning the identification of the body, which included a scar on the neck, the initials "JWB" tattooed on the left hand, a broken left leg and two dental fillings.

Still, the descendants of Booth couldn't be swayed. They presented further evidence with statements made in 1922 by two soldiers who had been at the Garratt farm that fateful day. In affidavits, they had sworn that the body carried out of the barn and placed on the porch was not the actor, John Wilkes Booth, but a man in a Confederate soldier's uniform.

After weighing the evidence on both sides, Judge Joseph Kaplan ruled against exhuming the body. Kaplan explained that the evidence of the body being that of Booth far outweighed evidence that it wasn't. He also stated that, since several other graves in the 13-grave plot would be disturbed upon such an exhumation, it was critical that there be hardly any doubt before such a procedure could be allowed.

MURDER

BRAINWASHED TO KILL
AMOS BABCOCK

Mercy Babcock was born in 1750, the daughter of Jonathan and Lydia (Larkin) Babcock of Exeter. At the age of 22, she married Abner Loomer and probably expected to live out a happy life. But Mercy Babcock's life was anything except happy. It was, in fact, an existence shrouded in overwhelming pain and despair.

At the age of 41, Mercy was overcome with a serious fever. After being bed-ridden for several days, the illness began to subside. But the fever had affected her brain and she would never be the same. In Abner's eyes, this mentally incompetent woman was not the person he had promised the rest of his life to. Distraught, he decided to leave her.

As Mercy was unable to take care of herself, her brother Amos intervened. Amos had recently married Dorcas Bennett and the couple was living in Shediac Bridge, New Brunswick, Canada. Amos made plans to take his ill and abandoned sister into his home.

By 1804, Amos was taking care of not only his sister Mercy, but his wife and the nine children his marriage had brought him. Financial difficulties were arising and Amos sought some type of religious strength to help him through it. That so-called strength presented itself to him in the form of an Evangelist preacher named Jacob Peck. So powerful were the sermons of Peck that Amos's 12-year-old daughter Mary fell strongly under the preacher's spell.

Amos and Mary's belief in the words of Peck soon became an obsession, as Peck convinced Amos that Mary was an angel sent here to earth.

Mary then began to give sermons of her own to anyone who would listen, her preaching based on the teachings of the man who had pushed his way into the Babcock family's lives.

The apocalypse was coming, Mary warned. For this revelation had been given to her by Peck. The revelation had conditions, however. Peck assured Amos and Mary that the Bacbock family would apparently be saved from destruction only if the mentally ill Mercy was destroyed first.

Peck convinced the family that Mercy was not ill, she was possessed by the devil, and that if Amos had any hope of saving the rest of them from eternal damnation, he had to rid himself of the evil he had taken into his home.

On February 3, 1805, Amos entered his house, where his 55-year-old sister sat idly. With his bare hands, he killed her in front of his wife and children. He was quickly arrested, brought to trial for murder and found guilty. Four months later, he was hanged behind Dorchester Jail and then buried beneath the gallows there.

Peck remained free to live out his life, never being held accountable for ordering the murder of a mentally ill woman.

A NEIGHBORLY SHOOTING
HENRY ANDREWS

A flock of sheep being pelted with rocks led to murder.
Photo from the collection of United States Department of Agriculture.
Image provided courtesy of Wikipedia.org: public domain photo.

During the 18ᵗʰ century, Charles and Mary Andrews were living out a peaceful life in East Greenwich. Eventually they had children, and their children had children. Luckily they didn't know what fate had planned for their family history.

Henry Andrews, the grandson of Charles and Mary, was born in Vermont in 1812. After marrying, he and his wife Harriet settled in Sheldon, New York and started up a large farm where they would bring up seven children. Across the street was the farm of Royal P. Case and the two men did not exactly become friends.

In the morning hours of June 10, 1866, Case ventured out to his cornfields to check on their well-being. It was common for him to find Andrews' chickens tearing up his corn and the two had argued over the situation many times.

As Case walked about his fields, Andrews was walking around his own property. Suddenly the men became aware of each other's presence and the curses and threats began to fly as usual.

Finally Case gave up the argument and returned to his house, as it was time to feed the sheep. He summoned his young farmhand to help lead the flock down the road where they could graze. Case stuffed a pistol into his jacket before leaving the house, vowing that if any of Andrews' chickens were into his corn, he would make sure it was their last meal.

Seeing Case and his farmhand headed down the road, Andrews fetched his sons, 22-year-old William and 13-year-old Frank, and the three of them snuck through their orchard in the same direction Case was going. Once they arrived in close proximity to where the sheep were grazing, Andrews and his boys began throwing rocks at the animals. Startled, the sheep dispersed in all directions.

An enraged Case began yelling and Andrews yelled back, finally jumping over the fence that separated them and tackling Case to the ground. Case struggled but could not break free of the hold until Andrews relented and allowed him to get up.

Stumbling backwards a few steps, Case pulled his pistol from his pocket and aimed it at Andrews. He warned his neighbor not to ever come near him again. Taking this as a challenge, Andrews charged at Case once more. As the two men fell to the ground, the pistol went off, sending its ammunition into the neck of Andrews.

Case went to the authorities and swore the shooting had been an accident. Andrews received quick medical attention and it was expected that he would recover, but he died of his injuries a few weeks later.

Case was then arrested, charged with manslaughter and sentenced to two years in jail. All was finally quiet between the two farmers.

SHOT BY WIFE
DENISON HEALY

The quiet town of Hope Valley was shaken by news of murder.
Photo courtesy of Gladys Segar Collection at Langworthy Public Library.

June 29, 1885 started out as a beautiful day in Hope Valley. But things were about to change.

Ruth Elizabeth (Wright) and Densison Healy, a married couple well-known throughout town, lived in a farmhouse which stood a short distance behind St. Joseph's Church. Denison was seventy years old and married for the second time. His first wife, Mary M. (Gardiner) had died on May 10, 1872 from consumption, at the age of 56. His new wife was a mere twenty-eight years old.

At 9:30 on that warm June morning, William Woodmansee from nearby Richmond stopped to visit the couple. The three of them talked and laughed until Woodmansee left to go to work.

At 11:30, the Healy's had another visitor, Silas Tefft, who lived next door. Taking to the sitting room, the

Healy's conversed happily with Tefft until he bid them good-bye and headed to his own job.

An hour later, Tefft returned, in need of purchasing some of the cabbage plants that Dension had for sale. He loaded the plants into his carriage and mentioned that he was now on his way down to the gravel bank to get a load of gravel. Saying their goodbyes again, the company was parted.

When Tefft had finished his business at the gravel bank, he was preparing to leave the site when his friend Gideon Cyrus pulled up alongside him. "Healy's shot himself," Cyrus announced.

Tefft immediately returned to the Healy house with Cyrus. Lying face down on the kitchen floor was Denison Healy. His head was beneath an iron sink that was propped up on two poles. His left arm was under the weight of his body, and his back displayed a gaping gunshot wound, encircled by the burned edges of his shirt.

A lounge chair near Denison's body was spattered with blood, as was the kitchen door and a washboard beside the sink. The sink itself was filled with blood-tinted water.

On the floor in front of the lounge chair, Denison's hat lay. And propped up against a pole was a buckshot gun, spotted with blood.

Both in shock, Tefft and Cyrus stared down at their lifeless friend.

"Do you think he is dead?" Ruth asked. When they assured her he was, she quickly turned and began to leave the house, explaining that she needed to go look for someone. Minutes later, she returned with Tefft's mother, Desire. "My husband has shot himself," Ruth explained to the other woman.

By 2:30 that afternoon, news of the tragedy had spread through town and several people had gathered at the Healy House. David Kenyon of Richmond and

Cyrus's wife Edna were among those who tried to comfort the emotionally distraught Mrs. Healy in the sitting room.

At 3:00, Ashaway medical examiner Alexander Briggs arrived to examine the body. He was soon joined by Dr. E.P. Clarke of Hope Valley. The two men discovered that, in addition to the gunshot wound, Denison had several broken ribs. They also noticed that beside his body lay broken pieces of china and a large rock.

F.B. Bennett of Hope Valley arrived at the Healy house at 4:00. "How did this happen?" he asked.

"Well, we have been having trouble with hawks preying on our chickens," Ruth explained. "He took the gun down and was going to go outside and shoot at the hawks. He picked up the gun and held it like this..." Ruth picked up the blood-stained gun and held it behind her back to demonstrate how her husband had allegedly been standing. "I went into the other room," she continued, "and I sat down at my sewing machine. The machine was running so I didn't hear the shot. But when I stopped the machine, I heard him groan."

Ruth said she then ran onto the kitchen where her husband was reeling about, moaning, "I think I have shot myself." She said she helped him over to the lounge where he could lay down and then she ran for help.

Bennett asked if Denison had been drinking. "No," Ruth answered. "He has not had a drink for three years."

Although Ruth gave detailed explanations to those present at the house that day, many of them did not believe her story. One even pointed out things that looked suspicious, asking, "How did the gun get propped up against the pole?" Ruth replied that she had picked it up and put it there. "I didn't think I was doing anything wrong by that," she said.

A couple of the men picked up the gun and found it to be in somewhat faulty condition. Half-cocked, the trigger would catch, and the only way it would fire was if the trigger was pulled again and again until it was unstuck. Though no one said anything that day, the alleged suicide appeared to be more like a homicide. And the victim's wife appeared to be the likeliest suspect.

After an official investigation, Ruth Healy was arrested and brought to jail. She could not afford to pay the $2,000 bail so was imprisoned in Richmond while awaiting the trial, which began on October 9th in Kingston.

Ruth pled not guilty and several people testified in her defense. William F. Joslin, a Hopkinton store-owner, told the court that he saw the Healys often and that he never once witnessed any sign of discord between them.

Benjamin Barber, a boarder at the Healy house, said that Mr. and Mrs. Healy were always very loving toward each other in his presence. He testified that he regularly saw them out in their yard together and they were always laughing and conversing. Barber added that he had often gone shooting with Denison and that Dension usually brought along faulty guns that he was not very careful with. And he claimed that Denison had indeed been very concerned lately about hawks going after his chickens. "He would stand at the kitchen window with his gun waiting for them," he told the jury.

Other witnesses, however, had a different story to tell about the nature of the relationship between the Healys, and it was not one of love and laughter.

Thirty-two-year-old cotton mill worker Joseph Cherry, of Arcadia, told the court that he had been passing the Healy house at about 2:00 on the day of the shooting. He said he saw Mr. Healy angrily throwing dishes through an open kitchen window. "I stopped and asked him if everything was alright," Cherry testified. "He said that his wife was inside drunk and that she'd locked him out." At that moment, Cherry went on, Mrs. Healy appeared at the kitchen window and told Denison she would let him back in the house on the condition that Cherry come with him. "She seemed scared of him," Cherry explained to the jury. "And I told her that I believed she had no reason to be scared. She said that he had threatened her life. Mr. Healy then called her a drunk."

Only a few people actually heard the gun go off that day. Addie Reynolds of Hopkinton was walking past the house with the Larkin sisters and their dog when they all heard a loud noise come from the structure. Reynolds explained what she witnessed prior to hearing the shot. "I saw Mr. Healy throwing things at the house and I heard him swearing," she testified. One of the Larkin girls took the stand to tell how she saw Mr. Healy "crawl through the basement window." She said that a few moments later, she "heard a sound as if something fell."

Ruth Healy was not put on the stand to defend herself. Her attorney felt that she had not been treated respectfully thus far and he did not want to submit her to further attack. Instead, she sat silently in the courtroom, occasionally fidgeting with her red fan. She was described by court reporters as being "unmoved by the presentation of evidence" and as "a neatly attired woman whose face does not indicate intelligence or refinement. It indicates a woman with a coarse nature and uncommon nerve."

On October 22nd, the jury retreated into the back room of the courthouse at 2:45. One hour later, they returned with a guilty verdict. When Mrs. Healy was asked if she had anything to say, she replied, "Nothing. Only that I am innocent."

Ruth Healy was sentenced to twelve years imprisonment for the crime of manslaughter.

Shortly after being released from prison, Ruth married again. This time her husband was John Browning of South Kingstown, 27 years her senior. But by 1922, Ruth was under the care of the town asylum in South Kingstown. On March 2, 1923, she died at the RI State Asylum in Cranston. There, the 66-year-old woman was buried in a pauper's grave, marked only by a numbered concrete block.

HANGED BY THE NECK
THOMAS CARTER

1908 postcard of the Pettaquamscutt River.
Public domain image

When we think of gallows and nooses, and townspeople gathering to watch evil-doers pay for their crimes, we may not picture our local counties as a backdrop for the scene. But there was a time when even our little hamlets played hangman.

The first execution in Washington County happened on May 10, 1751, the culmination of a murder trial that was the talk of the town for many years. It was also the culmination of the life of Thomas Carter.

Carter was a privateer from Newport, assigned to a ship that suddenly floundered along the Long Island coast, leaving him stranded and miles from home. With nothing but the clothes on his back, Carter set out on foot back home to Newport. Along the way, he must have passed many people. But for one William Jackson, that intertwining of paths on New Years Day 1751 would prove fatal.

Jackson was a leather salesman, selling tanned deer hides on horseback to merchants who would construct over-alls and mittens out of his material. A resident of Virginia, Jackson made his New England sales rounds every year, passing through Washington County on his way to Newport.

Upon noticing that Jackson had a horse, worthy goods and over 400 pounds of silver, the down-on-his-luck Carter quickly devised a plan. He explained to Jackson that he was on his way home, was terribly sick and desperately needed assistance.

Jackson took pity on the man and climbed down off his horse, insisting that Carter ride comfortably while he walked alongside. Several hours later, the men began to get hungry and decided to stop at Nash's Inn on Old Post Road in Wakefield for food. Jackson paid for both their meals and asked Mrs. Nash to replace a missing button on his vest before they left.

Continuing on their way, Jackson and Carter walked about ten more miles before they reached Tower Hill. By that time, it was nearing midnight and Carter decided to get off the horse and let Jackson ride. Moments later, Carter picked up a large rock and threw it at Jackson, striking him in the head and knocking him to the ground. Still alive and conscious, Jackson pulled himself to his feet and ran to a nearby vacant building. Carter followed, caught up with him and stabbed him with a dagger.

Dragging the body behind him, Carter hurried to Pettaquamscutt Cove, one mile away, and threw Jackson into the water. Now in possession of both material goods and money, he jumped on the horse and rode off into the night.

Several days later, a local man fishing for eel at the cove pulled up more than he was expecting. The body of Jackson lay there before him.

Mrs. Nash came forward to give the identification of the body. She recognized the button she had sewn onto his vest. She also identified Carter as having been with the deceased at her inn.

Thomas Carter was taken into custody, brought to trial and found guilty of murder. His sentence was handed down on April 6, 1751. He was sentenced to be hanged by the neck until dead on May 10, between the hours of 11 a.m. and 2 p.m. From inside a small jail cell, he awaited his execution.

The hanging took place at a tree at the foot of Tower Hill, near the Pettaquamscutt River. The rope was then removed and his body was suspended in chains from a nearby gallows. According to legend, the body hung there, swinging back and forth in the wind, for years, until the gallows began to disintegrate and was dismantled.

AND THE JUDGE SPOKE TO MOSES
THE GRINNELL FAMILY

A dispute over the rightful ownership of chicken coops led to the murder of Charles Thomas.
Photographer: Kelly Sullivan Pezza

Benjamin Grinnell and his friend Charles Thomas spent the afternoon of November 9, 1880 taking the coops out of the henhouse at the Grinnell farm in Tiverton.

Family strains had caused 37-year-old Benjamin to seek legal advice and he had been told that it was probably in his best interest to move away from the farm and find a new residence. Since his mother Hannah's death, in 1861, virtually everything was under the control of Benjamin's father Moses. Hannah had left her husband a life estate and he allowed Benjamin to live there rent-free. But the two men did not see eye to eye.

As Benjamin had paid for the building material and constructed the coops, he decided he had every right to take them with him. So with Charles's help,

347

they dismantled the contents of the henhouse. This plan didn't set well with Moses.

Just two days prior, Benjamin and his 31-year-old wife Ellen had been arrested for assaulting the elderly Moses, and now Benjamin had returned to the property. To aggravate the situation even more, he had brought Charles with him, the one man Moses had absolutely forbidden to set foot on his land.

Charles had spent sixteen years of a twenty-year sentence in a Taunton Jail for highway robbery. As far as Moses was concerned, he was now committing another act of robbery by helping Benjamin take the coops away.

Upon seeing what the two men were up to, 68-year-old Moses grabbed his gun and went out to the henhouse. Stopping just fifteen feet from the door, he aimed his gun. Charles was bent over and oblivious to the landowner watching him, but Benjamin saw his father standing there and yelled, "Don't shoot, Father, don't shoot!"

No sooner were the words out of Benjamin's mouth when he saw his friend crumble into a heap on the floor, blood gushing from his body where the bullet had passed through his lung. Attempting to get out of harm's way, Benjamin ran out of the henhouse and quickly headed toward the road. His father was hot on his heels, chasing him about thirty-five yards as he threatened to shoot him as well.

Eventually, the Grinnell family would be facing each other in court. Moses, who had been locked up for eighteen months as he awaited trial, was represented by attorney Nicholas Hathaway.

Benjamin's 11-year-old son Edward testified that he had witnessed the entire event that fatal afternoon. He claimed that he had been standing out near the henhouse when he saw his grandfather come out of the farmhouse with a gun, approach the henhouse, point his gun inside and shoot.

A neighbor, Ann Maria Lake, testified that she had overheard the scuffle and Moses telling one of the men, "I am going to shoot you and I am going to kill you!"

Moses's 21-year-old grandson John Wilcox, son of his daughter Elizabeth, also testified against him, stating that he had gone to the farm that day with Benjamin and Charles and that his grandfather had come out and told him to go away. He said he hadn't gone far when he heard his uncle tell Moses not to shoot.

Yet the story Moses gave to the court was entirely one of self-defense. According to him, he had ordered Charles off his property that day and Charles refused and came after him with a club. He said that since he had been in the yard shooting hawks when he noticed the men were taking the coops, he just happened to have his gun in his hand. Shooting the recently released felon was all he could do to thwart the attack, he said.

It was Moses belief that his children and grandchildren had put together a plan to get the farm away from him. Police records backed up his claims that he had been assaulted by his children on numerous occasions.

Moses' brother Nathan testified on his behalf, telling the court that Moses, who suffered from painful Rheumatism, had long been afraid of his children. He said that, the night before the murder, he had given Moses the gun to defend himself in the event his life was threatened.

The defendant's testimony was loud and straight-forward as he sternly maintained his plea of not guilty. But the story, with its two entirely different sides, was hard to weigh.

Old postcard of the front entrance to the Rhode Island State Prison. Public domain photo

Finally Moses daughter Christina took the stand and laid the straw that broke the camel's back. She testified that she had gone to her father's house right after the shooting and that he had greeted her with the warning, "Get off this property or I will shoot you too!"

Moses Grinnell was found guilty of murder and sentenced to life in prison. His family got the farm, yet not everyone concerned was happy. Christina was left to mourn the loss of her fiancé. For she and the former train robber Charles were to have been married in the coming weeks.

Moses spent the remainder of his life in the Rhode Island State Prison. He died there at the age of 95.

LACK OF EVIDENCE
FRANK LARKIN

When William Larkin of Hopkinton was lying on his deathbed in 1882, he surely never imagined that in just two years his well-respected grandson Frank would be sitting in a jail cell. The charge hanging over his head: murder.

It was about half past midnight on February 20, 1884 when James Pendleton of New London, Connecticut was awakened by the ferocious barking of his dogs. Climbing out of bed, he peered through the window to witness someone throwing an object toward the dogs in an apparent effort to silence them. Who the person was and why they were outside sneaking around wouldn't be a real concern until morning. Shortly after sunrise, his neighbor, 74-year-old farmer Harvey Chappel, was found murdered.

After authorities questioned residents, it was discovered that a known criminal had recently been in the vicinity. Thirty-five-year-old Oliver Kingsley was a petty thief who had spent more time in jail than out. When not incarcerated, he boarded with anyone who was kind enough to take him in. Several people had seen him in the area of Chappel's house on the night before the murder. A few others had seen him looming about the location at approximately 6:30 p.m. on the night of the murder.

But those who came forward with this information didn't believe it was going to help solve the crime. No one really thought that Kingsley was the kind of person who could murder someone. His conscious didn't prevent him from stealing, but taking a life was a different story.

Kingsley was living with the Wilcox family, about two miles from Chappel's house when the murdered occurred. The family told police that he had been absent from their house for most of that evening and didn't return until late.

Kingsley was placed in jail but even the sheriff had doubts about his guilt and continued to seek out other suspects. Another man, not from the area, had been seen loitering around New London right before the murder. His name was Frank Larkin and he lived in Narragansett. Three years before, Larkin had worked as a hired hand on Chappel's farm so locals knew his identity.

When visited by police, Larkin claimed to know nothing about the elderly man even being dead. But then he admitted that he *had* heard the news. When asked if it was true that he had been in the vicinity of Chappel's house recently, he said no. Then, again, he relented and admitted that he had been in that area in the days preceding the murder. The sheriff placed Larkin in custody and transported him to the jailhouse.

Larkin's story, after that point, didn't waver. He claimed to have left Rhode Island for Connecticut on the night of February 15th. When he reached New London later that evening, he stayed at the home of a relative, harness-maker James H. Stedman.

He said that he stayed with Stedman until the night of the 17th when he went on to stay with 41-year-old James Pendleton, who lived right across the street from Henry Chappel. The following day, he went on to his planned destination, the New London home of his uncle Welcome H. Larkin.

Larkin told police he left for home early on the morning of the 20th because an auction was taking place in Green Hill and his uncle had asked him to attend and bid on a piece of farm equipment for him.

Due to a lack of evidence positively linking Larkin to the crime, he was released. For the same reason, Oliver Kingsley was also released. History doesn't tell us who the murderer of Henry Chappel was.

Was it Larkin? Was it Kingsley? Or was it another who was never even suspected? Time will never tell.

HOMICIDE IN CRANSTON
AMASA SPRAGUE

Amasa Sprague
Photo used courtesy of the Cranston Historical Society.

Nearly half a foot of snow covered the ground on New Year's Day 1843. But the large house at 1353 Cranston Avenue was warm and comforting, and inside Amasa Sprague enjoyed a hearty dinner with his wife Fanny and their four young children.

The only worry on Amasa's mind that afternoon was the welfare of his livestock at the family farm about a mile away. Because the cows had no shelter, he was concerned about the frigidity of the weather. After dinner, he decided that he would walk down to the farm and check on the well being of his animals. He bundled up and set out at half past three that afternoon.

The Sprague family was highly respected and influential in Rhode Island. Amasa's grandfather had begun a small dye factory, which his father William expanded into one of the largest corporations in New England. In 1790, William built the ornate house which Amasa would one day raise his own children in, and thoroughly enjoyed the wealth that all his hard work had brought.

SPRAGUE MANSION

The house of Amasa Sprague in Cranston.
Photo courtesy of the Cranston Historical Society.

In 1836 however, while eating dinner with his wife, a fish bone became lodged in William's throat requiring surgery to remove it. It was an ordeal he would not survive.

Amasa and his brother, William Jr., inherited the house as well as the Sprague textile and dye factories and that year they formed the "A & W Sprague Company," a complex of print works, spinning mills, stores and tenement houses.

William, not as interested as his brother in the politics of business, was more content to be involved in the politics of government. So while Amasa ran the factories, William served as a Rhode Island congressman. Once again, it mistakenly appeared that life would be wonderful for the Sprague family.

At 4 p.m. on New Year's Day 1843, Michael Costello, a servant of the Sprague household, was returning to his own home after work. Trudging through the snow, he left Amasa's yard and headed toward the footbridge, which led over Pochasset Brook. But halfway across the bridge, Costello stopped and looked down at the snow, which was heavily spotted with a deep red color. He followed the trail of blood to the end of the bridge where another shocking sight met his eyes. Lying face down, sprawled out on the ground, was the body of a man.

Costello ran to the nearest house for help, returning to the spot with a group of men. Upon turning the body over, it was discovered that the victim had been beaten unrecognizable. A blunt instrument had in fact been swung against both the right and left sides of his head with a force that ruptured his brain. There was also a gunshot wound near one of his wrists that had broken the bone of his forearm.

Dr. Israel Bowen was summoned to examine the body. During his examination, it was discovered that the dead man was Amasa Sprague.

Rumors began to fly around Rhode Island. Because sixty dollars in cash and an expensive gold watch had been found on Amasa's body, it was obvious the attack was not a robbery. There were unfounded rumors of politics, adultery or business issues being the motivating factor in the crime. But the truth was that no one knew for sure why Amasa was murdered, or who took his life.

The elaborate grave of Amasa Sprague at Swan Point Cemetery in Providence.
Photographer: Kelly Sullivan Pezza

Nicholas Gordon, an Irish immigrant, arrived in Rhode Island in 1836. He established a small store, which sold groceries and other desired goods such as liquor. By 1843, business had become so profitable for Nicholas that he was able to send passage money for his brothers William, Robert and John, and their mother Ellen to sail from Ireland and join him in America. But the summer of that year, things took a downward turn.

Amasa Sprague, upset that his employees were arriving at work intoxicated after visiting Nicholas's store, convinced the Town Council to deny him a renewed license to sell liquor. As it was the liquor sales that brought in most of the money for Nicholas, he was enraged and confronted Amasa. An argument ensued which was overheard by many townspeople. Nicholas threatened to get even with the man who had interfered with his business.

On the morning of December 31, 1843, William Gordon was at work in the mill where he was employed when his brother Nicholas visited him to ask if he would like to have New Year's Eve dinner with the family. William accepted the offer but his supervisor informed him that he could not leave work until dusk. William assured his brother he would join the family later and Nicholas departed for home.

Later that day, on his way to his brother's house, William passed a group of men gathered at the end of the footbridge. He inquired as to the occasion and was informed that a crime had occurred and that two of his brothers had just been arrested in connection with it.

William began to cry as he made his way toward Nicholas's house where his mother was also in tears. Suddenly, William remembered that Nicholas owned a gun. In Ireland it was a crime to be in possession of a firearm. Certainly, he thought, if the brothers were under suspicion for a crime, the police would search the house and find the gun, which William assumed the possession of to be a crime in itself.

William took the gun from his brother's shop room and pulled up the carpet in an upstairs bedroom, removing a floorboard and concealing the weapon beneath it.

A $1,000 reward was put up by the Town Council for information leading to the arrest and conviction of the murderer. William Sprague appointed himself overseer of all aspects of the murder investigation.

A blue coat, found by police in a swamp near the footbridge became one of the first pieces of recovered evidence. Bloodstained, the coat also had a gunshot hole in the elbow. Another item found in the swamp was a gun, battered and broken in two pieces.

William Gordon decided he had best put his brothers' minds at ease by informing them he had hidden Nicholas's gun. But on his way to the jailhouse, he was interceded by the sheriff. Not only was he arrested and committed to a cell of his own, but his sickly mother and her youngest son Robert were also taken into police custody.

Mrs. Gordon and Robert were released later that day after authorities searched their house where they found a blood-spotted shirt and wet boots beneath one of the beds. All fingers were now pointing at the three oldest Gordon brothers as the murderers of Amasa Sprague.

On April 8, 1844 Nicholas, William and John Gordon began their trials for murder and conspiracy. The first to be brought into court was William, who was quickly acquitted, never mentioning the weapon he had concealed in the floor of his brother's house. John, the next to be tried had been told about the hidden gun. Both he and William decided it best to keep the weapon a secret, as it was still possible that the brothers would be found not guilty and should the jury learn of a hidden weapon, it may look bad for their defense.

However, John was not happy that his brother had hidden the gun in the first place. "It is you that will hang me," he whispered to William in the courtroom.

The prosecution worked to prove that the gun found in the swamp was the same gun purchased by Nicholas from Tillinghast Almy's store just a few months before the murder. The main objective of the prosecution was to show that Nicholas had planned the murder and John had committed it. Several witnesses were called in to support that theory. Many of them were friends of the Spragues who recalled hearing Nicholas threaten to get even with Amasa. But others were prostitutes and alcoholics who could not even correctly identify the accused men.

Ellen Gordon, who was very sick and feeble at the time of her testimony, did more to harm her sons' defense than help it. With a failing memory and overwrought with depression, she often contradicted herself in her statements.

On February 14, 1845 John Gordon was sentenced to death by hanging for the murder of Amasa Sprague.

At 10 a.m. on the scheduled day of the execution, William and Nicholas were allowed to visit their brother in his cell for the last time. Before the sheriff and Catholic priest arrived to walk John out to the scaffold, John urged Nicholas to be brave during his own trial.

Sixty people attended the execution, which was held in the yard of the Providence County Jail. Another one thousand stood atop the hill beside the prison, straining to see over the high walls.

The priest officiated the event with rites of execution, as the crowd awaited a confession from John that would save his soul. But a confession to murdering Amasa Sprague never came from John Gordon's lips. "I hope all good Christians will pray for me," were his last words. He was 29 years old.

The trial of Nicholas then began. In his testimony, he fully admitted to owning a gun, which he purchased at Almy's. However, he swore it was not the gun that had been recovered from the swamp, the alleged murder weapon. He implored authorities to search his house, explaining to them that they would find the gun in his shop room. Police searched the house but found no gun. Neither they nor Nicholas knew it was secretly concealed beneath a bedroom floor.

This was a point for the prosecution, but the defense began to score some points of its own. Several witnesses testified to seeing a man with a gun in the area of the murder who did not resemble any of the Gordon brothers. Still others began to change their stories, admitting that things they had been certain about during their testimonies in John's trial, they weren't so certain about now. Maybe the gun in the swamp wasn't Nicholas's as had been previously sworn to. Maybe the "blood" found on the clothing in the Gordon house wasn't really blood at all, but dye from the mills Maybe the footprints at the murder scene didn't match exactly to the boots found at the Gordon house. All statements and evidence now had to be re-examined.

Even more shocking for the community was the discovery that some of the prosecution's witnesses may have been paid off by William Sprague. Others may have simply been out for the reward money. It was learned that the prosecution had ignored vital pieces of evidence that pointed the finger away from the Gordon brothers, and in the direction of William Sprague.

But what was the jury to do? John had already been found guilty and hanged. If the brothers were now decidedly innocent and Nicholas was freed, a severe miscarriage of justice had taken a man's life. At 10:30 a.m. on April 17, 1845, the jurors informed the court that they were unable to come up with a verdict. Nine out of twelve jurors were now having serious doubts about the Gordon brothers' involvement. Finally after 15 months of incarceration, Nicholas was released on $10,000 bail.

Upon the release of his brother, William Gordon sent an affidavit to the courts, informing them of the gun he had concealed in the house. Police searched the dwelling and found the weapon right where he said it would be.

William Sprague took over the family businesses. For years he had argued with Amasa about expanding the business but never won the argument. Now it was his alone to control.

William Gordon died of Typhoid Fever on October 19, 1856. Nicholas Gordon died just 18 months after his release from jail.

As for John, his execution played a major part in the abolishment of the death penalty in Rhode Island. His execution was the last before a vote was taken on February 11, 1852 to stop capital punishment. Roger Potter, the man who had hanged John spoke out in favor of the abolishment, stating that he had never recovered from the experience of ending John Gordon's young life.

Over 1,400 people took part in the procession at John's funeral. Others lined the streets, some cheering and other's protesting the punishment that had taken place. His coffin passed Amasa Sprague's house and the courthouse where he had been convicted, his final journey ending at the North Burial Ground in Providence.

Was the murder of Amasa ever truly solved? Some believe it was his own brother, propelled by jealousy or greed, who brought about Amasa's brutal death. Others believe the murderer may have been a disgruntled employee or a political opponent. Still others believe justice was fairly served to John Gordon.

Was John Gordon a cold-blooded killer? Or was he merely a pawn in a deadly game? A Catholic, Irish immigrant who would make the perfect suspect in a time when Catholic, Irish immigrants were not readily accepted by the majority. A man whose reputation was already marred by the fact that he sold alcohol, or that he had the nerve to argue with the highly respected Amasa Sprague. A man who would make the perfect scapegoat in a conspiracy plan.

The murderer of Amasa Sprague may well be interred at the North Burial Ground. Or perhaps he lies somewhere else, never having claimed the notoriety nor the punishment for killling one of the most wealthy men in Rhode Island.

LETTERS

A LOCAL LOVE STORY
TELL ME WHEN YOU GET ANOTHER GIRL

Found in the attic of a house in Charlestown, a box of nearly one hundred old letters tell a nineteenth century love story:

September 1882

"Well, Herbert, the young people around here are all getting married. I'd smile if you were married before they were. I don't know whether I shall live to be an old maid or not. Do not let that string get out of your pocket for fear of losing it. Isn't any one heart to carry around for five years quite a burden, or did you keep it in a box?"

Enclosed in the tattered envelope which held this letter was a piece of bright pink string and a scrap of paper which read, *"I will send you this to give to some other girl in a year or two."*

Apparently that other girl never came along.

December 1882

"Herbert, I had never believed you would leave me to go with another girl. I always knew you loved me and, before you commenced going with me, I knew you may be provoked with me at something or other. Herbert, no one has seen any of your letters but me. I have been knitting this evening and your picture was watching me. I carried it down for Grandma to see and then I turned it around to watch me."

While 23-year-old Herbert lived in Shannock, his beloved lived in Kingston, quite a vast distance at the time. The two constantly tried to make arrangements through letters to see each other.

January 1883

"I dreamed of seeing you last night, right before I dreamed of being with you."

By Valentine's Day of that year, it appeared that distance was not the only thing coming between them. Even in the 1800's rumors flew and hearts got broken.

February 1883

"Ed told me that you went home with Ida from singing school. Why is it, Herbert, that people can not let you and I alone? Well, Ed was not positive whether that was her name or not. You say you have been thinking of me for the past few days more than common. I should think you would be thinking of Ida. I know, if it is so, you will tell me because you will not want two girls. And you said you will tell me when you get another girl."

There were no letters from Herbert included in the box so it is not known what his responses to these allegations were. But there was indeed another girl pining after him, and her letters *were* in the box.

"Herbert, I should like to see you but it would not be best for you to come over my house now that Jo is here. For he would soon spread the news and in less than twenty-four hours it would be all over the town. But I will have nothing to do with anyone else. If I only behave as I had ought. I do not blame you for not wanting to go with me right now. From the one who loves you."

Another letter from the heartsick "other girl", who resided in Alton, makes it apparent that she was an ex-flame of Herbert's who was still carrying a torch for him.

"Herbert, I received your letter. I would not have answered it, for you did not seem to care for me. I should have stopped and talked to you but you did not seem to care for my company. S.G. is, nights, down his grandmother's so he is often in. And it is true that he

was in the night before I came, but he did not stay until ten o'clock nor did I sit on his lap. You say that you never will go with a girl who, when you are not around, goes with someone else. Can you think of one time that, when you went with me, I went with someone else? You can do just what you please. I want the privilege to love you just the same. I never loved but one."

Although the Alton girl seemed to realize, over time, that Herbert's affections lay elsewhere, she didn't give him up easily.

"Herbert, I now write to know what you mean by writing to me in this shape. Is it because you have got someone else? I have been true to you through all. Why should you leave me? If you should think more of someone else, it's best for you to say so. I thought that if you had another girl, I would have all the fellows that I could get, and I have got a pretty good lot of them. But I care for none of them. There is only one that I ever think of."

But apparently Herbert was not the only one with a secret admirer. His sweetheart had one of her own. A letter addressed to her was coated with sweet sincerity.

"You must not let anyone see this letter. But I must say some things that I believe and they are these things: I can say that my love is yours and I hope you will accept of the letter from me. Your affectionate friend, Levi."

Apparently Levi's affection was not returned. Nor was the interest that the Alton girl still had for Herbert. And the letters from Kingston continued to come.

"Herbert, I carried that picture of yours to church tonight and put it in my pocket. Just now I pulled it out."

Carefully folded into most of her letters were pressed flowers, four-leaf-clovers and pieces of pink string. All in their envelopes, neatly stacked in the box, carefully packed away.....sometime after Herbert married her in 1884.

A WHALING VOYAGE
THE ATLANTIC WILL CARRY OUR LETTERS

Casks of whale oil unloaded from whalers at a Rhode Island dock. Originally published in the 1902 book State of Rhode Island and Providence Plantations: A History.

The smallest item in a large box full of old documents and photos was a brown envelope about two inches long and three inches wide. Discovered at a flea market, the envelope was addressed to Squire Carr of Adamsville, RI. A pink stamp costing one shilling and a green stamp costing sixpence were affixed to the envelope which was postmarked "Seychelles", a small group of islands in East Africa. Extravagant black script fills the time-worn pages of the enclosed letter.

June 10, 1869

At Sea

Dear Brother, I now take my pen in hand to let you know that I am well and I hope these few lines will find you enjoying the same good blessing, and all the rest of the folks. We ain't had much sickness so far and I hope that we shant.

The old cook has been sick with a fever. The old fellow came pretty near going for it. He had it about four months ago and he ain't got well yet and I don't think he ever will. For he is a very old man. And the old woman has been sick some but not dangerous. She has spells of raising blood. She gets so sometimes that she can't speak out loud but she don't seem to get frightened about it. I expect it is because she has had it so much.

I feel sorry for her, For she is a nice woman. She never troubles our business, nor the old man. Whether they are a good match, they never fall out and they get along first rate. And, take comfort, that is the way I like to see people do. They are very good-hearted folks. We shalt never starve to death as long as they are around.

She says that the men ought to fair just as we do in the cabin. I did think when I left home that I should not because he took his wife. But it don't make any oats.

We ain't had much trouble yet. Our first mate is a very fine man but don't cross his wake if you don't want a brushing. I and him get along first rate. We never had a hard word as of yet.

I have had a few words with the mate and will have a few more if he ain't careful. He must keep his nose out of my dish if he don't want to lose it. I could tell you a big story about him. When he left home, he told the old man that he was a religious man. But it turned out queer after we left. He got so that he had fits and I thought he would die but got over it. All hands was frightened about him. We watched him and found out what the matter was. I went in his stateroom and took all the liquor that I could find and gave it to the captain and told him if this happened again this voyage that we could not sail together any longer. We ain't been where he can get anything.

We are now off the Banks. We came here to have a game with the ships. For we ain't seen a whale ship for nine months. It looks good around here now. We gamed the Elizabeth and gamed the John Lawson. She has got nine hundred of sperm, and bound home I saw that man that you laughed so much about. He is fourth mate now. The Atlantic will carry our letters in and bring the others out. I am glad that we have got a chance to send for our letters.

We was at Johanna last month. I wrote to Delilah from there and we shall go there next September and I shall write again from there. I ain't had any chance to write before. After we got around the Cape, we went to a place on the coast of Delagoa Bay, for water, and that was all we could get there.

I ain't heard from home yet, but I shall in a few days if anybody has wrote. I want to hear from some of you before we go north. We shall start for the coast of Arabia, where we got our oil last voyage. There was two ships that got ambergris up there last year, so I think that we shall get some. So just keep your eye on the shipping list after we come from there.

We was six months out clean but we have done very well this side. We have 350 sperm. There ain't much chance to get oil here now. For it is very bad for the last two months.

A great deal of rain, but I hope that will be better soon as we have got some provisions coming out of Zanzibar next spring.

I want you to find out when it will start. You can go over to New Bedford early next spring and see the owner, Mr. Wilkens, and he will be able to tell you, then you will know what time to send your things.

I want you to send me one small box of tobacco and I will be responsible for it. It will be a good time and you can send anything you want and it won't cost you anything. Put all your things in a box of letters and papers and nail her up and let her slide. You can let the rest know so they can send if they want to.

You can write until next March, then write one in April to Joanna Comora Island, Indian Ocean. And be sure and pay postage enough. If you don't, they won't come. And send them by the way of Marseilles.

I will write again soon so you can give my best respects to all of the folks and tell them to write. So I must close my letter by bidding you good day.

Yours truly, Squire Carr. From your true brother, John Carr.

A LIFE REMEMBERED
TEACHER NEARLY KILLED ME

The following letter was discovered in a box of old paper items at a local flea market. It was most likely written right around the turn of the century by a girl named Catherine (Tourgee) Tucker.

My dear reader,

The writer of this story is only a poor uneducated person, that is to say only summer school learning. My earliest memory is when about six years of age. The house we lived in was one of the old historic, out of the way places. I being born in the house in the year 1873, July 8 makes it more dear to me.

My parents were just common every day people, working hard to get an honest living, which was quite a struggle. In fact, we had no luxuries same as children have today. But we had plenty of good, wholesome food and were probably happier for all that.

There were seven of us children, two girls and four boys living. One boy died at five years old.

My father was a regular Yankee, born in South Kingstown. My mother was Irish. The old house we lived in, they say was haunted. The old Indian burying lot was on the farm and there were ropes hanging from the beams upstairs and we were told they were the beams they hanged the Indian slaves on, years before we lived there.

Well, anyway, I believed it and when I went to bed nights I used to cover my head and tremble and shake until I went to sleep. Old-fashioned people told ghost stories every time any friend happened in.

When I was six years old, the village schoolteacher nearly killed me. She beat me so my father had her arrested and it was tried in court and her certificate was taken from her. I never went to school again for a year. I was not able.

371

In 1881, we moved to the village and I was some pleased. For there I found playmates which I yearned for. There was one girl in particular I played with, and many happy hours we spent together. Never had a word in all our life, and today I love her dearly.

For eight years I went to Peace Dale School and then I moved again in the lonesomest place on earth, where the nearest school was two miles away, which I attended, my two brothers and I.

When I was fourteen years old, my only sister got married, which seemed to me one of the greatest events I ever knew. Mother cooked a wedding cake and pies and all kinds of good things and we cleaned the whole house from top to bottom. For there were to be invited guests from out of town. My schoolmate was at the house and I was some happy girl. I had a new dress for the occasion and the first long one. Done my hair like a young lady and I realized all of a sudden that I had grown up. My friend had to have her white collar done up and, as Mother was busy, I done it and I wish you saw it. I ironed it on a red tablecloth and turned it red.

Well, the day of the wedding come and cold enough to kill you, three below zero. My sister looked beautiful in brown silk with everything to match. Her bridesmaid was sweet looking too and was as happy as if it was her.

Just before they left, Mother had a wedding dinner and, believe me, she knew how to cook one.

The groom was handsome with lovely brown curly hair and blue eyes and one of the best fellows ever walked. I'll say they were some happy.

I was confirmed that summer and I looked just like a bride with my wreath and veil.

The years I spent in this isolated place was the happiest ones I ever spent. My beau idol came along and then my life was complete. In fact the stars seemed to be brighter and the sun gave out more golden glow, or I just imagined it, who can say? I was happy, that's all I know. He was an ardent lover. He was the kind of fellow any girl would wish for and handsome too. His hair was black and curly and his eyes was gray and cheeks of rosy red. Something out of the ordinary but of a jealous nature. Things did not run too smoothly, for I liked to plague him. So the outcome of it all was a quarrel. We never spoke for four whole months. Well, after punishing ourselves, we made up again and at last got married. Went to New Hampshire on our honeymoon. I even teased him on that. On our way there, I held some fellow's hat that sit in the seat opposite us. He asked me to so what could I do? So George took me in the next car and I never saw my admirer again.

I enjoyed New Hampshire very much with its lovely mountains and woods that have no underbrushes. The only thing I did not like was thunder storms, which they have every day.

A SOLDIER'S LETTERS
MY DEAR DAUGHTER

Postcard of National Soldier's Home in Hampton, VA.
Public domain photo

The establishment of National Soldiers Homes began shortly after the Civil War, providing a place for wounded soldiers to recuperate and relax. Eventually Soldiers Homes existed in Maine, Wisconsin, Rhode Island, Virginia and Ohio.

In 1930, the Veterans Administration took over ownership of the Soldiers Homes, continuing to provide rehabilitation and recreation for disabled soldiers. In 1989, ownership passed into the hands of the Department of Veterans Affairs.

The following letters, discovered at an East Greenwich flea market, were written by a man who was injured in World War I. They are all addressed to his daughter:

March 16, 1921
The National Soldiers Home
Hampton, Virginia
"My Dear Daughter,

You must excuse me for not writing before. I was waiting to see how long it would be before I could get away from here. With the help of God, it will be between the 24th and 26th. If I was in good health, it would be one of the most delightful trips that I ever had since I became the age of man. It is to go see you, the only female that ever haunted my mind. I could write square miles of paper to you but it would not do me any good. I have to see you myself. Don't worry. I will see you if I am living."

December 11, 1922
The National Soldiers Home
Bristol, Rhode Island
"This is Father. I want to let you know that my brother is not living where he was, He moved. I do not know the address. Remember, I may see you in spring."

Postcard of National Soldier's Home in Bristol, RI.
Public domain photo

January 5, 1925
The National Soldiers Home
Bristol, Rhode Island
"Dear Daughter, I intended to go and see you before Christmas but luck went again. I would be glad to see you every day. I am going to see you before long. I have

lots to tell you. Be careful about your health. Do not get your feet wet. I am apt to leave here any time. I never had any luck since I came here."

January 12, 1926
The National Soldiers Home
Dayton, Ohio
"I received your letter but you did not give me the right count. You did not tell me how you were living, with your son or alone. I wish you would give me more correct news if you want to hear from me. Do not forget that. I will not tell you anymore. You will find enclosed in this letter the sum of ten dollars. When you get it, let me know. I am not well myself. I had to go to Washington to operate on my nose and eye. Goodbye. From, Father."

November 1, 1927
The National Soldiers Home
Hampton, Virginia
"I write these few lines to find out how yourself and family and the kids are getting along since I left. When I got to Providence, I found my brother dead and buried about three weeks before I got there. So I did not enjoy the trip very well. When I got to New York, I found things very bad. I done my share of talking if it will do any good. If this time don't do any good, I give up."

December 15, 1927
The National Soldiers Home
Leavenworth, Kansas
"These few remarks I am going to tell you. I do not like how your friends kept you in the dark as much as they did. But when I will get to you, I will enlighten you between the dark and the right. Daughter, I could fill a big book of arbitrary questions and answers that other people talk about which they know nothing about. I

would not write this kind of letter to you, only for fear I might meet with accident and couldn't see you. I am going to you very plain. I will not be dressed very good, so I will not deceive you. You say a few prayers for me, to carry me safe to you."

Postcard of National Soldier's Home in Leavenworth, Kansas.
Public domain photo

ETC.

LOST SHOES & MAD DOGS
NEWS

Usually newspapers try to be fair and accurate in their reporting. But in olden days, things were apparently a little different. Old newspapers often show us they were the stage for free-for-alls, where neighbors could argue with each other publicly or chastise other residents. There also wasn't a lot of privacy when you could read about everyone else's businesses in the weekly paper. The following items appeared in the Wood River Advertiser during the 19th century:

The letter to the editor from Charlestown, signed 'Cook' is laid over until next week. The one from Kenyon's Mills will go into the wastebasket unless subscriber sends his real name.

The town treasurer is short of funds. The taxes have not been paid.

Any person who shall willfully send to the publisher of any newspaper a fraudulent notice of the birth of any child, or the marriage of any parties, or the death of any person, shall, upon conviction thereof, be punished by a fine not exceeding one hundred dollars.

Letter to the editor concerning the Richmond Town Council's vote not to allow the circus to come to town: To the editor, the people of this village as well as elsewhere are greatly excited over the matter and say at the next election that the council, which is composed of old fogeys who neither want pleasure themselves or anyone else to enjoy themselves, will step down and quit.

*Notices were circulated calling for a meeting of the citizens last Saturday evening to make some arrangements about the decoration of the soldiers' graves. As but two or three seemed to have any interest in such matters, we presume the day will pass and nothing will be done.

*An eyewitness wishes to request that those young men who are accustomed to attend the Sunday evening services at the Baptist Church in Shannock for the purpose of creating a disturbance with their rude behavior, be more orderly.

*A party of four or five, one night recently went from this village to the Long Woods to dig for money that one of the number had dreamed was buried there. But they don't wish anything said about it.

*Mrs. P. Smith of Mystic, an insane Irish woman, cut her throat last week and is not expected to recover. Her insanity has been supposed to be harmless.

*A man at Shannock Mills broke one of his toes by kicking at a cat and hitting a table instead.

*A mad dog was killed in a Woonsocket barbershop Friday evening.

*Last Wednesday, a man named Matteson, belonging to Arcadia and of unsound mind, wandered from his home barefoot and bareheaded. He was found under a shed at Rockville about 2 o'clock the next morning.

*We have no local reporters and are in great measure obliged to rely on our readers and the public for items.

*The new house of Stephen J. Reynolds is fast approaching completion. He has just introduced water into it from a spring nearly a thousand feet distant, through a siphon.

*The largest cheese ever made is on exhibition at Providence. It weighs nearly twelve hundred pounds.

*Professor Bateman has been examining heads at the Union Hall during the past week.

*Ann Elizabeth, the well-known wife of Brigham Young, entertained the people of Wakefield with her troubles on Saturday evening.

*On Tuesday of last week, Patrick Roony of Clarke's Falls fell from a wagon and a wheel passed over his head, inflicting a serious scalp wound and nearly severing one of his ears.

*Fourteen petitions for divorce were presented in the court at Kinsgton.

*The person who lost a rubber shoe last Friday night in the mud near the residence of E.T. Burdick, can find the same by calling this office.

*The following cases were heard at the Richmond Trial Court: Susan M. Jaegar vs. William T. Collins on the charge of slander, RI State and Mike Baudett vs. Celena Baudett on the charge of bigamy, RI State and Mike Baudett vs. Joseph Snow on the charge of adultery.

*No license granted by any town council shall authorize any theatrical performance, or rope or wire dancing, or any other show or performance, or any wrestling, boxing or sparring match, or exhibition to be given on the first day of the week.

*Amos A. Whitford was last week sentenced to five years in the state prison for robbing George A. Wells of Exeter.

*In consequence of their horse falling, Mrs. H. Phillips and Miss Emma Gardiner were thrown from a sleigh near the Baptist church last Friday evening. Both ladies were considerably bruised.

*Remember that land requires feed just as regularly as animals do. Don't pretend to cultivate more than you can feed.

*George Sisson accidentally changed overcoats with someone and would be glad to change back again. So if this meets the eye of the other fellow, he will know where his coat is.

*A tin peddler, carrying his stock on his back, passed through town the other day.

*James Prince has left the Ownedale Mill and removed to Potter Hill where he has secured a position of increased pay.

*Last Saturday evening, Mrs. Clark A. Brown met with a serious accident by being knocked down and run over by a passing carriage. Mr. Brown and his wife were coming to this village and she started out on foot. Just below the residence of H. Austin, she heard a carriage *coming and stepped to one side to let it pass. She stepped into the path again just to be struck by another.*

John F. Palmer and Lloyd Tyler went to Grassy Pond Thursday and picked a bushel of blueberries.

Warren Tourgee has a very sick horse.

Sunday afternoon, as Georgie Hadley was returning to Hope Valley, Thomas Kenyon's dog ran into the road and bit him in the back. The dog is a large St. Bernard.

Henry Crandall has put in a new pump at his residence on High Street.

Dr. J.D. Jillson's offers permanent sets of gum teeth, either upper or lower for $12 and a fit guaranteed. Also, taxidermy in all its branches. Pet birds and animals stuffed.

G.E. Greene, druggist, Wyoming: Pure wines and liquors for medicinal purposes only. Also sold, revolvers and cartridges.

E.P. Clark, M.D., Hope Valley: Owing to the continued hard times and the low prices received for labor, I'm willing to share with my patrons in adversity as well as prosperity. On and after this date, my price will be fifty cents for each professional visit to Hope Valley, Locustville or Wyoming, instead of seventy-five cents.

A.C. Burdick, Hope Valley: Picture framing. Pictures hung, if desired, without extra charge. Also serving oysters in a first class manner.

*Mrs. N.B. Card of Charlestown was slightly injured by being thrown from a carriage on Sunday of last week. Mr. Card and his family were returning from church when the horse suddenly startled. The back seat, which was not securely fastened, fell over the hind end of the carriage, throwing Mrs. Card and two children, who escaped unhurt, to the ground.

HERE & THERE
TOWN NAMES

Carolina: Named after Caroline Newbold Hazard, the wife of Rowland Hazard, who developed the village.

Arcadia: Named for the Greek word which means tranquil, rural abode.

Shannock: Named for the Indian word Mishanneke, which means squirrel.

North Kingstown: Incorporated in 1674 as Kings Towne, changed to Rochester in 1686, then attained its present name in 1722.

Ashaway: Called Cundall's Mills, then Temperance Valley due to residents' strong opposition to alcohol use. Derived its current name in 1850 from the Indian word Ashawaug meaning cold spring.

Hopkinton: Incorporated in 1757 and named for Governor Stephen Hopkins.

Charlestown: Incorporated in 1738 and named for King Charles II.

Westerly: Called by the Indian word Misquamicut until incorporated as Westerly in 1669. Name changed to Haversham in 1686, and then back to current name in 1689.

Foster: Incorporated in 1781 and named for the Honorable Theodore Foster.

Cumberland: Incorporated in 1746 and named for William, the Duke of Cumberland.

New Shoreham: Called by the Indian name Manasses until renamed Block Island by navigator William Block. Incorporated in 1672 under its current name.

Little Compton: Called by its Indian name Seacomet until incorporated in 1746.

Tiverton: Called by its Indian name Pocasset until incorporated in 1746.

Johnston: Incorporated in 1759 and named for attorney general of the colony Augustus Johnston.

Cranston: Incorporated in 1754 and named for RI Governor Samuel Cranston.

Barrington: Called by its Indian name Sowams until incorporated in 1717.

Jamestown: Called by its Indian name Quononoqutt until incorporated in 1678 and named for King James.

Lincoln: Incorporated in 1871 and named for President Abraham Lincoln.

Burrillville: Incorporated in 1806 and named for the Honorable James Burrill.

Bristol: Incorporated in 1681 and named for Bristol, England.

North Smithfield: Incorporated in 1871 as the town of Slater. Changed to its present name 16 days later.

Providence: Incorporated in 1637 and named by Roger Williams for the Supreme Deliverer.

Warren: Incorporated in 1746 and named for Sir Peter Warren.

Gloucester: Incorporated in 1730 and named for Frederick, the Duke of Gloucester.

Warwick: Called by the Indian name Shawomet until incorporated in its current name for the Earl of Warwick.

Middletown: Incorporated in 1743 and named for being the town in the middle of the island.

East Greenwich: Incorporated in its current name in 1677. Name changed to Dedford in 1686 but changed back in 1689.

THE LOVE THEY LEAVE BEHIND
EPITAPHS

Gravestone in local cemetery.
Photographer: Kelly Sullivan Pezza

Words carefully carved onto a gravestone have long been a way of saying a final good-bye. Reflecting grief and sorrow, hope and adoration, the messages upon grave markers reflect both love and loss, etched in stone. The following epitaphs grace markers in local cemeteries:

Grace Tillinghast, died 1878 at age 74
Mother has fallen asleep in Jesus, they have met beyond the river.

Gilbert Tillinghast, died 1878, at age 53
To live in the hearts we leave behind is not to die.

David S. Woodmansee, died 1863, at age 2
Sleep on, sweet babe.

William T. Barber, died 1861, at age 6
Oh, Mother dear, weep not a tear for me, put your trust in Jesus and there the Lord you'll see.

Lilla Johnson, died 1862, at age 5
Sleep, little Lilla, free from sin. Too fair for the earth thy are.

387

Mary Anstis Card, died 1868, at age 28
Good night, loved ones. Remember it is only good night. We'll meet again in the morning...Let me go.

Volney Clark, died 1873, at age 41
We loved him.

Catherine Potter, died 1852, at age 17
Tis true my flesh lies beneath this stone and soon will waste away, but my soul is living with my God which never will decay.

Mary T. Hoxie, died 1855, at age 39
Weep not for me, beloved friends, though here my body lies. My spirit has gone to dwell with Christ, beyond the starry skies.

Albert L. Richmond, died 1880, at age 28
A light from our household is gone, a voice we loved is stilled, a place is vacant at our hearth that never can be filled.

Mary E. Potter, died 1861, at age 8
Loving Mary now has left us, thou art gone as thou did desire, to sleep in the arms of Jesus, where no one will disturb thee there.

Elizabeth Potter, died 1861, at age 83
My mother now has left the shore that is by sin uneven, her days are past, her suffering over, afflicting scenes disturb no more, me thinks she's gone to Heaven. How often, dear Mother, you have mourned and labored for your children, lest they should never have their sins or ever prepare for Heaven.

George W. Eldredge, died 1878, at age 35

Rest, soldier, rest. Thy suffering over, sleep the sleep that has no waking.

Noah S. Tanner, died 1880, at age 57
We love thee still.

Charles H. Lowe, died 1852, at age 45
Farewell my children and partner dear, if aught on earth could keep me here, it would be my love for you, but Jesus calls my soul away, Jesus forbids my longer stay, my dearest friends, adieu.

Francis Drysdale, died 1905, at age 90
God's finger touched him and he slept.

Sarah Olney, died 1862, at age 62
Mother, thou art not forgotten.

Thomas H. Barber, died 1819, at age 1
Our little bird has flown.

Julia A. Fenner, died 1837, at age 23
Although dear Julia slumbers beneath the grass green sod, her spirit still may humbly bow before her father God.

Emily A. Burdick, died 1878, at age 40
Her example is our inheritance.

Coming Soon from Finca Publishing:

Books by Kelly Sullivan-Pezza:

Maggie
THE ROCKY POINT MURDER

Murders in Quiet Villages
(series):

Book I.
Maggie - The Rocky Point Murder

Book II.
Because I Loved You – The Kenyon Murders

Now available from Finca Publishing:

SNOWGLOBE

KELLY SULLIVAN PEZZA

ISBN 0-9764715-0-7
Copyright 2005 by
Kelly Sullivan Pezza